DI006572

BUFFALO
SOLDIERS

BUFFALO ✦ SOLDIERS

Tom Willard

A TOM DOHERTY ASSOCIATES BOOK
New York

This is a work of fiction. All the characters and events portrayed in this novel are either fictitious or are used fictitiously.

BUFFALO SOLDIERS

This book is printed on acid-free paper.

A Forge Book
Published by Tom Doherty Associates, Inc.
175 Fifth Avenue
New York, N.Y. 10010

Forge® is a registered trademark of Tom Doherty Associates, Inc.

Book design by Patrice Sheridan

Library of Congress Cataloging-in-Publication Data
Willard, Tom.
    Buffalo soldiers / by Tom Willard.
        p. cm.—(Black sabre chronicles ; bk. 1)
    "A Tom Doherty Associates book."
    ISBN 0-312-86041-2
    1. United States—History, Military—19th century—Fiction.
2. United States. Army—Afro-American troops—Fiction.   3. Frontier
and pioneer life—West (U.S.)—Fiction.   4. Afro-American soldiers—
History—Fiction.   I. Title.   II. Series: Willard, Tom. Black
sabre chronicles ; bk. 1.
PS3573.I4445B84   1996
813'.54—dc20   95-53295
                                                                                          CIP

First Edition: June 1996

Printed in the United States of America

0   9   8   7   6   5   4   3   2   1

For Special Agent John L. Gales, U.S.A.F., and his lovely wife, Pamela, and their children, Johnathan, Marques, Christopher, and Cayla, an African-American military family.

Thanks, John and Pam, you were with me from start to finish on this novel.

For Mary Williams, Park Ranger and Historian at the Fort Davis, Texas, Historic Site, once the home of the 9th and 10th Regiments of the United States Cavalry—the "Buffalo Soldiers."

Thank you for your help in the research of this novel.

For Jerry Johnson, Los Arcos de Oro Ranch, Alpine, Texas, a member of the Friends of Fort Davis, who was greatly helpful in providing information on the Battle at Rattlesnake Springs.

My family and I look forward to joining you one day for a wonderful horseback ride and camping trip through the Big Bend of west Texas!

For my father and mother, Norman and Faye Smith, Friendswood, Texas, who have always been my supporters.

And especially for my wife, Laura, and our children, Sean, Ryan, Alissa, and Brent, whose patience during the writing of this novel is appreciated.

For my agent, Julian Bach, who believed more than any other in this story; and my editor, Harriet McDougal, Tor Books, who has been a patient friend.

For Sergeant Major Leo "ABU" Smith, USA Ret., now the curator of the Medal of Honor Museum, Chattanooga, Tennessee, and CWO-4 Charlie M. Musselwhite, St. Petersburg, Florida, HHC 1/327 Airborne Infantry, 1st Brigade, 101st Airborne Division, who took the time to teach a young paratrooper how to survive the jungles of Viet Nam and made certain I was put aboard a Med-Evac chopper after being wounded during Operation Valkyrie.

You were the heroes of my youth . . . and still are thirty years later. "Above the Rest!"

Thank you all.

A country with no regard for its past, will do
little worth remembering in the future.

—*Abraham Lincoln*

Foreword

In 1862, the First Regiment of South Carolina Volunteers was formed under the command of Colonel T. W. Higginson of Massachusetts. This regiment, composed of former slaves willing to fight for the Union, was the first all-Negro military unit in the history of the United States. Though composed of Negroes, it was led by white officers, and never saw combat during the Civil War.

The war would see numerous other Negro units in the Union forces, and they would prove their valor and dedication on many battlefields. Fort Wagner, South Carolina; Milliken's Bend, Louisiana; Point Lookout, Maryland; Fort Pillow, Tennessee; and Cold Harbor and the bloody "Crater" at Petersburg, Virginia, are a few of the most notable of their 449 military engagements against the Confederacy. More than 180,000 Negroes served with the Union during the Civil War; more than 33,000 gave their lives.

With the end of the Civil War the Union army was faced with two problems: providing troops to garrison the south during Reconstruction; and pacifying the western frontier, locked in a vicious Indian war, while concurrently holding back the onslaught of bandits and revolutionaries pillaging along the vast Mexican border.

On July 28, 1866, the United States Congress, realizing the value of the Negro soldier, but fearing the repercussions should Negro troops be introduced into the south during Reconstruction, passed an act authorizing the creation of six regiments of Negro troops, four regiments of infantry, and two regiments of cavalry. Upon receiving the authorization, General Ulysses S. Grant ordered General Philip Sheridan, Military Division of the Gulf, Commanding, and General William T. Sherman, Military Division of the Missouri, Commanding, to organize the two cavalry regiments and to deploy them to the west for immediate service on the frontier. These three generals determined that the Negro soldiers would be led by white officers.

The two cavalry regiments were designated the 9th Cavalry Regiment (Colored), with organizational headquarters at New Orleans, Louisiana, under the command of Colonel Edward Hatch; and the 10th Cavalry Regiment (Colored), with organizational headquarters at Fort Leavenworth, Kansas, under the command of Colonel Benjamin H. Grierson.

Grierson, a favorite of both Sheridan and Sherman, had led the famous Grierson Raid, which struck more than six hundred miles behind Confederate lines to Vicksburg, Mississippi. During the raid, Grierson's regiment had disrupted telegraph communications, destroyed railroad lines, and burned vital bridges, as well as wreaked havoc upon the general population and created panic with the penetration into territory the south believed was safe from Union attack.

Colonel Grierson was confident that the 10th Cavalry, who were to be deployed alongside the 7th Cavalry under the command of Lieutenant Colonel George Armstrong Custer, could provide security on the western plains and in the Indian Territory.

Colonel Hatch, who had served with Grierson during the Civil War, and taken part in the Grierson Raid, was confident his 9th Cavalry could provide security for the settlers of west Texas.

This service differed significantly from service in the Civil War, when Negro troops fought for their personal freedom. The troops of the 9th and 10th cavalries would fight for the freedom and security of white settlers, who treated the troopers with disdain and hatred, and even murdered them for sport.

These gallant troopers were called the Buffalo Soldiers, a name given them by the Cheyenne, who compared their dark, wiry hair with that of the buffalo, the central creature of Cheyenne lives and culture.

The Spanish-American War brought about another colorful page in the history of the Negro soldier, as it offered the first opportunity for Negro military units to fight alongside their white comrades on foreign soil. At Kettle Ridge and San Juan Hill, the 9th and 10th cavalries made the famous charge alongside Colonel Theodore Roosevelt's Rough Riders. Additionally, several Negro volunteers were squadron members of the Rough Riders.

But it is the Buffalo Soldier, standing in iron stirrups with drawn sabre at full charge, who began a long tradition that continues through the generations and into the sands of the Persian Gulf.

Into the annals of American history.

THE MONUMENT
1992: FORT LEAVENWORTH

☆ ☆ ☆

On July 25, 1992, thousands of Americans gathered at Fort Leavenworth amid a sea of blue cavalry hats and tunics; children ran and played on the grass and steps while old soldiers lounged on the benches, sharing decades of memories. Some good. Some bad. Most were real.

They stood on hallowed ground, where ancestral and spiritual descendants mingled with ghosts from the past.

They had come to dedicate a monument to the memory of men who sacrificed themselves in order that others might enjoy what they fought so valiantly to build and protect: a free nation.

They were called the Buffalo Soldiers.

One only had to see the monument to understand the price they paid.

Upon entering the Buffalo Soldier Monument, which rises above the once mosquito-infested site where the 10th Cavalry established its first headquarters on the western frontier, the visitors passed a three-flag rostrum where Old Glory fluttered between the regimental colors of the 9th and 10th cavalries. A path wound toward what appeared to be a descending figure eight, the upper circle a natural pond surrounded by prairie grasses and wildflowers, to the stairs that led to the lower elevated circle, a reflecting pond. Between the two ponds a mounted Negro trooper sat poised on his horse on a pedestal of hand-cut stones, his Spencer rifle gripped in one hand, the reins of his horse gripped in the other, his Kossuth hat pushed back at the brim. Benches surrounded the reflecting pond, allowing the visitors a place to sit and enter into the solitude and dignity of history.

Suddenly, a jolt of excitement threaded through the crowd as a tall man dressed in an army uniform approached the podium. He was recognized at once, and greeted by applause that was long, loud, but polite.

General Colin Powell, the highest-ranking African-American in the history of the United States military, and Chairman of the Joint Chiefs of Staff, stepped to the podium, waved to the crowd, then began to read from the farewell speech of Colonel Benjamin H. Grierson to his troops of the 10th Cavalry Regiment.

" 'The officers and enlisted men have cheerfully endured many hardships and privations, and in the midst of great dangers, steadfastly maintained the most gallant and zealous devotion to duty, and they may well be proud of the record made and rest assured that the hard work undergone in the accomplishment of self improvement and valorous service to country cannot fail sooner or later to meet with due recognition and reward. Benjamin H. Grierson, Colonel, 10th Cavalry.' "

Powell went on:

"And now, one hundred and four years later, on July 25, 1992, his dream of recognition and reward has finally come true. And so has my dream.
"Beginning with the Buffalo Soldiers in 1866, African-Americans would henceforth always be in uniform, challenging the conscience of a nation, posing the

question of how could they be allowed to defend the cause of freedom, to defend the nation—if they themselves were to be denied the benefits of being Americans?

"The great liberator Frederick Douglass made the same point. Douglass said . . . 'Once let the black man get upon his person the brass letters of "U.S.," let him get an eagle on his buttons, and a musket on his shoulder, and bullets in his pocket and there is no power on earth which can deny him his citizenship in the United States of America.'

"So look at this statue. Look at him. Imagine him in his coat of blue . . . on his horse . . . a soldier of the nation . . . eagles on his buttons . . . crossed sabres on his canteen . . . a rifle in his hand . . . a pistol on his hip. Courageous iron will. He was every bit the soldier that his white brother was. He showed that the theory of inequality must be wrong. He could not be denied his right. It might take time—it did take time. But he knew that in the end he could not be denied.

"The Buffalo Soldiers were not the only ones in this struggle . . . the 24th and the 25th infantry regiments . . . the 92nd and 93rd infantry divisions . . . the high flying Tuskegee Airmen . . . the parachuting Triple-Nickels . . . our navy's Golden Thirteen . . . the Montfort Point Marines . . . and thousands of other brave black Americans have gone in harm's way for their country since the days of the Buffalo Soldier. Always moving forward and upward . . . step by step . . . sacrifice by sacrifice.

"But we are not here today to criticize an America of a hundred and fifty years ago, but to rejoice—to rejoice— that we live in a country that has permitted a spiritual descendant of the Buffalo Soldier to stand before you today as the first African-American Chairman of the Joint Chiefs of Staff.

"And I am deeply mindful of the debt I owe to those who went before me. I climbed on their backs. I will never

*forget their service and their sacrifice. And I challenge
every young person today . . . don't forget their service
and sacrifice . . . don't forget our service and sacrifice and
climb on our backs to be eagles.*

*"And so the powerful purpose of this monument must be
to motivate us. To motivate us to keep struggling until
all Americans have an equal seat at our national table.
Until all Americans enjoy every opportunity to excel . . .
every chance to achieve their dreams . . . limited only by
their imagination and their own ability.*

*"We will leave this beautiful monument site today
knowing that caring Americans made a modest dream
come true. But let us also leave, my friends, determined
that the most important dream in the world—the
American Dream—of progress and full equality has
gained today with this monument a new vision.*

"A new strength.

"And a new tomorrow. . . ."

PROLOGUE

1866: THE SERGEANT MAJOR

✯   ✯   ✯

A cold November rain pelted the dining car attached to the rear of the westbound Kansas Pacific train, streaking the outside of the windows, but through the watery sheen a young Colored porter could clearly see a soldier standing near the open platform, and it was obvious he was not an ordinary Colored man.

Newly appointed Regimental Sergeant Major Roscoe Brassard, 10th Regiment, United States Cavalry (Colored), stood at attention, clutching a leather valise in his left hand; in his right he held a heavy metal scabbard, sheathing a long, curved three-foot sabre. His face was smoothly shaven, except for the thick mustache that flowed from beneath his broad nose to join his sideburns. Over his uniform he wore a greatcoat bearing the gold stripes and rockers of his rank. His highly polished cavalry boots, the tops nearly touching his knees, were sprinkled with drops of rain.

The train gave a lurch, the signal that it was preparing to leave. Through the frosted glass the porter heard the muffled cry, "All aboard!"

On the platform, Sergeant Major Brassard turned and motioned to forty Colored men he had been assigned to accompany to Fort Leavenworth, Kansas, the training center of the 10th Regiment.

Brassard's face tightened as he looked at the men, then relaxed, like that of a man resigned to a distasteful task. A man who had made a decision he knew he could not back away from.

Most of the men were in their twenties; a few were older, and one even had gray hair. They all appeared confused.

And why not! God Almighty! thought Brassard. This is not the way to treat soldiers who might die for this country!

The recruits were dressed in an assortment of clothing, none of which was standard U.S. military issue. They looked tired, and scared to death.

That was to be expected. What he didn't like was that they were also filthy and had not been properly fed, and since he had not had time to requisition rations for the men, they would not be fed until they reached Fort Leavenworth.

That was when he thought of the order given him earlier that morning, an order he found distasteful and offensive. "You will draw from the armorer a pistol and cartridges. Should any of the recruits attempt desertion . . . you are authorized to shoot to kill."

Specifically, he didn't like the idea of shooting a young man for what, in the circumstances, might seem a natural act.

Brassard had expected to find the men in some semblance of military formation, with proper noncommissioned guidance. What he found was a drunken white infantry corporal standing alone on the platform.

"Where are the recruits?" Brassard had demanded.

The corporal spat, then nodded over his shoulder. "They're over yonder." The corporal belched, snorted with laughter, and walked away.

Brassard had only to follow the smell drifting on the cold air to locate the new recruits. They had been assembled in an area near a cattle pen. Some of the recruits had been there for days, Brassard knew, after filtering into St. Louis from all over the country. Leaving the recruits to fend for themselves, the white corporals either returned to their assigned recruiting stations, or decamped to one of the many saloons along the riverfront.

Since Coloreds were not permitted to wait for the train on the platform, Brassard kept the men near the cattle pen until the last moment. But now he chose to march them through the middle of the platform, past waiting passengers, wanting all to see how these men, sworn to fight for their country, had been treated.

At the conductor's signal, Brassard led the men onto the train with relief, since there was little feeling in his cold feet.

Brassard found himself on a bench seat he was forced to share with two other recruits. The car was designed to carry thirty passengers and now held forty.

By noon the two wood-burning stoves stationed front and rear began warming the inside of the passenger car, and as the heat rose, mixing with the smell of unwashed bodies and clothes soiled with cattle manure, the stench became unbearable.

Sergeant Major Brassard knew that if these men were to be molded into a cohesive fighting unit, they must begin to embrace the first maxim of the profession of arms: Pride!

At that moment something inside the man broke. Years of discipline gave way to a boiling rage.

Brassard stood up and looked around at the recruits. They sat staring at him sloe-eyed and dumbfounded, like so many Colored troops he had seen during the Civil War. They were malnourished, some were sick, and all sat waiting to be told what to do.

Told what to do!

Men without initiative. A trait that had been beaten from them over years of slavery.

If they are to be men, he told himself, they must have an example. The men must learn to think for themselves if they are to survive!

"Men!" Brassard's voice boomed through the stench of the passenger car. "I want you to listen to me. I am Regimental Sergeant Major Brassard, of the Tenth Cavalry. You are ordered to strip off your clothes. Immediately. You may not get to Fort Leavenworth with full bellies, and you may be butt naked, but by God . . . when you do get there you won't be smelling like a troupe of dancing bears!"

A loud burst of laughter rose from the recruits as worn-out trousers and tattered shirts came off; filthy drawers—from those who wore them—followed. The windows were lowered and loose articles of clothing began to sprinkle the landscape along a one-mile stretch of the Kansas Pacific Railroad.

In the dining car, as he leaned over a passenger to serve tea, the porter saw the clothing flashing past the window. He stopped serving tea and nervously made his way to the COLORED ONLY car. What greeted him was almost more than he could fathom.

Forty men sat naked on the hardwood benches.

The windows were down and the men were shivering, but they all wore smiles, except the tall soldier with all the stripes on his immaculate uniform.

The tall, uniformed man thrust an angry finger at the porter. "I want forty blankets. Do you understand, boy?"

The porter nodded slowly, then carefully backed out of the car. He returned minutes later with the chief conductor, who was apoplectic.

"What the hell are you doing?" the conductor demanded.

Brassard flashed a quick, menacing smile and then stepped so close to the conductor that the shorter man withdrew several steps.

"I'm imparting instruction in personal hygiene. These men stink. Their clothes stink. This passenger car stinks. Army regulations state that soldiers of the United States cavalry are not permitted to stink—except in the field."

The tall man looked around, and stated a conclusion even the conductor could understand.

"We are not in the field."

A thin dribble of tobacco juice slid from the conductor's frozen, open mouth, disappearing into his beard. "You must be insane."

Brassard's face hardened into a demonic mask. "You may be right. But I still want forty blankets."

The conductor left, only to return again in a few minutes accompanied by a young white officer who wore the same type of forage cap as Sergeant Major Brassard. On the cant were the crossed sabres indicating cavalry; above the sabres was the number ten. Tenth Cavalry.

A thin smile crept across Sergeant Major Brassard's mouth as he stood to attention.

Second Lieutenant Jonathan Bernard O'Kelly, in the company of his bride of two weeks, was enroute to his first posting since his graduation from West Point. He had had no idea that recruits he might one day lead into battle were aboard the train.

"What's the problem, Sergeant Major?" asked O'Kelly. He was a lean young man with blond hair and bright blue eyes; the trace of a mustache was beginning to grow over his top lip. The sergeant major guessed the young man had been cultivating the blond down ever since learning of his posting to the cavalry. The mustache was as essential to the cavalry officer as his horse.

It was tradition.

Another tradition was looking after your men.

The conductor pushed through, saying, "What do you mean, 'what's the problem?' Are you blind! There's forty-two niggers in this passenger car and there ain't but two of 'em got clothes on!"

"I can see that," O'Kelly replied. "Will the sergeant major please explain?"

Brassard nodded at the recruits. "Sir, these men are enroute to Fort Leavenworth, to begin their cavalry training."

"Are you posted at Fort Leavenworth?"

"Yes, sir. I'm the new regimental sergeant major."

Then O'Kelly asked, "Why are these men without clothes?"

Brassard explained the conditions in which he had found the recruits. "They smell. They're hungry. And—as you can see—they are without proper apparel. I've instructed them that they can go in search of food—or whatever—once we reach Kansas City."

Laughter rolled from the hardwood benches. O'Kelly gazed at the men severely, then looked back to the conductor.

O'Kelly said to the conductor, "We have a problem, sir."

"You're damned right we do—"

O'Kelly cut off the conductor with a wave of his hand. "The problem is clearly yours."

"Mine!" The conductor, a squat, balding man with a heavy beard, stared wide-eyed at O'Kelly. "What the hell do you mean?"

"I mean, if forty naked Colored men get off the train in Kansas City—to search for food, or whatever—a riot could follow."

The conductor nodded. "I guaran-damn-tee a riot will follow. Sure as you're wearing Yankee blue."

O'Kelly continued, "I'm certain there will be a great many people—women included—waiting at the depot in Kansas City. Not to mention those people presently aboard. The Kansas Pacific Railroad will, no doubt, be held responsible. Along with the United States Army. The army will survive. The Kansas Pacific Railroad will survive. I dare say Kansas City will survive. My question is . . . will you survive?"

The conductor's eyes narrowed as he tried to comprehend. "What are you trying to say?"

"In searching for someone to blame, your company will blame the army, who will blame the sergeant major. But from what I've observed, he seems to have already accepted his fate."

Brassard clicked his heels and snapped to attention. "Yes, sir."

O'Kelly nodded at Brassard and looked back at the conductor. "That leaves you to explain to your railroad why this incident was not avoided. No doubt, you'll point out that it was beyond your control. As an officer, I know that that defense is sometimes possible. However, as an officer I also know that blame must ultimately find a place to rest. The civilian blame will quite likely rest with you. Unless, of course, you find what the sergeant major requires to straighten out this situation."

"But what can I do?" moaned the conductor.

O'Kelly thought for a moment. "Is there a stop on the line where we can find a telegraph operator?"

The conductor nodded.

"I'll telegraph Colonel Grierson at Fort Leavenworth, requesting he order the quartermaster to meet the train in Kansas City with trousers, boots, tunics, and greatcoats."

"What about when we reach Kansas City?" the conductor pleaded.

Brassard cleared his throat. "My men will stay aboard the train until the quartermaster arrives with proper clothing. In the meantime, all they'll need is food and blankets."

As though beginning to see some light at the end of this very dark tunnel, the conductor asked meekly, "Do you think your colonel will agree?"

O'Kelly flashed the conductor his best West Point smile.

The train made an unscheduled stop at a small town where the conductor found what Sergeant Major Brassard required. The sergeant major signed a voucher for the blankets, and he signed another voucher for the eight smoked hams and two dozen loaves of bread. Lieutenant O'Kelly wired Colonel Grierson at Fort Leavenworth and received the reply he expected; then he, Brassard, and the conductor brought several buckets of soapy water that the men used for bathing.

Sergeant Major Brassard showed them how to make a poncho by slitting a hole through the middle of the blanket. Though they did not realize it, the recruits had been given their first lesson in becoming troopers of cavalry.

All the recruits, including a young white officer sitting with his bride in the forward passenger car, had learned that becoming troopers would not put them on equal footing with the white soldiers and citizenry of this hostile country.

That would be a more difficult campaign to wage.

*   *   *

Three cars forward, Second Lieutenant Jonathan O'Kelly took a journal from his valise and began writing his impressions of the day. The writing of letters and the keeping of a journal were a professional requirement, providing a tangible reference for observation, reflection, and evaluation.

The first entry was carefully thought through, with O'Kelly noting his theories on leadership of Colored troops. But the day had taught him a lesson in leadership from the sergeant major that transcended race, and followed the strictest teachings of West Point: A good officer looks after his troops.

With that, Second Lieutenant Jonathan O'Kelly began by comparing the elements that he knew were now destined to clash on the western frontier:

> The red Indian on the frontier is no longer tolerable and must be wiped from the earth or subdued on reservations where he can be closely maintained and scrutinized. The use of Colored troops to achieve this mission is ironic and paradoxical, for the government intends to strip one race—the red Indians—of their human and natural rights, and property, by the use of force carried out by soldiers who have historically been denied human and natural rights, and were considered property, and only after a great Civil War were made free. Now these men are to be used tactically to deny the very same freedoms to the red Indian.
>
> The red Indian was in America when the first white man arrived; the Colored race was brought by force to America, and enslaved. As a nation we are now expecting the red Indian to go eagerly to enslavement and are willing to use former slaves to carry out that doctrine. That is the irony and the paradox, for how can we as a nation say to one race that you must lose your freedom and property or die? While on the other hand we incurred such tremendous loss of life during the Civil War to remove the bonds of slavery from the slaves?

Do we not have a moral obligation to both races? Or are we merely hypocrites in our policy? A policy that denies direction to the red Indian, except internment, while at the same time uses former slaves to enforce the very type of misery they were forced to accept?

The difference, as I see it, lies only in the fact that the red Indian stands ready to fight and die for his freedom and property and has no choice, while the former slave will fight not only because he is told to do so but also because he knows he has freedom and can now acquire property and does have a choice.

The red Indian stands to lose his culture; the Colored hopes to build a culture.

Who will fight the hardest? The culture that will be destroyed? Or the culture that will build?

That answer will only be found on the field of battle.

PART 1

1869: FORT WALLACE

1

In January 1869, the major problems standing in the way of the Kansas Pacific Railroad were the Arapaho, Cheyenne, Comanche, and Kiowa nations. Which was, ostensibly, why regiments of the 7th and 10th cavalries were assigned to the western frontier: to protect the railroad and railroad work crews and freight companies, as well as the stage lines running east and west. However, that was not the true purpose of the regiments' deployment: The true purpose was to eradicate the four Indian nations living in that region under the auspices of the Medicine Lodge Treaty of 1866.

The Medicine Lodge Treaty granted certain areas of the plains to the four tribes, and promised that those lands would not be trespassed upon by white settlers or buffalo hunters.

Which was not the case this afternoon. Heavy-caliber rifle fire broke the silence on the plains every twenty seconds, the time Trooper Darcy Gibbs, H Troop, 10th Cavalry, figured it took the buffalo hunter in the distance to reload, aim, and fire.

Trooper Gibbs, a Buffalo Soldier as the plains Indians had named the Colored cavalry troops, was on patrol northwest of Fort Wallace with orders to warn settlers and buffalo hunters that the Cheyenne were raiding the work camps along the Smoky River line of the Kansas Pacific Railroad.

Gibbs watched as another buffalo dropped to the frozen plains. "Pretty good shootin', Sarge." Gibbs sat back in his saddle, chewing on a twig, watching Sergeant Moss Liberty study the situation through a telescope.

Liberty sat astride his horse, the reins held tight in his gloved hands. He had sat there for nearly ten minutes, giving careful thought to his next move—if there was to be a move. Liberty was not a man of indecision, but at thirty-five he knew there was a time to exercise patience. There had been a time in his life when he had had to wait to be told what to do; that had been required of him, as a matter of fact.

At that time he'd been a slave in Tennessee.

Liberty had escaped from bondage in 1852, making his way north by following the Big Dipper, which the slaves called the Freedom Cup. He had traveled at night, sleeping by day in the trees to prevent discovery, until he swam the Ohio River near Owensboro, Kentucky, and came ashore to freedom in Indiana. That was sixteen years ago; ten of those years had been spent in uniform following his enlistment in the 54th Massachusetts Infantry. He had fought at Fort Wagner, South Carolina, where he was wounded in the final charge that had cost the life of commander Colonel Robert Gould Shaw. Liberty had learned firsthand that the price of liberty was not cheap.

That was why he had chosen Liberty for his last name.

Moss, his first name, had been given to him by his mother because his dark hair was curly and soft like moss growing in a wet, dark place. Now a sergeant of cavalry, he was tall and muscular. A quiet man by nature, in the two years he had served on the plains he had learned to spot trouble and avoid the situations that often drew Colored soldiers into conflict.

He was now confronting one of those difficult situations, one that pulled at his guts as he again extended the telescope and surveyed the hills in the distance.

The plains stretched endlessly toward the west, where the sun was beginning to settle onto the horizon. A light breeze blew easterly, carrying the smell that Liberty knew came only from a slaughter. And a slaughter was what lay before him.

He had been watching the growth of what the buffalo hunters called a "stand," a large cluster of dead buffalo lying at the edge of the herd, a herd that stretched as far as Liberty could see.

"Must be more than fifty in his stand," Liberty said, looking again through the telescope.

"How many in the party?" asked Gibbs.

"A gunner and a skinner."

"Just one gun?"

Liberty nodded but wasn't impressed; he knew it took no particular talent to build a formidable stand, except a steady hand on the trigger and a constant supply of bullets. The other buffalo would not run or move so long as the shot felled the creature; a wounded buffalo would generally start a panic and the herd would bolt. He also knew the buffalo were their own worst enemy because they were predictable. The buffalo always moved into the wind; therefore, the hunter had only to position himself crosswind and begin shooting.

Not that the sight of a large stand bothered him. He knew this area, called the Republican, was prime hunting grounds for the buffalo hunters, who would strip the hide from the animals, then stake the hides for fleshing and drying, marking the snowy landscape with dark splotches, leaving the meat to rot on the prairie, carrion for vultures and other predators.

Predator. The word seemed to have special meaning as Liberty heard the thunder of a Sharps rifle and saw another buffalo drop nearly one quarter of a mile from the gunner, who lay a half mile from Liberty on the top of a knoll.

Liberty examined the hunter again, making certain he was seeing the unbelievable truth.

There were some things a man could not walk away from.

Augustus Talbot was eighteen years old, tall and wiry, his skin and eyes the color of charcoal. He wore leather breeches that were coated with dried buffalo blood, and was wrapped in a heavy buffalo robe as he lay atop a hill on the open prairie south of the Republican River, his leg tied to a stake driven into the frozen ground. Smoothly, he inched over the mound of snow that he had built to support the long barrel of his fifty-caliber Sharps buffalo gun, took aim and fired the "Big Fifty," as it was called by the buffalo hunters, and watched as another buffalo fell dead.

Charlie Calhoun, a skinner with failing eyesight, always knelt behind him, a Colt .45 pistol ready should Augustus violate the single rule that kept him alive: Keep the barrel pointed toward the buffalo.

"You're shootin' too slow, boy. We're losin' daylight." Calhoun thumped Augustus in the back with the heel of his boot, then leaned forward, checked the rope attached to Augustus' leg, and gave it a sharp tug. The stake held firm. Calhoun spit a long stream of tobacco juice and wiped his beard with the heavy sleeve of his buffalo robe.

To Augustus's immediate front, low on the side of the hill where he was positioned, twenty-four buffalo lay still, their legs jutting parallel to the ground. Steam rose off some of the bodies in twisting, ghoulish clouds as the crisp cold began to cool the carcasses.

"Come on, boy. Shoot!" Calhoun slapped Augustus in the back of the head just as he pulled the trigger, throwing off the shot. A buffalo screamed, tumbling into the snow, but wasn't dead. The herd bolted and, in the moment of madness, turned toward the buffalo hunters.

"Damn your black ass!" Calhoun jumped to his feet, running toward the wagon filled with hides.

Augustus pulled desperately at the rope; the stake held fast as the buffalo herd thundered closer. Again he kicked, pulled, and thrashed, but the stake wouldn't break free. He turned to the herd and saw the lead buffalo closing on him, no more than twenty yards away, followed by thousands more, their great heads plowing in imperfect rhythm.

In that instant Augustus fell calm, as though death would be a blessing. He stared directly into the buffalo's eyes. Suddenly, from the corner of his eye there was a flash of blue. He

looked up and saw what he thought could only be a dream:
Two Colored men dressed in army uniforms were riding toward him, the tallest of the two gripping a long, curved sabre.

The tall soldier leaned over and, as he swept past Augustus, swung the sword, cutting the rope. The second soldier followed close behind but didn't stop, merely reined in sharply
next to Augustus and extended his hand.

"Come on, boy!" he shouted.

Augustus gripped the hand and swung onto the back of the
horse. The soldier spurred the horse toward the wagon, where
Augustus saw Calhoun hiding behind a wheel as the buffalo
charged closer.

Augustus could see the tall soldier race toward the wagon,
but wheel diagonally when he saw there wasn't enough time
to reach the skinner.

Augustus' eyes met with the eyes of Calhoun, who then disappeared beneath a sea of black fur.

An hour later the earth appeared to have been plowed by
some great machine in a long path to the edge of the horizon.
The wagon lay in splinters among buffalo hides strewn like
black boils; the air was still, but the ground continued to trem-
ble though the herd was no longer in sight.

Liberty could only shake his head in amazement while
Gibbs and Augustus walked among the ruins.

There was little left. Calhoun's mangled body lay in four
separate pieces over a fifty-yard stretch of broken ground.

Augustus looked into Calhoun's dead face, what was left
of it, staring emptily to the sky, his head severed at the throat.
He suddenly reached to the ground and retrieved the Sharps
rifle. It was covered with mud, and the stock was cracked
nearly in half.

"Ain't much good now," Liberty said.

Augustus wiped at the mud, sighted down the barrel, and
replied, "The barrel's straight, and I can fix the stock."

This brought a laugh from Liberty. "How you going to do
that?"

Augustus smiled as he picked up a buffalo robe.

Gibbs approached, carrying a cartridge belt he'd taken from Calhoun's body. He handed it to Augustus.

They slept that night in a thicket of trees around a fire pit dug low in the frozen ground to prevent the flames from giving away their position. Over the sunken fire they roasted a piece of buffalo hump, and the Buffalo Soldiers watched Augustus work on the rifle stock.

He cut strips of buffalo hide and stretched them over the fire until the fat began to bubble; next, he slowly worked the hot fat into the cracks of the stock. He wound the strips tight around the stock and soaked them with water. Augustus then turned the stock slowly over the fire, patiently drying the strips until the hide formed a rigid cast around the wood.

This mightily impressed Liberty. "Where'd you learn that, boy?"

"From the Kiowa," Augustus replied softly.

"Kiowa!" Liberty exclaimed. "What were you doing with the Kiowa?"

Augustus shrugged. "I was a slave."

Liberty chuckled. "I didn't know the Kiowa bought Colored slaves."

"They didn't buy me. I was captured by a raiding party just after the end of the war."

Augustus' comment spurred Liberty's curiosity. "You want to tell us about how you come to be here on the Republican?"

Augustus nodded slightly, then spoke in a low, deliberate voice. "I come from west Texas. I was captured by the Kiowa three years ago. The Indians sold me to Charlie Calhoun last year for three horses and a rifle."

Liberty waited, but Augustus said nothing more.

"Is that it?"

"That's all I want to say."

"What about your folks?" asked Gibbs.

"Both my mama and papa are dead. They died during the war."

"I expect you learned a lot of things living with them Injuns," said Gibbs, who was cutting off another piece of meat.

"I learned many things, Mr. Gibbs."

"Did the Kiowa teach you how to shoot?"

Augustus shook his head. "My massah in Texas taught me how to shoot. He said I had a natural eye with a rifle."

This prodded Liberty further. "Can you ride as good as you can shoot?"

Augustus nodded, then held the stock up for closer examination. He was pleased with what he saw.

The stock would hold firm.

The next morning they rose from the stiff buffalo robes and stretched their muscles. Noting that the fire was out and fresh snow had fallen during the night, Augustus took a robe, cut off a square the size of his hand, turned it fur side up, took kindling, and began scraping his knife against a piece of flint he carried in his leggings. The fur from the robe began to slowly burn, throwing off a stinging odor, but as he added more wood he had a good fire going within minutes.

Liberty and Gibbs glanced at each other. Liberty grinned. "This here Augustus Talbot knows a few tricks, Trooper Gibbs."

"He sure does," Gibbs replied admiringly.

When they finished what was left of the buffalo meat, Liberty said, "We best be moving. We're going to Fort Wallace, Augustus. Come with us; you can make plans from there. If you want to hunt buffalo, the Goddard brothers are hiring shooters out of Hays to fill government contracts on land the Injuns don't own."

Augustus shook his head. "I'd rather starve to death."

2

The trio reached Wallace, Kansas, the next afternoon. Wallace was a sprawling community of canvas tents, mud huts (called "soddies"), and Conestoga wagons now trapped along the frozen tracks of the Kansas Pacific Railroad.

It was the first town Augustus had seen since being captured by the Kiowa, and he found Wallace uglier than a boil on a sow. He had seen many prettier Kiowa villages. Wooden saloons and sporting houses lined the main street, a soggy bog splattered with manure. They rode along, the mud sucking at their animals' hooves.

Liberty turned to Gibbs. "Let's spend a few minutes over with my family. Then we'll stop off at Philadelphia Phil's place before we head out to the fort."

Gibbs grinned broadly. "That sounds particularly proper, Sergeant."

They turned off the main street and rode into a neighborhood of old wagons and worn tents. Augustus saw Colored children playing in the snowy streets; heard the voices of women singing hymns. Smelled chitlins, ham and beans, and roast buffalo hump. It smelled good!

"Must be Sunday," Gibbs said.

"Where are we, Sergeant?" asked Augustus.

"This part of town is called Buffalo Bottoms, on account it's where all the Coloreds live. Coloreds who have families and served in the army. Colored soldiers are called Buffalo Soldiers by the Injuns, you know. They says our hair looks like the fur of the buffalo. So we call this Buffalo Bottoms, 'cause living here is about as close to being at the bottom a Colored man can get."

"We called something else by the white cavalry. Everything from brunets to moacs to nigger," snorted Gibbs. "We at least got some pride in being Buffalo Soldiers."

"My wife and daughter live right down yonder." Liberty pointed at a tent that was more patchwork than canvas.

In front of the tent, steam rose off two large cauldrons of boiling water, carrying from one the heavy smell of lye soap.

"My wife, her mama, and my daughter, Selona, are laundresses. They take in laundry from the fort. It helps, adds some money to my pay. Twenty-four dollars a month for a sergeant with a family don't make ends see each other, much less meet." He stopped his horse as a young girl ran from the tent.

"Daddy! Daddy!" She ran and jumped up and threw her arms around Liberty, startling the horse.

"Whoa, girl, you going to scare my hoss to death." He was grinning as he pulled her up onto the saddle and gave her a great hug. "How's my baby?"

"I ain't no baby. I'm almost twelve years old. Almost a woman grown. Besides, you married Mama when she was fifteen."

Augustus looked at her and saw that her face was mature beyond her age.

Liberty started to say something, when the voice of his wife interrupted. "It's about time you come home. Off gallivanting like some crazy man."

Della Liberty looked worn to the bone; the skin appeared loose on her cheeks and thin arms. The post doctor called her illness the consumption, Liberty had told Augustus.

An older woman, probably the grandmother, stood at the flap of the tent, a corncob pipe clamped tightly in her toothless mouth. She reminded Augustus of a horse that had been rode hard and put away wet too many times.

Gibbs whispered to Augustus, "That old woman's named Miss Marie. She's meaner than a two-legged dog and watches over the girl like a hawk."

Moss lowered Selona gently to the mud street and swung his leg over the saddle. He removed his kepi, placing it over his heart, and walked smartly to his wife. He pulled her to him slowly. Carefully.

Augustus stared at Selona; her right eyebrow raised.

"Where you from?" she asked.

"Texas."

"Don't they have soap and water in Texas? You're so dirty, I can smell you from here."

He had never spoken to anything so beautiful and been embarrassed so deeply at the same time. "Smell washes off. Manners are something that must be learned with time," Augustus retorted.

Her eyes widened. "You the one that needs manners, boy."

"I'm not a boy. I'm a man."

Selona harrumphed, then turned and hurried into the tent. The old woman followed, cackling with laughter like an old hen.

Augustus sat there, realizing he had said both the right and wrong things in the same breath.

Moss hugged Della and remounted, telling her, "I'll be back tonight."

The moment the trio stepped through the door in Philadelphia Phil's, a woman ran to Gibbs, throwing her arms around him.

"How's my buffalo gal?" Gibbs started to kiss the woman when a booming voice interrupted.

"If you ain't going to pay for it . . . you ain't going to taste it."

Loud laughter from the dozen soldiers in the tent nearly

buckled the rickety wooden framework supporting the canvas exterior of the saloon.

Augustus peered from behind Liberty, both of them standing at the door. His eyes widened at the source of the voice. Philadelphia Phil was the biggest Colored woman Augustus had ever seen in his life. She wore a buffalo robe draped over her shoulders; several mink furs, laced together with rawhide, formed a scarf around her neck; and her head was covered by the cowl and cape of a timber wolf.

"How you doing, Phil?" shouted Liberty.

Behind the bar, constructed of split railroad ties mounted on huge wooden telegraph-wire spools, Philadelphia Phil wagged her finger at Liberty.

"Don't you 'how you do' me, Sergeant Liberty. I done told you and your men, before their fingers start dancing on my girls, I want their money dancing on the table!"

The sound of Gibbs slamming two dollars onto the bar made her smile. Her teeth were black as coal.

"There's your money. Now leave me and Gerdie be," Gibbs said.

The two hurried through a hole in the back of the canvas to one of the "pleasure tents" behind the saloon.

"Who's that woman with Trooper Gibbs?" asked Augustus.

"That's Gerdie Jenkins. She's a buffalo girl."

"A buffalo girl?"

"A sporting woman," he replied.

Augustus didn't understand.

Liberty explained, "She sells her body to the soldiers." He shook his head slowly, then added, "Gerdie's worked every saloon from Fort Leavenworth to Fort Riley to Fort Hays, and now Fort Wallace, the end of the track. She was pretty there for a time, but now she looks older everytime I see her. Bad whiskey and broken promises from bad men can age a woman beyond her years."

The piano music started up, and more laughter echoed through the thin walls of the saloon.

Liberty bought Augustus a drink. "You ever drink white mule whiskey?"

Augustus looked at the glass of clear liquid. "I've never drunk any kind of whiskey."

Liberty grinned. "To the regiment." He downed the drink in one swallow.

Augustus did the same; at once his gut burned, his eyes glazed, and his legs gave slightly.

Liberty slapped him on the back. "You'll do. C'mon over to the piano."

A young trooper from the 10th sat at the keys. Liberty leaned on the piano, and said, "This is Augustus Talbot."

Augustus stuck out his hand. The trooper played with one hand as he shook, saying, "Haymes. Trooper Isaiah Haymes. I'm from Georgia. Pleased to meet you."

Someone entered. The room suddenly fell silent, and all eyes turned to the front door of the saloon.

Liberty, like the other soldiers, was slipping on a ring that Augustus recognized as a bent horseshoe nail. When their fists tightened, the rings jutted from their knuckles like sharpened pitchforks.

The newcomer was a short man, with blond hair and beard that framed cold blue eyes shining with mischief. He was dressed in an army uniform. Behind him stood several more white soldiers, all obviously drunk.

Haymes whispered to Augustus, "That's Sergeant John Armitage from the Seventh Cavalry. He's a galvanized Yankee."

Augustus shook his head, not understanding.

"He used to be a Secesh, a secessionist. Now he's in the Union army." Then a bitter truth was revealed. "He was at Fort Pillow with Nathan Bedford Forrest."

Augustus knew about Fort Pillow, and the massacre of hundreds of black Union soldiers who had tried to surrender to the Confederate general. Forrest had ordered his officers to "kill everything blue 'twixt water and sky."

This was taken to mean the black soldiers, many of them wounded. Their bodies were piled near the hospital like cords of wood and set afire.

"Howdy, boys!" Armitage shouted. He staggered in, followed by the other soldiers.

Liberty stood, motioning the others in the room to remain seated.

"We don't want no trouble, Sergeant," Phil said.

Armitage leered. "We just thought we'd stop in for a drink." He eyed one of the black saloon girls sitting on a trooper's lap and added, "And some entertainment."

"Why don't you boys go on back to your side of town, Sergeant? This place is off limits to the Seventh Cavalry, and you know that as well as any man here."

At that moment Augustus met Armitage's eyes for the first time. Armitage stared long and cold, reminding Augustus of the hatred he had seen from the Kiowa when he was first captured.

One by one, chairs creaked on the floor, and the Colored troopers rose.

A voice yelled, "Now that's enough!" Phil stepped forward cradling a shotgun leveled at Armitage's stomach.

"I told you the last time you come in here I didn't want you coming back, Sergeant. Now take your men and git on out of here before there's trouble."

One of the 7th troopers whispered to Armitage, and whatever was said had instant effect. Carefully, the white troopers eased out the door as a blast of cold air roared in from the street, and then there was silence.

Haymes quickly resumed playing the piano, and the soldiers' relieved laughter, nervous at first, grew into a happy roar.

He slipped off the ring and put it in his pocket. Augustus looked at Liberty's ring.

Liberty saw him do so. He shouted over the music, "This is called drinking jewelry."

"What's that for, Sergeant?"

"Our boys have to take a lot of guff from the white cavalry around here. This ring is what we wear to say we're ready to fight. It keeps a lot of the white boys from starting anything."

Augustus shook his head in amazement. "I've never seen Colored men ready to stand up against whites."

Liberty nodded as he poured another drink. "There's lots you don't know. Maybe you'd like to find out?"

"How?"

Liberty swirled the white whiskey around in his glass, saying nothing, the way a man does when he's hatching a careful plot.

3

Sergeant Major Brassard was sitting at his desk when the door to the regimental headquarters orderly room flew open, admitting a blast of cold air followed by Liberty and what Brassard could only describe as the filthiest human being he had ever seen in his life.

The young man was wearing a heavy buffalo coat; his face was coated with a sheen of buffalo fat, blood, and dirt. Brassard rose slowly, noting that despite his dirt, the boy had a certain bearing.

"Boy, when's the last time you had a bath?" Brassard asked.

"Don't call me 'boy.' My name is Augustus Talbot," Augustus snapped.

Brassard swallowed a grin. "Very well, Augustus Talbot. When's the last time you had a bath?"

"About three years ago."

Brassard's eyebrows rose as he looked at Liberty. "What's going on here, Sergeant?"

Liberty bit into a plug of chewing tobacco. "We found this here boy—this here Augustus Talbot—yesterday afternoon up on the Republican."

"Buffalo hunter?" asked Brassard, not taking his eyes off Augustus as he slowly moved around the desk.

"Yessuh. And one helluva buffalo hunter. This man can shoot better than any man I ever seen. Except he didn't have no choice in the matter."

"What's that suppose to mean?"

"He was captured three years ago—"

Augustus cut him off. "I can speak for myself, Sergeant." He stared into Brassard's eyes. "I was captured by the Kiowa three years ago. The Kiowa sold me to a buffalo hunter last year."

"Sold! You was a buffalo hunter's slave!" Brassard's voice nearly shook the building.

"Yes, sir. Born a slave. Set free and captured by the Kiowa. Probably would have died a slave had it not been for your men."

"Talbot? That's your last name? You keeping the name of your massah? Most Colored men have picked a new name since freedom."

Augustus shrugged. "I hadn't give that much thought in the past three years, Sergeant Major. I had other things on my mind."

"Can you read and write?"

"Some. My massah was a rancher, but he was also the local preacher before he went off to the war. He taught me."

"Can you cipher?"

Augustus said, "My massah's wife had to teach me ciphering after the massah went off to war."

"Why's that?"

"Her health was too poorly for her to take care of business. I did it for her."

"What about the overseer? He could have done the business."

Augustus shook his head. "There wasn't an overseer. Massah didn't have the money to hire one."

"What about your family? You got any kinfolk left alive?"

Augustus's eyes hooded with sadness. "No, sir. My mama and papa died during the war."

Brassard sat back down, planting his boots on top of the desk. "I expect you must have a powerful hatred for Injuns."

"More than you can know." Augustus' eyes were like banked coals.

Brassard understood that kind of hatred; hatred that could destroy or, if channeled properly, be of great use. "You got any plans?"

Augustus replied, "I'd like to borrow some soap and take a bath."

Brassard laughed. "You surely need a bath. You smell like death warmed over." Brassard motioned to Liberty. "Get this buffalo hunter a hot tub, some soap, and some clean clothes."

"Yessuh." Liberty spat into the spitoon. "Come on, Augustus. Let's get that buffalo stink off you."

Augustus Talbot stood six feet tall; he was scrawny from malnutrition, but strong and sinewy. The hot bath was a wonderful experience. Once he'd lowered himself into the tub, he scrubbed for nearly an hour. Liberty brought him some fresh clothes, laughing in a secretive way as he placed a pair of black boots atop the blue trousers and tunic.

Once dressed, Augustus headed out to the parade ground. Mounted troops came and went through the main gate; the air was filled with the sounds of the military. His pace quickened as he saw Brassard walk out of the orderly room. They shook hands.

"You hungry?" Brassard asked.

"I could eat a horse."

Brassard led Augustus to the mess hall. When Augustus stepped through the door he heard the crisp bark from a soldier, "Atten-hut!"

From their tables, the troopers rose sharply, standing at attention as Brassard led Augustus to a table. Brassard studied the men for a moment, then nodded and said smartly, "As you were."

The men sat down and returned to eating; then a soldier brought two plates of food for Brassard and Augustus, who began eating like a wolf. Brassard ate slowly, watching Augustus, saying nothing until three plates of food had vanished.

"You thought about what you're going to do, Augustus?"

Augustus sipped hot coffee, shaking his head. "I suppose I'll have to find a job."

"Not many jobs in these parts for a Colored man, unless you want to go back to hunting buffalo."

Augustus exhaled heavily. "No, sir. I'd rather starve."

Brassard came to the point. "You don't have to starve. I know where you can get fed, clothed, and give yourself a chance to get your feet on the ground."

Augustus chuckled, as though he already knew what would be Brassard's next words. "You mean the army?"

Brassard replied, "I mean the Tenth Cavalry. It's a chance to do something important. Important for you . . . and our people."

"Why important? And why would I want to risk my life as a soldier?"

Brassard went into his recruiting pitch. "This nation just finished a bloody civil war to set slaves free. A lot of good men died, mostly white men. Now we're a country again, and if the Colored man is going to stand shoulder-to-shoulder with the white man we're going to have to pitch in and do our share." He paused for effect. "Besides, it'll give you a chance to settle your account with the Kiowa, and we need young men like you. Hell, boy, you just spent two years with the Kiowa and on the plains. I expect you got a lotta Injun in you now."

"I learned how they fight. How they think."

"That's what I mean. You'd make a perfect scout for the regiment."

"A scout?"

"Among other duties. But most of all, you know Injuns."

"What other duties?"

"Do you know who does most of the paperwork in this regiment?"

"I couldn't say."

"The white officers, and a few noncommissioned officers like myself who can read and write. There ain't many of us, either. You could be very valuable to the Tenth."

Augustus had been watching the troopers in the mess hall. They appeared confident, self-reliant, and carried themselves with an obvious pride.

"I don't know anything about being a soldier."

Brassard grinned. "I do. You'll train right here, under my supervision."

"You can do that?"

"Damn right I can do that. I told Colonel Grierson about you while you were cleaning up. He ordered me to enlist you into this regiment by reveille tomorrow morning . . . or he'd have my stripes."

"What about my rifle?"

"The Sharps?"

Augustus nodded. "I'd like to keep it."

Brassard thought for a moment, then said, "Troopers in the Tenth carry the Spencer rifle. I reckon we can make an exception. But you'll have to carry the regulation Spencer as well."

Augustus wolfed down more food, then said, "That'll give me more to shoot with, Sergeant Major."

"You'll have to supply your own Sharps cartridges. The army don't issue them. You can buy them in town."

That sounded fair to Augustus. "I'll buy my own cartridges."

Brassard took an enlistment form and asked, "Do you know how to sign your name?"

"I know."

Brassard pushed the form across the table and handed him a pencil. "Sign your name, Augustus Talbot, and you'll be a member of the Tenth Cavalry."

Augustus signed, but not the name Brassard was expecting.

"You signed this form with the name Augustus Sharps. Is that for the rifle?"

Augustus thought about the other freemen cutting their ties with the past, and said, "The Sharps has a good sound. A good feel. Most men know the Sharps is a serious rifle. A name should be the same. Sharps is a name that stands for pride."

4

Reveille echoed across the parade ground, welcoming Trooper Augustus Sharps harshly into his first full day of army life. The thirty-man barracks was dark and quiet, except for the bugle; then the darkness was swept away by a chain of dancing lanterns hurrying along the aisle between the rows of bunks, the quiet shattered by the barking voice of a corporal.

"On your feet! Move! Move!" The corporal stopped at Haymes' bunk and turned him out with a forceful pull on his leg.

Haymes hit the hardwood floor, rubbed his sleepy eyes, and looked at Augustus, who was sitting on the edge of his bunk, bewildered. "Just think, Trooper Sharps. Me and you done volunteered for this man's army."

Augustus wasn't sure of what to say, except, "Is it always like this in the morning?"

Haymes stood and started making his bunk. "Every day that we ain't in the field. Come on. Let me show you how we make the bunk. That's the first thing we do every morning."

Augustus watched as Haymes stretched the blanket across the bunk, then tightened the corners until the blanket was smooth. "Then you got to check the bounce."

"The bounce?" asked Augustus.

Haymes took his horsehoe-nail ring and threw it onto the blanket. The ring bounced a few inches into the air. Haymes smiled, "Tighter than a frog's butt in water. That's the way it's got to be, otherwise Sergeant Liberty puts you on mess detail."

"What's mess detail?"

Haymes shook his head. "That's worse than fightin' Injuns—if we ever get to fight Injuns. Mess detail means you go to the mess hall and work in the kitchen all day. From three in the morning until eight at night, or later. Come on, now, get that bunk made up. Inspection comes in ten minutes."

Augustus hurriedly made up the bed, then looked around. It was obvious by his expression that something was missing.

Haymes immediately saw the problem and reached under his bunk to a small box where he kept his personal belongings. He then tossed a small object to Augustus. "I've got an extra."

Augustus took the ring and bounced it off the blanket. The ring popped up several inches and he knew the bunk was tight.

"Keep it."

Augustus looked at the ring. He tried to slip it onto his finger but the ring was too small.

"When we get over to the stables we'll have the farrier to open it up for that big finger of yours. But now, get dressed. We ain't got much time."

Augustus was nearly dressed, when the door suddenly opened.

"Atten-hut!" a voice boomed.

The troopers hurried in front of their bunks and stood at attention. Augustus followed suit as he heard the voice of Sergeant Moss Liberty dress down the first trooper he inspected.

"Look at them boots. They covered with mud, Trooper. If you ever stand inspection with muddy boots again, you'll be wearin' your ears on the tops of your boots!" Liberty jerked his head to the corporal and said, "Two days mess detail!"

Down the line Liberty went, chewing out each of the men. Perhaps there was no way possible to pass inspection.

Augustus was staring straight ahead when Liberty's face suddenly appeared before his eyes. Augustus swallowed as he looked into the fiery eyes. This could not be the same man who had rescued him on the prairie and brought him to meet his family. Liberty was now hard-faced, his fists balled, and his voice harsh.

"Eyes straight ahead, young soldier!" barked Liberty.

Augustus froze, but he could see Liberty reach into his pocket and step to the bunk. He heard the faint sound of the ring bounce off the tightened blanket.

Liberty again was in Augustus' face, his breath hot as he snapped, "You best learn to tighten that bunk, do you understand me, boy?" He said "boy" with an obvious delight in his voice.

Augustus nodded meekly.

Liberty's eyes widened. "When I ask you a question you say 'Yes, sir!' or 'No, sir!' Is that understood?"

"Yes, sir."

Liberty shook his head. "I can't hear you, boy!"

"Yes, sir!" Augustus shouted.

Liberty's eyes slowly scanned Augustus' area, then settled on the Sharps rifle leaning against the wall. "After inspection you take that Big Fifty to the barracks armorer and have it stored with the other weapons. Is that understood?"

Augustus stammered, "Sergeant Liberty, the sergeant major said—"

"Don't fat mouth me, boy. Just do as you're told! Is that understood?"

"Yes, sir!" Augustus shouted.

"When you finish morning mess, you report to the orderly room at regimental headquarters. Sergeant Major Brassard wants a word with you. You got that?"

"What kind of word?"

Liberty's nostrils flared; his eyes widened, and he bit off another piece of the young soldier. "He didn't bother tellin' me, boy. You're in the cavalry. You don't ask—you just do!"

"Yes, sir!" Augustus shouted.

Liberty turned and marched down the aisle and out of the barracks.

A voice shouted, "At ease!"

A heavy sigh of relief issued collectively from the troopers, followed by nervous laughter.

Haymes slapped Augustus on the back, nearly knocking him over as he stood on shaking legs. "Welcome to the cavalry, Augustus."

Augustus picked up the Sharps and walked to the front of the barracks, where a corporal was already unlocking the weapons rack. Thirty Spencer rifles were stacked in the rack, with several empty slots still available. Augustus handed the rifle to the corporal and started to walk away, then paused and looked again at the buffalo gun.

Since his capture by the Kiowa, the only pride he had known was his accurate firing of the Sharps; the only comfort, the sudden kick against his shoulder, reminding him he was still alive.

To Augustus, the Sharps was more than a rifle: it was a trusted companion.

Augustus stood in the cold blackness with the other members of H Troop, 10th Cavalry, wearing his freshly issued boots and uniform, which included a heavy coat made from a buffalo robe; on his head he wore a pile hat made from buffalo fur with ear flaps that could be tied beneath the chin.

The Buffalo Soldiers truly looked like dark buffaloes, standing at attention as the platoon leaders took the roll from each platoon sergeant, then turned and faced Sergeant Major Brassard. In numerical order the platoon leaders reported the status of their platoons until they reached Augustus's platoon, where Lieutenant O'Kelly reported, "All present and accounted for."

When the complete roll was reported, Brassard turned and saluted Captain Louis Carpenter, a short, rotund man with a thick white walrus mustache. Carpenter had been one of the

first officers to join the 10th. A Civil War cavalry commander, he was breveted for gallantry. Augustus had heard the men
speak highly of Carpenter, but not higher than the officer to
whom Carpenter then saluted and made his report.

Colonel Benjamin H. Grierson was the regimental commander of the 10th, whose headquarters were now at Fort
Wallace. Grierson, who had led the famous Grierson Raid,
was a tall, heavyset man with a thick, flowing beard that hid
a massive scar on his cheek where he had been kicked by a
horse while growing up in Illinois. During the Civil War he
had volunteered for the infantry, but later was assigned to the
cavalry, where he was forced to overcome the fear of horses
that had haunted him since childhood. He had been a music
teacher before the war and was a violinist, and one of his first
tasks during the organizing of the 10th was to form a regimental band.

The formation was dismissed and Lieutenant O'Kelly approached Haymes and Augustus, who were starting for the
mess hall.

"Trooper Haymes," said O'Kelly.

Haymes saluted, and glanced at Augustus, an urgency in his
eyes that Augustus didn't understand. Finally, Haymes said,
"Salute the lieutenant."

Augustus saluted. O'Kelly smiled lightly, then returned the
salute, saying to Augustus, "You must be the new recruit the
sergeant major told me about."

Recalling the earlier incident with Liberty, Augustus
shouted, "Yes, sir!"

O'Kelly looked at him in astonishment. "I can hear quite
well, Trooper. There's no need to shout." Then he turned to
Haymes. "Trooper Haymes, after you finish morning mess,
requisition a horse and buggy and report to my quarters."

Haymes saluted, and O'Kelly walked off. Haymes started
for the stables.

"Ain't you going to eat, Isaiah?" asked Augustus.

Haymes shook his head. "I best get that hoss and buggy for
the lieutenant."

Augustus went to the mess hall, ate quickly, then reported to the regimental orderly room.

Sergeant Major Brassard was sitting at his desk when Augustus entered the orderly room. Brassard rose and led him into the small office where Captain Carpenter was talking with Colonel Grierson.

Brassard nodded politely at the two officers, then said to Grierson, "This is Trooper Sharps. He's the young man I was telling you about, sir."

Grierson studied Augustus for a moment. In a voice that almost sounded gentle, he said, "I understand you were captured by the Kiowa."

"Yes, sir!" Augustus shouted.

Grierson chuckled. "I'm not deaf, Trooper Sharps."

"No, sir." Augustus's voice was now lower.

Grierson went to a large map that included Kansas and the Indian Territory. Grierson swept his hand over the map, then asked, "Do you know this territory, Trooper Sharps?"

Augustus looked at the map, then shook his head. "I don't know how to read a map, sir."

"Do you think you could recollect the areas you might have traveled?"

Augustus didn't have to think about the answer. "Yes, sir. From the Canadian River, north to the Republican, and west into Colorado Territory."

Grierson appeared pleased by this answer. "How was it this buffalo hunter was able to avoid being seen with you? Surely he must have had to go into towns or settlements for rations."

Augustus didn't want to remember, but he knew it was a part of his life that couldn't be avoided. "He would tie me up and leave me on the prairie, or in a thicket of trees. He once hid me in a cave for three days."

"Three days without food and water?"

"Yes, sir. I thought I was going to die."

"It must have been a difficult experience."

Augustus looked at Grierson. "The biggest fear was that he'd get drunk and killed in some scuffle."

"I understand. Then you would have been left alone to die."

Augustus' mouth tightened, and he said, "No, sir. I was afraid when he died I wouldn't be there to see it . . . or be the one to kill him."

There was a long silence as the men stared at Augustus. Then, Carpenter said, "I understand you're a fair shot with a Sharps rifle."

Augustus grinned. "Yes, sir. I generally hit what I aim at, sir."

The officers laughed, then Grierson asked, "What's the longest shot you figure you've ever made?"

Augustus thought for a moment. "I couldn't rightly say, sir."

Brassard said, "Sergeant Liberty saw him kill a buffalo at more than a thousand yards."

Grierson was visibly impressed. He told Augustus, "I might have use for your shooting talent in the next few days, Trooper Sharps. Meanwhile, the sergeant major will supervise your training."

Brassard snapped to attention. "Yes, sir." He took Augustus by the elbow and steered him from the office.

"What was that all about, Sergeant Major?"

Brassard only said, "Report to Sergeant Liberty. He's going to start your training this morning."

Augustus put on his pile cap and left; Brassard, with a huge grin, winked at the clerk.

"You got no imagination what it's like to be a slave," Marie would always say as they started the morning fires beneath the huge black kettles.

"I was born a slave," Selona Liberty always replied, then she would bend down and stir the fire, being careful to bring up a burning ember to light Marie's pipe. "But I know you're going to tell me how lucky I was not to have lived in slavery."

Then she would listen to the litany she had heard every

morning since the day she could remember: the life of a slave; the life of a camp follower; the hardships suffered by Colored people on the frontier. The whole list. But on this day her grandmother added something new to the conversation.

"You got to own a piece of land," Marie said, puffing on the pipe while throwing more wood on the fire.

"What piece of land?"

"The piece of land you're going to own some day."

"I ain't ever going to own a piece of land."

Marie took a long draw from the pipe and stared at the frozen street of Buffalo Bottoms.

"You will if you want it bad enough."

Selona had britches and blouses to wash; she threw a large batch of dirty drawers into the cauldron, stirred the clothes with a stick, and said softly, "I can't give no never mind to ever owning a piece of land. I just want May to come so we can go and pick flowers."

Lieutenant Jonathan O'Kelly knelt by the bed in the roughly hewn cabin on Officers Row. He gazed fondly at the small woman in the bed and saw her hands, reddened and rough, move from beneath the covers to rest against her alabaster face. Her long dark hair gleamed in the pale lantern light, and he wondered again if he shouldn't have stayed in Illinois and worked with his father instead of going to West Point.

Camille O'Kelly had wanted to be a soldier's wife, but she soon found it was not what she had expected. Parades, cotillions, and tea parties with other officers' wives were not what she found here.

She had found a life that was hard at best, cruel at worst.

She had tried hard, he told himself, since they arrived at Fort Wallace; but now the truth was clear: She needed help.

He kissed her lightly on the cheek, watching her stir with the delight he had felt as a boy seeing a baby bird for the first time.

Her eyes fluttered open, and she saw him, dressed in his uniform.

"I'd better start breakfast," she yawned, but he gentled her back into the bed as she tried to rise.

"I'll eat at the officers' mess," he said soothingly. She said, "Let me up. There are dirty uniforms lying in the closet. There's washing to be done."

He shook his head. "No. You're not going to do any more washing. From now on, we'll use the Colored laundresses."

"We can't afford to hire a laundress."

O'Kelly smiled. "We can afford a laundress." He laid a piece of paper on the dresser, saying, "Here's the name of a family that'll do the washing. Trooper Haymes is waiting outside with a horse and buggy. He'll drive you into Wallace and you can make the arrangements."

He kissed her on the forehead and left, his sabre dancing lightly from its harness.

Camille O'Kelly, at twenty-four, in this desolate wasteland, had realized that life in the military would not bring comfort.

She was living among savages—Colored people and Indians—and terrified to the bone, especially now, as her buggy approached Buffalo Bottoms.

Trooper Isaiah Haymes had said nothing on the way, having been born into slavery in Georgia and taught never to look a white man or woman in the eyes.

Camille stared at the mixture of ragged tents and shanty shacks, wondering how human beings could live in such squalor, when the buggy lurched in a muddy rut and swung sideways, throwing her into the mire.

"God Almighty," Haymes moaned. He stopped the horses, jumped down, ran to where she lay, and offered his hand.

Her eyes flashed as her words bit through the cold morning air, "Leave me be. You've done enough harm." She tried to rise but couldn't.

"Let me help, Missy," a voice said softly. Camille looked up and saw a young Colored girl standing nearby, reaching out to her. Behind her a crone puffed on a corncob pipe, and

Camille thought she saw a glint of enjoyment flash in her old dark eyes.

"What you doing down here, Missy?" asked the girl, gently pulling her to her feet. "You got no business coming down to the Bottoms."

Camille was covered with mud.

The old woman hurried into a nearby tent, all too obviously no longer able to contain her laughter.

The girl followed, guiding Camille inside the heavy flaps. The hot, sweltering tent didn't look fit for animals to live in. That cackling old crone sat on a bed near the stove next to a sickly looking Colored woman.

Camille said nothing as the girl began unbuttoning her coat.

"I'll get this washed for you in quick order, Missy," she said.

The girl gingerly stripped her dress and pantaloons, and left Camille sitting beneath a buffalo robe on a wooden crate as she raced back outside.

Near the kettles, Haymes stood frozen with fear.

"Lord, Miss Selona. What am I going to tell the lieutenant? He'll skin me for sure."

"Just go on back to the fort. Leave the buggy and I'll drive her back when we've got her cleaned up."

Trooper Haymes hurried off, wearing the look of a doomed man.

Selona threw the dress and pantaloons into the boiling cauldron and walked back to the tent and the whimpering Camille O'Kelly.

Lieutenant O'Kelly returned to his quarters immediately after Haynes' report of the incident; the trooper had been so terrified he could barely speak.

The place was cold and dark, except for the slight glow in the hearth, where the fire had been neglected. He started for the bedroom when his boot kicked something metallic. He reached down and picked up a metal flask engraved with his initials. She had given it to him upon his graduation from West Point.

The flask was empty.

"Where have you been!" Camille's hysterical voice shrilled. She was standing at the bedroom door, still dressed, and as she walked toward him she swayed, then stumbled and fell. O'Kelly caught her and sat her in a chair by the hearth. Her breath smelled of brandy, and in the dim light her features appeared mean; her delicate mouth curled in a cruel leer as she screamed again, "Where have you been!"

"I had to take a patrol to one of the line camps. We just returned a few minutes ago. I came as soon as Trooper Haymes told me what happened."

She grunted, "I want that Goddamned nigger court-martialed."

O'Kelly stiffened. He had never heard her swear an oath, nor speak of Colored people in such fashion. "He didn't commit a court-martial offense, darling."

She whimpered, and looking defeated said, "You love your niggers more than you love me."

"That's not true. Trooper Haymes explained what happened. He said the wheel hit a rut and you fell out of the buggy." O'Kelly then looked at the empty flask and asked, "Had you been drinking again?"

Her eyes flashed, and she snapped, "What do you mean, 'again'!"

He held up the flask. "I filled this last week, Camille. Now it's empty, and we both know it's not the first time."

There was a sudden wildness in her eyes as she stammered, "One of your niggers drank it. I saw him sneak in through the back window. I was so terrified I ran into the bedroom, but he found me." Her voice rose to a wail as she said, "He made me drink the brandy, then he put his hands on me."

O'Kelly stood slowly, then walked to the back window. The windows could be opened outward to allow air in during the summer, but in the winter they were tightly sealed with a thick caulk of mud and straw to insulate against the cold. He released the wooden catch on the window and pushed, but the window held fast. He pushed again, this time with greater force, until his hand broke the heavy glass and sliced his palm.

Camille shrieked, then jumped to her feet and ran into the bedroom.

O'Kelly watched her disappear. He walked to the hearth, where he slowly unwound the yellow scarf from his neck and wrapped his bleeding hand in the dim light.

He didn't feel pain from the wound; but pain was in his eyes, reflected in the mirror on the mantel.

5

The first time Augustus threw his leg over his newly issued horse and settled into the McClellan saddle, he felt as though he were riding a whirlwind.

"How does it sit?" asked Liberty, who was standing next to his saddled horse.

Augustus stretched out his legs, then stood in the saddle. "The stirrups are too long."

Liberty adjusted the straps, and Augustus tried again. This time he was satisfied.

Liberty then mounted and motioned Augustus to follow. They rode onto the far side of the large parade field to where poles stood in the frozen ground. In the distance, beyond the walls of the fort, there was the sound of firing from the rifle range.

Liberty drew his sabre from its scabbard, telling Augustus, "Being a cavalry trooper means you got to show pride. Always show pride. No matter what you're doing, whether on parade or in a fight with the Injuns." He raised the sword and executed a salute, then motioned Augustus to do the same.

Augustus sat at attention, drew his sabre, and saluted. Exhilaration flooded through his body.

"When making the charge, you draw your sabre, then spur your hoss. There are three basic manuevers: thrust, slash, and parry." Liberty demonstrated each maneuver, first thrusting forward, then slashing at each side. Finally, he parried an invisible attacker. Then he sat at attention for a moment, and when ready, released a loud yell as he spurred his horse to a gallop and charged toward a pole, where his sabre cut a deep notch into the scarred target. Without breaking stride, he wheeled his horse, struck the pole again, and rejoined Augustus.

Liberty motioned toward the pole. "Give it a try, young soldier."

Augustus saluted with the sabre, then spurred the horse to a gallop. He rode first in a straight line, standing in the iron stirrups, sabre extended over the head of the horse, gripping the reins tightly in his other hand. He brought the sabre back and with a vicious swing cut a chunk from the pole, then wheeled the horse and charged at the oblique. To the amazement of Liberty, he pulled his pistol from his holster, gripping the reins in his teeth, becoming a charging flash of fury with both weapons extended to the ready.

Augustus came abreast of the pole, cut another notch, passed the pole, turned, and pointed the pistol at the pole, but did not fire.

Suddenly, from one of the 10th barracks, troopers started cheering and clapping.

Brassard was standing on the front steps of the orderly room, but he wasn't watching Augustus. He was studying a group of 7th Cavalry troopers on the far side of the parade field, noticing that their attention was on Augustus. A coldness icier than the air cut at Brassard's stomach as the young trooper rode closer to what was called "the line," which divided the parade ground between troopers of the 10th Cavalry on one side, troopers of the 7th Cavalry on the other. There was no clear line drawn in the frozen ground, but the colors of their skin built a wall higher than the sharpened logs that rimmed the fort. Augustus was now riding dangerously close to what all Buffalo Soldiers considered enemy territory.

Suddenly, a roar rose from the 7th side as a trooper charged toward the center of the field.

Trooper Jeremy Davis was from the Dakota Territory and had been in the 7th for nearly a year; he was redheaded, with piercing blue eyes that were now aflame as he rode toward Augustus, his sabre extended.

Augustus' stomach tightened. He holstered his pistol and prepared to meet the challenge.

Trooper Davis came at Augustus from his right, sabre extended, and their cold steel met with a shrill that resounded over the parade ground.

All fell silent, except for the sound of eight pounding hooves, the strained breathing of two charging horses, and the joining of two cold sabres.

On the next pass Davis tried a different tactic, thrusting the sabre dangerously close in this mock battle, but Augustus parried to the outside and slapped the flat of the blade across Davis' back as he passed.

This brought a thunderous roar from the 10th troopers, who by now had emptied the barracks to watch the duel.

Trooper Davis wheeled his horse and charged again, not realizing he had crossed the line into 10th territory, driving Augustus into 7th territory. Neither cared as their eyes met in challenge. Augustus saw the slash coming and prepared to parry to the outside, but at the last possible moment Davis feinted to the outside, leaning hard into the neck of his horse, and as Augustus passed, slashing at empty air, Davis rose quickly and slapped the flat of his blade across Augustus' back.

The roar from the 7th Cavalry was nearly deafening.

The back-and-forth duel continued for nearly twenty minutes, with every eye in the fort trained on the two troopers, until, finally, the horses began losing strength in the bitter cold. Both troopers reined up, facing each other. They saluted with the sabres and simultaneously returned the blades to their scabbards with a resounding *zzzilch!*

Trooper Davis kneed his horse forward to Augustus and extended his hand. They shook, and Augustus realized this was the first white man ever to offer him his hand. Davis said nothing; he merely nodded and rode toward the stables of the 7th Cavalry horses.

Augustus dismounted and was walking his mount toward the stables of the 10th when he heard a voice commanding him to halt. Turning, he snapped to attention when he saw a sharp-faced, long-haired officer wearing the shoulder bars of a lieutenant colonel.

"That was a daring piece of horsemanship, Trooper." Lieutenant Colonel George Armstrong Custer stood with another man who also wore his hair long.

Augustus saluted sharply. "Thank you, sir."

The other man, dressed in buckskin, added, "Maybe you ought to have this trooper give your Seventh boys a few pointers, Colonel."

Custer stared hard at the man, then said, "My men couldn't learn anything from the Tenth Cavalry, Mr. Hickok."

Augustus' eyes widened, for he knew the name of the famous frontiersman. "Are you 'Wild Bill' Hickok, sir?"

The man nodded. "My name is James Hickok. I'm a scout for Colonel Custer. Some folks call me Wild Bill, though I don't know how they came up with the 'Bill.' " He paused for a moment, then seemed to realize something important. "Are you the shooter that worked for Charlie Calhoun?"

Augustus stiffened. "I didn't shoot for him because I wanted to, Mr. Hickok. But I was there when he was killed."

Hickok said with unconcealed pleasure, "The world won't regret his passing."

"No, sir."

Colonel Custer asked, "Where did you learn to ride and use a sabre, Trooper?"

Augustus took a deep breath, his thoughts tumbling back to darker moments in his life. "I was a Kiowa captive for nearly two years. After a few months they let me take part in their games. Instead of using sabres, they used a short spear. Or tomahawks. The tactics are much the same."

Custer nodded. "I've joined in the games myself, only it was with the Cheyenne." Custer started to walk away, but stopped, a gleam in his eye. "You were a buffalo hunter?"

"Yes, sir."

"I'd wager you're a fair hand with a rifle. Is that correct?"

"Yes, sir."

Custer merely nodded and walked off.

Hickok started to leave, but turned and warned him, "You best watch yourself now, son. Them Seventh Cav boys ain't gonna take lightly to eatin' this much mud." There was mischief in his eyes as he hurried along and joined Custer.

Augustus didn't understand; but when he looked to the far side of the stables, to the 7th Cavalry section, he understood.

Trooper Davis was not being treated politely. Sergeant John Armitage was dressing him down, pointing at Augustus with an angry finger. Then Armitage stormed away, pausing to glare at Augustus with a heat he had never seen from another man, even as a slave.

Augustus was eating noon mess when the door flew open and the shout of "Atten-hut!" brought all the troopers to their feet.

Colonel Benjamin Grierson strode through the door, followed by Captain Carpenter, Lieutenant O'Kelly, Sergeant Major Brassard, and Sergeant Liberty.

Grierson looked around briefly until his eyes found Augustus. The colonel started forward, slowly removing his gloves, then said, "Go back to your eating, men."

The troopers sat down, but Grierson kept coming toward Augustus, followed by the officers and non-coms. Grierson stopped in front of Augustus, who quickly rose and started to salute, but was stopped by the sudden warning in Liberty's eyes, who had told him a soldier doesn't salute indoors except when reporting to an officer.

"Yes, sir," said Augustus.

Grierson slowly peeled off his gloves, then nodded at an empty chair.

Augustus quickly pulled out the chair and seated Grierson.

Stone silence filled the mess hall; some mouths were clenched, some agape, filled with food.

Grierson came straight to the point. "Trooper Sharps, do you know what is the most important quality of a military regiment?"

Augustus thought for a moment, then replied, "Courage?"

Grierson shook his head, then said, "Pride. Esprit de corps. It's the very core of a fighting unit."

"Yes, sir." Augustus swallowed the bit of fatback he still had in his mouth.

"This morning you gave the Tenth Cavalry a moment of pride. It was greatly appreciated by the officers and men of this regiment."

"Thank you, sir. But I didn't mean to start something with that boy from the Seventh, Colonel Grierson."

Grierson quickly said, "You didn't start anything. The Seventh has continuously made this regiment eat their dust for some time. What you did today gave them a well-deserved come-uppance." He paused, as though for effect. "A short while ago Colonel Custer came to me with a challenge."

"A challenge, sir?"

Grierson's deep eyes seemed to peer into Augustus' soul as he softly asked, "Do you know what a challenge is, Trooper Sharps?"

Augustus nodded. "To see if one man is better than another."

Grierson shook his head. "No, son. A challenge is to see if one man can overcome an obstacle that stands before him."

"I don't understand."

Grierson stood and put on his gloves, and without saying another word, turned and walked out of the mess hall, followed by the officers and Brassard.

Liberty stayed, staring at Augustus with the strange look

Augustus had once seen on a jackass who had its mouth filled with briars.

"What is he talking about, Sergeant Liberty?"

Liberty simply said, "Go to the barracks and fetch your Sharps rifle. I bought you some cartridges."

6

Low gray clouds hung heavy over Fort Wallace, barricading the sun from the rifle range. A light wind drifted from the west, sliding over a thick crust of frozen snow lightly powdered by a soft snow from the night before, giving the range a misty appearance. It would not be taken for a rifle range except for the eight shooting stations, less than a hundred yards from the fort.

Each station had a specific target positioned downrange, a different distance. The first station was fifty yards; the second seventy-five yards; the third, one hundred yards. The targets were wood planks set upright in the ground, bearing a round orange circle; behind each was a ten-foot-high berm designed to stop errant bullets.

The stations graduated to four hundred yards, where, as seen through Augustus' binoculars, the orange circle was unmarked by bullets.

Colonel Grierson stood off to one side, with the men of the 10th, more than a hundred, gathered around Sergeant Liberty. There was a sudden roar as Liberty walked from the group toward the 7th Cavalry, who were gathered around Armitage.

The two sergeants met in the center, each holding a fistful of money. Armitage glared at Liberty, then spat, saying, "We've got five hundred dollars. What'd you and your niggers come up with?"

Liberty smiled that soft smile he always offered when insulted by a white man. "We'll match your wager." Liberty looked around, noting aloud, "But we don't see your shooter."

Armitage turned and looked toward the fort, where a lone rider could be seen slowly approaching the large gathering. When the rider stopped at the 7th group, a loud roar went up. The man stepped from the saddle and shook hands with Custer.

Armitage spat again, saying to Liberty as he walked toward the 7th, "I reckon he's here. You best get your boy ready."

Augustus watched the rider chat for a few moments with Custer. Then the two men approached the firing line.

The shooter for the 7th had long flowing hair, with a thick, sagging mustache; he wasn't in army uniform, but he wore fringed buckskins and a heavy buffalo coat. In his arms he cradled a Sharps rifle.

Augustus saw Grierson bristle as Custer and the shooter approached the firing line. "I must protest, Colonel Custer. I thought we agreed that the contestants would be members of the regiments."

Custer removed his pile cap and swept it toward his shooter, replying, "This man is a member of the Seventh Cavalry regiment. As a matter of fact, as you know, he's our chief scout."

Augustus studied the man, whose eyes were piercing and steady; his gloved hands held the rifle with the ease of an artist holding a paintbrush.

The shooter removed his gloves and extended a hand to Augustus, saying simply, "My name is Bill Cody."

At that moment a chant went up from the 7th: "Buffalo Bill! Buffalo Bill! Buffalo Bill!"

Cody looked at Augustus for a long moment, then said, "I hear tell you're more than a fair hand with a Sharps."

Augustus was shaking, and didn't know if it was from the cold or the fact that he was about to have a shooting match with a frontier legend. "I hear tell you're more than a fair shooter as well, Mr. Cody."

Cody took a plug of tobacco from his coat, cut off a chew, and stuck it in his mouth. He offered Augustus a chew, but Augustus shook his head. Then Cody said, "I reckon we best find out."

Custer chimed in as the two walked to the firing line, "Gentlemen, I see no need for starting this contest at any distance less than six hundred yards. It is mighty cold, and my regiment prefers the quick kill to the slow death."

Grierson said to Custer, "The range doesn't have a six-hundred-yard marker."

Custer smiled, then suggested, "We'll move back two hundred yards."

Grierson wore a worried look as he turned quickly to Augustus, who nodded. Before he realized the words had issued, Augustus said, "I think seven hundred yards would be proper."

A gasp rose from the 10th, a cheer from the 7th.

Cody spat a stream of tobacco juice, and asked Augustus, "How does eight hundred yards sound, Trooper?"

Augustus said nothing. He merely hoisted his Sharps onto his shoulder and started walking toward what he figured would be eight hundred yards from the target. Cody followed as shouts from the 7th filled the air; stone silence had now settled upon the troopers of the 10th.

At eight hundred yards a target is barely visible, even to the keenest eye, as both Augustus and Cody had learned from shooting buffalo. But a buffalo is a large creature, and though it may be only a speck in the distance, the silhouette offers enough sight picture to give the shooter an aiming reference. After that, it is pure windage and elevation.

Custer took a twenty-dollar double eagle from his coat and said, "Eagle up gets the first shot. Since the Seventh made the challenge, we'll call the eagle."

Grierson nodded, then Custer tossed the coin into the air. The gold coin hit the hard ground, pitched upward, then settled, and Custer said, "Eagle up. Bill, you get the first shot."

Cody took his shooting rest, a steel rod with a U at the top for resting the barrel, and worked it into the ground.

Cody looked at Augustus and asked, "Do you have a rest?"

Augustus shook his head. "Never used one." Instead, Augustus began scooping snow with his boots, forming a mound the way he had always done when shooting buffalo for Charlie Calhoun.

Cody took his Sharps, snapped open the breech, and shoved a long cartridge into the chamber. He then laid the barrel into the rest, flipped up the rear sight and began the tedious process of adjusting to the distance by looking at the silhouette, figuring where the target lay in reference to the berm, then moving the sights the minute increments he thought would put him on target. Then he took a small pinch of snow, worked it into powder with his fingers, and let it fall, watching the direction it was blown by the wind.

"Little easterly, Trooper," Cody said, as he knelt on one knee, then nestled the butt of his Sharps into the well of his shoulder.

The wait seemed interminable, then Cody squeezed the trigger. A loud boom followed, and a cloud formed as the heat from the discharge met the cold air, and would have shrouded the frontiersman's view, except he had fired at a great distance in the cold on many occasions. The moment he fired, Cody quickly stepped to his left and gazed at the target.

Eight hundred yards downrange, a puff of snow kicked up in front of the target.

Augustus knew that Cody was getting the range, and had Cody stayed behind the rest he would not have been able to see through the frosty cloud, and would not have seen the bullet strike.

Custer was eyeing the target through his binoculars, as was Grierson. "Raise twenty yards, Bill."

Grierson watched Augustus stretch out on the cold ground and rest his Sharps on top of the mound. He tore a bit of fur from his buffalo coat, let the strands drift into the wind, then carefully adjusted his sights. Smoothly, he cocked the rifle, took a deep breath, slowly released half the air in his lungs, then squeezed the trigger.

The boom echoed, and Augustus rolled left and watched as a puff of snow kicked up downrange.

Grierson was watching through his binoculars and said, "Raise thirty yards, Trooper Sharps."

The match went on for another hour with each shooter slowly inching toward the target until Cody struck wood on his twelfth shot. A roar went up from the 7th as Custer danced a little jig, telling Cody, "You hit bottom right, but you hit wood. If Trooper Sharps doesn't strike wood, the match is yours."

Augustus lowered himself to the ground and slowly nestled the rifle butt into his shoulder, tested the wind, then studied the dark speck in the distance. He eared back the hammer, breathed in, released half the air, and slowly squeezed.

The boom echoed over the 10th troopers standing to his left, and not a sound was heard. Augustus had rolled left and did not see the snow kick as it had done on the previous eleven shots.

Grierson sat on his horse, studying the target, then said calmly, "Trooper Sharps has cut the orange."

The troopers from the 10th released a collective shout, then raced toward Augustus and raised him onto their shoulders. As Augustus became lost in the sea of jubilant Buffalo Soldiers, Cody shook his head admiringly, Custer cursed and kicked at the frozen ground, Grierson swelled with pride, and Liberty went in search of Armitage and the wager won by Trooper Augustus Sharps.

The Buffalo Soldiers were in a state of ecstacy that night. Augustus' barracks swelled to the point of collapsing as nearly a hundred troopers packed into whatever space could be found. Haymes was playing wildly on the harmonica, the cooks had brought food from the mess hall, and kegs of beer had been supplied by the officers.

When it seemed impossible to hear or allow another person entrance, the door opened and Gibbs, standing near the rifle rack, shouted, "Atten-hut!"

Colonel Grierson, Carpenter, O'Kelly, Brassard, and Liberty entered the barracks.

Grierson removed his pile cap as his eyes searched the quiet troopers. A smile came to his face as his eyes found Augustus. Grierson looked at Liberty and gave a simple nod.

The crowd of troopers parted as Liberty pushed his way toward the rifle rack. He unlocked the rack and removed the Sharps rifle.

Holding the Sharps above his head like a great trophy, Liberty worked his way through the troopers crowding the aisle.

Augustus was sitting on his bunk when Liberty leaned past Haymes, handed the rifle to Augustus, and said, "Colonel Grierson said you can keep the rifle by your bunk."

A cheer went up, filtering through the caulked walls of the barracks, and drifted across the cold night air above the parade ground, then finally settled in the barracks where troopers of the 7th Cavalry sat in silence.

7

By the end of March, Augustus' training was nearly completed, but his duties in the orderly room were now taking up most of his day. Which he disliked. Like most soldiers he had become accustomed to the regimen of army life. Life in the barracks wasn't as bad as some men thought, and for the first time in his life he was making friends.

Isaiah Haymes was a close friend, who wiled away the barracks hours playing his harmonica when he wasn't playing the piano at Philadelphia Phil's for a few extra dollars. Troopers were paid twelve dollars a month, but if they didn't drink or gamble they could usually stretch their wages from payday to payday, which came every four months.

"What you think, Augustus? We ever goin' to do any real fightin', or just guard the railroad line?"

Augustus was cleaning his Sharps on his bunk. "I'd say the fighting is going to get real serious, Isaiah. The Indians are being pushed farther and farther off their land. I don't think they'll take much more."

"Me neither. I'd sure like to get into a good scrap with them."

Augustus tensed for a moment, then relaxed, as though he was comfortable with what he was going to say. "Yes, that would suit me just fine, too."

Haymes grew serious. "You really hate them Injuns, don't you?"

Augustus sighted down the barrel. "More than you can ever know."

Haymes looked around the barracks at the other troopers, and recalled that many of them carried the burden of hate. Most of it was directed toward their white slave masters. Yet they were willing to die for people who treated them as though they were less than human.

Trooper Gibbs' back was a web of tangled scars from a whipping he'd been given as a boy; he had tried to run away but never made it beyond the plantation cornfield.

Trooper Moses Franklin walked with a limp. He'd had his leg broken by an overseer after he was caught trying to escape.

The one they called Trooper Done-Gots-My-Freedom spoke strangely, his tongue cut in half for talking back to the son of his master.

And they were all here, standing ready and willing to die in the name of Manifest Destiny, the doctrine that was gradually usurping land from Indians, land for farms and towns where the Coloreds wouldn't be welcome.

Augustus ran a cleaning rod through the barrel of the Sharps and returned the rifle to the weapons rack just as the door flew open.

Trooper John Bales stumbled through the door, holding his stomach. Blood seeped through his fingers; dark blood, which was freezing on his fingers.

"One of them Seventh troopers done killed me," Bales moaned as he fell to the floor.

Augustus and Haymes reached him first and hoisted him onto a bunk. "Get the sergeant of the guard!" Haymes shouted.

Bales' eyes were wide, staring emptily at the ceiling while his fingers clutched at his blouse. His coat was gone, as were the buttons on his blouse and the chevrons on his sleeves.

By now the bed was surrounded by the troopers, the anger etched deep in their faces.

"Let's get those sonsabitches," Moses Franklin said. He went to the weapons rack, jerked his Spencer free, and started for the door.

"I'm with you," Done-Gots-My-Freedom said. He, too, grabbed his Spencer.

A trooper at the door yelled, "Here's blood. Follow the blood." Then he was out the door.

Within seconds the barracks was empty except for Augustus and Haymes, who were trying desperately to stop the bleeding from the wound in Bales' stomach. Haymes tried to free Bales' blouse and reached under him. He brought his blood-covered hand up from Bales' back. "Good Lord, Augustus, he's been run clean through!"

Augustus gently removed the blouse, then peeled down the top of Bales' longjohns and saw the wound. A blade had entered just below the sternum and come out through the kidney.

It was unmistakably a sabre wound.

The night outside filled with shouts. Then there was the roar of a pistol, and then another, and then the baritone voice of Brassard:

"Get back in the barracks. Now! Move! Every damn one of you!"

The troopers backed angrily into the barracks, followed by Brassard, whose face bore a look of meanness Augustus had never seen on a man.

Across the parade field, the 7th troopers had emptied onto the parade ground; all except Trooper Jeremy Davis and Armitage, who sat on his bunk, running an oily rag along the length of his sabre. When Armitage had finished cleaning the sabre, he returned it to the scabbard, not noticing he had dropped the cleaning rag.

Davis saw that the rag was not only dirty from grime and oil, but soaked with blood.

*   *   *

The night had been long for O'Kelly, who returned to his quarters shortly after sunrise. Camille was awake and sitting at the small kitchen table.

"I'll fix you some breakfast," she said softly.

He shook his head. "There's no time. I've got to get back to the orderly room. Captain Carpenter wants to start an immediate investigation of the incident."

Camille shrugged. "I don't know why you're so concerned over a Colored being killed. They're soldiers. They're supposed to be killed."

O'Kelly could only look at his wife. "They're my men, Camille. My responsibility. Besides, this happened on the fort, not in the field."

"Do you have to assist in the investigation?"

"Yes."

"Do you have any suspicions?"

He sighed heavily. "I only pray that it wasn't one of the white soldiers. There's still a lot of hatred among the Colored soldiers and the ex-Rebs."

Camille spoke in alarm. "You don't think there could be trouble inside the fort!"

"There could be if it's a white soldier."

It was as though something trying to snap within her finally reached its limit of endurance.

"Then I won't leave this room. I won't be exposed to these savages anymore."

"That's absurd. You're not in danger."

Her voice rose to a shriek. "All the wives of the officers are terrified, Jonathan. Everywhere we go there's Colored soldiers. I can feel their eyes on me when I walk across the parade ground."

"You won't be harmed. I promise." He started to leave, then turned and said, "Try not to worry, dearest. I know these men. They're eager to prove themselves to this country. They take a lot of pride in the uniform. They won't cause any trouble."

When he had left she went to his desk in the corner and removed the metal flask bearing his initials.

As she drank the brandy she could feel its warmth, and she could feel it obscure the frightening images of Colored soldiers chasing her through the night.

As she had dreamed the night before.

Sergeant Major Brassard had been awake most of the night dealing with the aftermath of the murder. The men were ready to confront the 7th troopers with fists, knives, or guns, if necessary, to seek justice.

A quick discussion with Captain Carpenter led to a solution for cooling heated tempers: Send the troops into the field.

O'Kelly was unwilling to leave Camille alone when she was suffering such depression and fright, and he sought out Sergeant Liberty.

"Sergeant, I was wondering if it might be acceptable for your daughter to stay with my wife while we're in the field? I'd be glad to pay her. Ten cents a night and her meals."

Moss didn't like having Selona away from Della, but he understood from the look on O'Kelly's face that the man was truly concerned.

"I'll go to my quarters and speak with my family."

Selona stepped through the door of the O'Kelly quarters as though into another dimension. She had never known hardwood floors, only hard dirt, and she had never looked through glass windows except in the small store in Wallace; though the O'Kelly quarters were nearly uninhabitable to Camille, to Selona they were a palace.

A small bed had been set up in the kitchen for Selona, who, since she could remember, had slept on a pallet with Marie on the other side of the hanging blanket separating the tent.

"Oh, Missy. This is wonderful!" Selona squealed in delight.

Moss was standing by the front door, not about to take another step inside a white officer's quarters. He just smiled at Selona, then bowed slightly to Mrs. O'Kelly and hurried out.

"Daddy! Wait," Selona shouted. She ran through the doorway, threw her arms around Moss, and hugged him tightly.

"You best be a good girl," he whispered throatily. "And be sure to get up early and help your mama with the wash, then hurry back by noon to Miss Camille. She'll have chores waiting for you."

She kissed him on the cheek. "I will."

Then he was gone, swallowed by the thunder of horses tromping and snorting on the frozen parade ground.

That afternoon Selona had finished cooking supper and had washed the dishes when Camille came from her bedroom to the tiny sitting room near the front door. She appeared different to Selona, who couldn't quite understand why. Camille had said little to her that day.

Camille was holding a folded piece of paper and instructed her, "Take this to the Baxter store in Wallace. Tell Mr. Baxter it's for my medicine and please charge it to my account."

Selona put on her heavy coat made from buffalo fur, and walked into the cold air.

She passed through the front gate and began the short walk to Baxter's. The road was icy and slick, and the footing wasn't sure, but she reached the store and gave the clerk the paper. He read the order, then disappeared into the back and returned with a small wrapped package.

"You be careful, now, you hear?" he said as he handed the package to Selona. "Don't drop this, girl."

She started back to the fort, following the worn wagon wheel impressions in the frozen ground until she had the front gate in sight. Her feet were cold, her hands nearly frostbitten when, suddenly, a horse and rider bolted through the main gate and nearly trampled her.

She rolled away from harm, then slowly pulled herself to

her feet, and saw the package lying wet and broken in the
street. There was a strong smell of something she didn't rec-
ognize, but it made her nostrils sting.

Selona arrived at the O'Kelly quarters heartbroken, freezing, and terrified.

"I'm sorry, Missy." She held out the wet package to Mrs.
O'Kelly, whose eyes widened in horror.

Before Selona knew what was happening, she felt herself
being dragged toward the bed. She was thrown on the bed,
turned onto her stomach, and, too terrified to move, watched
in silence as Camille went to the kitchen and returned carrying a razor strop.

Selona saw the half-crazed look on her face, then the arc of
her arm, then the sting of the leather razor strop across her
back.

Fright and pain were sharp. Selona tried to rise but Camille
took her hand and held her tight, inflicting more and more
pain with each descending blow.

But the most frightening thing of all for Selona was the silence: Camille never said a word of admonition.

She merely smiled with each blow.

There was no hiding the beating from Marie, who had suffered
many in her life as a slave.

The craggy-faced old woman took warm molasses to a deep
welt on Selona's back, making certain she said something
soothing to help Selona's thoughts drift away from the stinging pain.

"That old sunshine bird with the black speckles'll be back
soon, and then comes the warm summer," she said gently. She
dabbed the molasses on another welt and felt Selona quiver as
the pain rushed through her body.

"It's called a meadowlark, Grams," Selona moaned.

"Meadowlark. Sunshine bird. Don't make no never mind
what folks call it . . . it'll be back and so will summer. You wait
and see."

Marie finished dressing the welts, and held her grandchild the way she had been held after her first whipping.

Then she put Selona in a long nightshirt, tucked her onto the pallet, and went to the small chair next to the hanging blanket. She struck a match and lit her pipe and listened to the whimpers until Selona finally fell asleep.

The nightmare jerked Camille from her sleep, and as she looked at the leathery face before her eyes she thought she had gone from one nightmare to the next. This was the more frightening.

"Who are you?"

"I'm the Devil, and the Good Lord, and the woman who nursed the wounds of a child you beat." Marie's eyes seemed to turn into two fiery bolts of lightning.

"What do you want? How did you get in here?"

"I wants you . . . and I can get in anywheres." Marie pulled a long sharp knife from beneath her heavy buffalo overcoat. She pressed the sharpened edge of the blade to Camille's throat.

"This evening you beat my child like a cur dog running the street. Well, Missy, let me tell you about a cur dog. You can whup it all over town, but when it gets under its own front porch and you try to whup it . . . that cur'll bite your leg off." Marie waved her hand around the bedroom. "This here is now my grandbaby's place of work. What me and you going to call her front porch. And I'm the cur!"

Camille felt the blade press even closer against her skin.

"If you ever take a strop to her again, or touch a hair on her head, I'll cut you the three ways the overseers did it on the plantation." Marie paused for effect, and added, "Wide, deep, and from your nose to your toes. And I ain't gonna give no never mind to the sheriff, or no lynching, 'cause I'm just an old nigger woman that's lived through being a slave and can' nothin' hurt me ceptin' someone hurtin' my baby."

Marie slowly straightened and then there was no movement except her hand, and the knife disappearing beneath the buffalo coat.

"You best remember that."

Then she was gone.

8

On Augustus' first patrol his squad was sent to scout an area south of the Arkansas River, desolate territory void of people and trees, except for those trees found in deep coulees. It was in a coulee that Gibbs, the patrol leader, ordered Augustus, Haymes, and three troopers to hole up for the night.

The men hobbled their horses on a picket line but kept them saddled and ready to mount; three slept while three stood guard.

It was during the guard change at midnight that Augustus began prowling uneasily around the camp, studying the sky, tasting the wind.

"Something wrong, Augustus?" asked Haymes.

"Bad weather coming our way."

Haymes shook his head, telling Gibbs, who lay near the fire, "Augustus is better than a beetle in a matchbox for predicting weather."

Gibbs stood and warmed his hands. Once Augustus was gone, he said, "We best build up this fire."

An hour later a heavy rain soaked men, animals, and equip-

ment; sleet followed, then a fine sharp snow driven by a heavy
wind that roared out of the northwest. The next morning,
standing in three feet of snow, the troopers ate hardtack for
breakfast, then mounted their horses and rode out of the
coulee and onto the freezing flatlands, moving north toward
the Arkansas River.

The wind whipped at them, shrouding them in a cloud of
piercing snow. The horses plowed slowly through deep drifts
that drained their strength. The horses' muzzles froze, then
their noses, until finally the first animal went down.

"We got to find a place to hole up, Augustus," said Gibbs.
It was the worst blizzard he had seen in his life.

There was nothing but frozen, snow-covered prairie in all
directions.

"We ain't going to make it!" shouted Haymes.

Augustus thought for a moment, then remembered a lesson
learned from the Kiowa. "We'll make a fort out of the horses."
Without another word he slid from the saddle and walked to
the front of his horse. He removed his pistol and fired between
the eyes.

"Get off that horse," he shouted to one of the troopers.
Then he pulled the horse near his fallen animal and fired again.

Minutes later the six horses lay dead in a circle. "Get your
saddle blankets and tie them off over the horses. That'll make
us a tent."

"Then what?" asked the trooper, who was staring wildly
at his dead horse.

"We get underneath and ride out the storm."

"How we going to get back to the fort? We ain't got no
hosses!" The young trooper, whose name was Thurman Luke,
was near panic.

Augustus gripped him by the shoulder. "First we have to
survive the storm. Then we'll worry about what comes next."

The men did as instructed; within minutes they lay on the
cold prairie, surrounded by dead horses and roofed by their
blankets.

Minutes later the horses and blue-blanket tent disappeared
beneath the snow.

The men huddled together; their bodies gradually warmed the small space as the snow provided insulation and protection from the wind.

Trooper Haymes took out his harmonica and began playing softly.

Outside the storm raged and the music from the juice harp was swallowed by the howl of the wind.

The sound of a train whistle stirred Augustus from sleep. He tried to move but felt as though he were buried beneath an avalanche of snow. Indeed, the snow had pressed the blankets down on top of the troopers.

"I hear a train!" Augustus shouted.

The six men began stirring until they were able to push the snow off the blankets and open them up. In the distance they could see a work train moving slowly across the white prairie.

"Grab your saddles! Can't be leaving General Sheridan's equipment behind for the Indians," Gibbs ordered.

The troopers grabbed their McClellan saddles and started toward the railroad tracks.

They had come within a quarter mile of the train when Augustus heard Gibbs yell, "Cheyenne!"

Augustus saw several dozen Indians on horseback moving swiftly through the trail the soldiers had slogged through the snow.

The situation was hopeless if they tried to run for the tracks. Augustus yelled, "Put the saddles in a circle. Get your rifles!"

The Cheyenne came at them straight on, firing rifles and filling the sky with arrows. The snow kicked up where the bullets struck; arrows thudded into the saddles.

"Hold steady," Gibbs ordered. "Don't fire until I give the command."

The Cheyenne warriors neared until their eyes were visible. Gibbs gave the command. "Fire!"

A fusillade of bullets from the saddle fort knocked several warriors from their ponies. There was a pause. Then the band broke into three groups, all on foot since the ponies couldn't move through the heavy snow with much speed. Augustus watched as one group of warriors approached from the front while two smaller groups began circling the soldiers.

Augustus crawled beside Gibbs, telling him, "They'll try to flank us."

"How do you know?"

"I know how Injuns fight."

"What we gonna do? We're outnumbered and on foot."

Augustus carefully raised his head and peered over his saddle, but was forced to duck as a bullet whistled overhead. Again he raised up and could see the warriors getting closer. He started to take aim when he suddenly realized the Cheyenne might have given the soldiers their only chance to survive.

Augustus pointed to where the Cheyenne had dismounted. The ponies waited in the care of two warriors.

"Shoot the ponies!"

Gibbs flashed a grin. He knew a Cheyenne's pony was more important to him than a squaw or a soldier's scalp.

The Sharps and Spencer rifles barked together, spitting six bullets, killing six ponies. Augustus raised his Sharps and fired. Another pony dropped through the cloud of smoky haze.

"Keep firing at the ponies," shouted Augustus. He killed another pony and watched as the terrified animals pitched and jumped, knocking the two warriors to the ground. By the third volley the attacking Cheyenne had broken off the attack and scrambled back to what was left of their mounts.

Minutes later the Buffalo Soldiers sat laughing as they watched the Cheyenne retreat, many of them on foot, some riding double.

That night they arrived at Fort Wallace, suffering from minor frostbite but alive.

Word of the ordeal spread through Wallace and into Buffalo Bottoms, where the battle was referred to as "the battle of the saddle fort."

Outnumbered, and outgunned, six Buffalo Soldiers of the 10th Cavalry had stood off dozens of Cheyenne.

9

"To the battle of McClellan's Fort!" shouted Brassard. He paused and looked around at the smiling faces, then loosened his ordinarily hard demeanor and said proudly, "It has a more military sound."

Philadelphia Phil's saloon exploded with laughter; Haymes' fingers danced on the piano keys as the packed house celebrated the victory. Small though the confrontation was, the six troopers had outfought, outwitted, and survived without a casualty against a force several times their size.

Brassard sat down with Augustus and several troopers. "It ain't much, but we need all the recognition we can get." He patted Augustus on the hand. "You did fine, son. This regiment's building itself a reputation to be proud of, and you're a part of that pride."

Gibbs gulped down a drink, then grumped, "One day at a time. We get to fight the leavings while the Seventh Cavalry gets all the prime pickings. Look at Custer on the Washita."

Augustus shook his head. "From what I heard, that wasn't anything to be proud of."

Gibbs still complained, "I don't believe Colored soldiers are ever going to get respect."

Brassard slammed his hand on the table. "Don't you talk like that. Our day'll come. You've just got to be patient. We can't get it all at once. By God, before long we'll make every Colored in the world proud of us. You wait and see."

Augustus nodded, then looked around. Someone was missing. "Where's Sergeant Liberty?"

Brassard shook his head. "Della's taken a bad turn. He's with her at their tent."

Augustus stood quickly and downed his drink. "I'd better go over there."

Brassard grabbed his hand. "There's nothing you can do, Augustus. The fort surgeon said she won't live out the night."

Augustus eased his hand loose. "He saved my life, Sergeant Major. I can at least be there in case he needs something."

Augustus left and walked his horse, a broken-down sorrel issued to replace his dead mount, to the front of Liberty's tent. He was tying off the reins when he heard a cry from inside. He started through the tent flap and crashed into Liberty's young daughter. She was crying as he put his arms around her and looked past her to the bed, where Moss and Marie sat beside Della Liberty.

"She's gone," was all Selona could say.

Moss slumped over the bed, holding Della's hand. Marie stood slowly and walked toward the door.

"Let them be for awhile," she mumbled, then took Selona's hand, led her out into the muddy street, and into the darkness.

The music and laughter from Philadelphia Phil's drifted on the night air, but Augustus felt no desire to go back.

He started back to the fort, and thought of his mother and father. He didn't think about how they died from a plague that swept west Texas. He didn't think about the fact that when they died he knew they loved him.

He thought about the fact that when they died—unlike Della—they had never enjoyed a precious moment of freedom.

*   *   *

The cemetery at Wallace was divided into white and Colored sections. Moss had dug a grave and found an old wagon wheel to use as a grave marker. He had carved his wife's initials into the dry wood. Now, for the funeral, Moss stood with his daughter. Nearly the entire company was present, including Captain Carpenter.

Augustus stood with Brassard and the other troopers. When the chaplain finished the short sermon, Haymes started singing a refrain from "Bound to Go":

> *"Oh free-dom! Oh free-dom! Oh free-dom over me!*
> *And befo' I'd be a slave,*
> *I'll be buried in my grave,*
> *An' go home to my Lord and be free."*

When the funeral was over, Moss said, "I didn't even have the money for a proper marker."

Selona took his hand and led him away, followed by Marie. It was the first time Augustus had ever seen Marie without her corncob pipe.

Looking around at the emptiness of the plains, he said to Brassard, "This sure is a lonesome place to be buried, Sergeant Major."

Brassard looked at him somberly. "Graveyards are supposed to be lonesome."

"What's wrong with that child, Marie?" Liberty asked one morning as Selona began the walk to Fort Wallace and the O'Kellys' quarters.

Marie shook her head. "I reckon she still sorrows for her mama."

Liberty's eyes followed her until she was out of sight. He wasn't convinced. "Maybe she's coming of age." He had the feeling that more than winter was turning into spring. "She's growing into a woman. I'd say she's coming into season."

When Selona arrived at the O'Kelly quarters, the light was dim, and from the door she could see the fire had not been properly stoked. She eased her way toward the hearth and reached for a piece of wood and threw it onto the glowing embers. She stood there, watching the fire catch, then turned and started for the kitchen when she collided with something and nearly fell.

That's when the fire blazed and she saw what was hanging from the overhead beam.

Camille O'Kelly's tongue protruded from her mouth. Her alabaster face was now purple, bloated by the rope cutting deep into her throat.

PART 2

1874: FORT SILL

10

★ ★ ★

Horst Bruner was a farmer; a quiet man with a cherubic face that seemed perpetually sunburned despite his wearing a floppy hat, which seemed to protect only the top of his balding head. Horst was a man who had raised cotton in the desert of Texas, and fruit trees in the Shenandoah Valley of Virginia. He was a man with a green thumb.

He had dug a garden behind his house, and it had become a habit of his to start off the day tending to his vegetables, mostly tomatoes, squash, and corn. This habit made the harder chores of the day more tolerable.

On the morning of May 8, 1874, he was in his garden when he heard his wife, Gertrude, scream, "Horst! Come quickly! Many riders are coming." Gertrude had spoken in German and that bothered Horst, for the family had agreed to speak only the language of their new country.

Stepping around the corner of the house he understood. A shaft of cold terror threaded through his body.

"Get to the house! Get the rifles!" he shouted as he charged toward the barn, where his son Ernst, a brawny fifteen-year-old, was saddling a horse.

"Get to the house!" again shouted Horst.

"What's wrong, Papa?"

Horst shook his head. "Go to the house and get a rifle. Lock the doors and don't come out." He looked around. "Where's Caterina and Mary?"

"They went for a ride."

"Maybe they'll be safe."

"Safe? Safe from what, Papa?"

"Comancheros. Riding this way."

Both started for the door, when there was the sound of horses moving at a slow pace.

"Thank God," Horst exclaimed. "They're back." He bolted toward the door, and as he stepped into the blinding sunlight he felt the cold steel suddenly slice through his stomach.

Horst slowly folded to his knees and thought he heard Ernst shout a profanity. Then he saw the bloody knife being wiped on his shirt and his eyes slowly raised until he was looking into a face that seemed to embody evil.

Then he heard his wife scream, and there was nothing but blackness.

Private Augustus Sharps was now twenty-four, a tall man with broad facial features, a flowing mustache that swept into long sideburns, and big strong hands. He was the chief scout for H Troop, which was now posted at Fort Sill, Indian Territory. He generally took three troopers along on patrol, because the Buffalo Soldiers of the 10th were responsible for maintaining lines of communications with the settlers pouring in from the east.

On this particular patrol he was accompanied by Haymes, Gibbs, and a very young trooper named Frederick Douglass Williams.

It was nearly noon when they reached the top of a ridge overlooking the Bruner ranch.

"Looks too quiet," Gibbs said.

Augustus took out his binoculars and scanned the tiny ranch house that lay in a grove of tall trees. "There's no movement around the house." He shifted the binoculars to the barn, then to the hog pen.

His face twisted with anger.

"Draw your rifles," Augustus ordered, snapping open the breech of his Sharps. "We'll go down in a two-by-two spread."

Augustus led off with Haymes; Gibbs and Williams held their Spencer rifles trained on the ranch until the two reached the barn.

Augustus waved Gibbs and Williams on, then swung down from his horse. "Cover me."

Haymes cocked his rifle. "You're covered." He pointed the Spencer at the barn door.

As Augustus opened the door, the stench of dried blood stung his nostrils; the buzzing of flies filled the hot air, and he felt his stomach might give way any moment to the nausea consuming him.

"Damn," he whispered. He stepped through the door and saw the mutilated body of Horst Bruner lying spread-eagled on the ground. Moments later he went back outside.

Haymes stared at him with a knowing look. "What'd you find?"

"Horst Bruner. He's been scalped. Looks like it was comancheros."

"What's a comanchero?" asked Williams.

"Renegades," replied Augustus. "Bands of white outlaws, Injuns, Mexican bandits. Nothing but scum."

"I thought Mr. Bruner was baldheaded," said Haymes, looking puzzled.

Augustus nodded slowly. "He *was* baldheaded. They scalped his beard from his face! Cut off his whole damn chin."

Gibbs shouted from the hogpen. "Mrs. Bruner is over here. What's left of her."

Gertrude Bruner lay naked, alone in the hogpen, her long blond hair thick with the evil-smelling mud.

Gibbs climbed the fence and went to the woman, who was lying on her stomach. He gently rolled her over, then, suddenly, bent over, ran two steps, and vomited.

"What?" Augustus asked.

Gibbs wiped his mouth. "They cut off her tits."

Williams blurted, "Why would someone do that to a woman?" He had been in the regiment only three months, and the cruelty of the frontier was still new to him.

Augustus looked at Gibbs, and then said, "Comanchero tobacco pouch."

Williams said, "What?"

"The comancheros cut off tits and make tobacco pouches out of them. They sell them down south in Mexico, where they take their captives to be sold as slaves."

Williams moaned. "What kind of men are these people?"

"The worst," said Gibbs. He looked around, spotted a shovel. "At least the bastards left something we can use to dig their graves."

Haymes had been looking around. He said, "What about the children? They had three children."

Augustus mounted, saying, "Spread out and look for them. But I doubt we'll find anything."

A ten-minute search produced nothing.

The Bruners were buried near the garden, with Haymes playing a soft tune on his harmonica. Augustus solemnly said The Lord's Prayer, and when finished, swung into the saddle and started riding in a circle around the ranch. West of the ranch house he found the trail that suddenly turned south toward the Red River.

After riding back to the other three, Augustus wrote a quick report, and told Gibbs, "Ride to the fort and give this to Captain Carpenter. I'm going to follow them if I have to ride to Mexico."

"How'll we know where to follow you?" asked Gibbs.

Augustus was quick with the answer. "I'll use rocks to make an arrow in the direction they're moving. Now, go! I want to get started while there's daylight."

The three rode off to the northwest; Augustus rode south and crossed the Red River late that afternoon. There he made his first rock arrow.

11

* * *

At the age of sixty-six, Marie was more than a living legend to the 10th Cavalry and the people at Fort Sill, Indian Territory. Corncob pipe and all, Marie was midwife to every newborn child, matrimonial counsel to couples trying to carve out a life in the harsh frontier, and without question the best cook around. She had even been called on over the years to help train the young soldiers assigned as cooks to the regiment.

This talent for turning rabbit into a gourmet meal had been passed on to Selona, along with the laundry chores that continued to bring them in a little money. Marie was a woman who never looked back except to see how far she had come, and on this particular June morning she didn't have to look too far in the past to see she had not come far.

There was something missing, and it would have to be set right one day if she and her granddaughter were to have any semblance of a normal life.

Selona was now seventeen years old, with long dark hair and dark eyes; tall and lithe, much like her father—who was now a first sergeant with the 10th at Fort Sill—she was no longer a child, but a frontier woman. She had learned to ride a horse and shoot a pistol, could sew and cook, and could wash more laundry than any of the other laundresses. She had even learned how to handle the advances of the young troopers, who buzzed around her tent when Moss or Marie were not present. Which wasn't very often.

Marie sat on the ground, laced her brogans, and smoked methodically, pausing occasionally to study Selona, who was working at the washboard.

Marie's steady gaze finally drew a sigh from Selona. "What you got on your mind, Grams?"

"You."

"Me?"

"And finding you a husband."

This brought a pause in Selona's scrubbing. "A husband? I don't need a husband. Besides, you're always talking about owning a piece of land."

"First you find a husband. Then you get you that piece of land. That way you got something solid to stand on when you start raising children."

"Children? Now I'm going to have children. First the husband, then the land, then children. Seems to me you got everything all figured out. There's just one thing I'd like to know?"

"What might that be?"

"Do I have anything to say about this, or are you just going to decide everything on your own?" Selona began stirring a kettle.

Marie didn't miss a beat. She was thinking and devising at full gallop now. "Every woman needs a husband. Look at that Vina Mae Jones. She done married up with Darcy Gibbs last fall and now she's expecting." Marie pointed some twenty yards away to a tent sitting in the same row as theirs.

These tents had become known as Suds Row, as similar rows were known on all the army posts, where the laundresses lived who followed the troopers from fort to fort. Beyond "the Row" lay another feature of all army communities: rickety wagons where bootleggers sold cheap whiskey, gamblers played with marked cards, and young Indian girls sold their bodies to the Colored soldiers.

"You going to be an old woman all alone like me if you don't start thinking about tomorrow."

"Tomorrow. Humph! All I can see is today." She stopped stirring the kettle and looked at Marie. "Who you got in mind for this husband who's going to buy me a piece of land and give me those children?"

Before Marie could reply there was the thunder of hooves pounding the hard ground. They both looked up and saw Trooper Gibbs, followed by Haymes and Williams, riding furiously through the main gate toward the regimental headquarters.

Sergeant Major Brassard was nearly fifty and had considered retiring, but he was determined not to leave the regiment until it was one that Americans of all colors would be proud of.

Unlike the 9th Cavalry, which was deployed along the Rio Grande in Texas, the 10th had known little glory and recognition, and sometimes seemed barely more than railroad and road guards.

The 9th Cavalry had fought against the Apaches, comancheros, Mexican revolutionaries, and cattle rustlers plaguing the Texas frontier, where Sergeant Emanuel Stance had received the Medal of Honor. Under the command of Colonel Edward Hatch and Lieutenant Colonel Wesley Merritt, the 9th had come to epitomize what the great Frederick Douglass envisioned as the perfect example of the Negro soldier, while the 10th had been relegated to nothing more than cleaning up after the white cavalry successes.

Brassard often gloomily pondered that fact, and wished the U.S. government had given the regiment more responsibility, or had stricken them from the roll of service.

He was sitting at his desk when he heard the horses approaching, and hurried to the front porch of the orderly room, where he saw Gibbs bring his horse to a skidding halt.

"Sergeant Major." Gibbs scrambled from the saddle and handed Brassard the note from Augustus.

Brassard read the note quickly, then hurried inside. Lieutenant Jonathan O'Kelly was working on the Returns at his desk when Brassard approached, saying, "You better read this, sir."

O'Kelly read the note. "What can we spare in the way of troopers?"

Brassard thought for a moment. "We have maybe thirty men we can put into the field."

"Get them saddled and ready." At that moment First Sergeant Moss Liberty came into the orderly room.

"First Sergeant, I want you to lead a patrol." O'Kelly knew Liberty couldn't read, so he read the note out loud to him.

" 'In pursuit of band of comancheros. Sign indicates twenty riders. Two settlers murdered. Three children taken hostage. Will mark trail with arrows formed by rocks. Signed, Private Sharps.' "

O'Kelly looked at Liberty. "You'll have to push hard to catch up, and I can't guarantee you'll have much success. The comancheros probably have better horses."

Liberty nodded. "Our stock is about give out, sir. These damn patrols has every hoss broken down."

"Make do, First Sergeant. Now, move out."

Liberty saluted and left, followed by Brassard.

O'Kelly stood at the door, watching the dust swirl as men and horses formed up on the parade ground. When the small detachment pulled out and the dust began to settle against the setting sun, a bright shaft of red-gray light flowed across his face. He went inside and sat at his desk and took up his journal.

12

His name was Red Travers, and his lip curled upward as he recalled the screams of the man and woman. Especially the man, whose beard he'd slowly skinned from his face before he cut his throat. The woman was dead when he took the knife to her; she had fought to save the three children and his men had grown impatient, so they shot her through the head after having their pleasure. Then they took their knives to her body.

It had been a good raid, he told himself. He was standing near the edge of their encampment south of the Red River. His men were drunk, and despite his better judgment they had encamped early. Travers was a thin man, wiry, with only a few strands of hair and a scraggy beard. He smelled of whiskey, horsehair, and death.

Travers walked about the camp inspecting the spoils of their raid. They had a dozen horses and several wagons loaded with goods taken from three families—two caught on the open trail, and the Bruners.

His cold eyes drifted to the greatest prize: three children sitting beneath the wagon, their hands and feet tethered to the wagon wheel.

Ernst Bruner would sell for a good price to a mine in Sonora.

Caterina was thirteen, starting to blossom, and Travers' greatest worry was keeping his men away from her. Virgins sold for a much higher price to the brothels in Chihuahua.

Mary was ten years old and would make a servant in a brothel until she was old enough for her virginity to be of value.

A good raid, he thought again. But there were hundreds of miles to go before they reached the border and safety from the soldiers and Texas Rangers. The soldiers would be mostly blacks, and everyone knew they couldn't last in a good fight. But the Texas Rangers—they were to be avoided.

Augustus lay two hundred yards from the encampment, huddled behind a large rock. Through his binoculars he could see the three children and a short man who came to check their ropes. He raised the Sharps and sighted the man as he walked through the camp, his body clear against the glow of the campfires.

They weren't afraid of being followed, thought Augustus. Or they didn't think they'd be followed so soon.

Augustus figured the latter, since they had not put out pickets.

He lay there through the night, listening until there was only the sound of coyotes howling in the distance.

When the moon reached its zenith, a full moon, he stripped away his pistol belt and shoved the Colt into his right boot; in his left boot he placed his sharp knife.

Then the long crawl began through thick buck brush, sharp rocks, and tall cactus.

Thirty minutes later Augustus reached the encampment, where the snores of drunken men gave him good cover as he slid between rocks, behind cactus, and over sharp fissures in the dry desert ground. The sleeping men wore rawhide breechcloths or Mexican garb, and one wore cavalry trousers.

He slowly crept toward the wagon. The night was draining fast now, the moon lower, and there was the first trace of purple light to the east as he crawled beneath the wagon to the children, who were tied on the camp side of the wagon.

Ernst awoke wide-eyed as Augustus clamped his hand over the boy's mouth.

"You must be quiet. I'm a soldier. I've come to help you, but you have to help me," he whispered.

Ernst nodded as Augustus took his knife and cut the ropes. Ernst rolled over to Caterina and woke her, covering her mouth as Augustus did the same to Mary. Augustus carefully cut the ropes, then motioned the three under the wagon. One by one the Bruners slipped under the wagon.

"Follow me," Augustus whispered.

Augustus had crawled on a few inches from beneath the wagon when he felt the wagon shudder, and the sound of snoring stopped. He froze as he felt the boot of one of the comancheros step onto his hand.

Augustus lay frozen. With the full weight of the man on his fingers, the stream of urine splashing against the side of his face, he didn't move, he merely controlled his breathing and could feel—taste—the fear in the children.

His own fear.

After what seemed an interminable time, the man shook himself, broke wind, and climbed back into the wagon.

Seconds passed slowly; then the snoring resumed, and Augustus again started to crawl, moving away from the wagon into the high brush surrounding the camp.

It was just dawn when they reached his tethered horse. He put on his pistol belt and tunic.

The sun broke over the horizon, flooding the desert with golden light.

"They'll know we're gone now," said Ernst.

"You only have one horse!" Caterina whimpered. She was dirty, her clothes torn, and Augustus could see she was terrified to the point of madness.

He took the Spencer rifle from the carbine boot.

"We can't all ride on one horse, children." He looked at Ernst. "You and I have to stay. We have to stay until your sisters get away and find the cavalry."

"When will that be?" Mary moaned.

Augustus looked at the sun. If the troop had done what he expected, ridden to the ranch and bivouacked the night before, then followed at a gallop now that they could see the trail, they would now be close. "An hour . . . maybe two," Augustus said.

"Can we hold out that long?" Ernst asked.

"We don't have a choice. We have to make a stand in those rocks." He handed the Spencer to Ernst, asking, "Do you know how to use this?"

"My father had a Spencer."

Augustus nodded. He turned to Caterina and handed her the pistol. "Just point and pull the trigger. But don't fire until they get close. If you don't want to be taken alive, save two bullets for you and your sister. Now, you and the little one get on this horse and ride straight north. Don't come back, no matter what you hear. Do you understand?"

"What if they follow us?" asked Mary.

Augustus hoisted the girls into the McClellan saddle and adjusted the stirrups for Caterina. "Remember . . . don't come back. Now, ride!" He slapped the horse on the rump and it bolted, with the girls holding on for dear life.

"What'll you use?" asked Ernst.

Augustus took his Sharps and started for the rocks. "If they come, and I think they will, we start with me firing the Sharps. I can take some of them before they get close enough to fire with any accuracy. I hope they don't have much fight in them, but we can't count on that. Once they get close in, you start with the Spencer. We can cut down the odds and hold out until the cavalry gets here."

The spot he chose for their defense was a small hill elevated some thirty feet above the desert; formed by huge outcroppings of boulders and tall cactus, it was good ground to defend against an attacking force. Through his binoculars he could see the camp was coming alive and he could hear the shouts and cussing of the comancheros. They were hastily saddling horses and they were heavily armed.

Within seconds a comanchero appeared, riding in a circle around the camp.

"What's he doing?" asked Ernst.

"Looking for our sign."

There was a loud war whoop, with the comanchero pointing to the north.

"They're on to us. Best get ready."

Ernst eared back the hammer of the Spencer.

Augustus looked at him. The boy had seen his mother and father slaughtered; had been taken a slave. It was as though they were now joined by a common hatred and it was then Augustus made a solemn oath: *He wasn't going to let them take this boy the way the Kiowa took him!*

The comancheros rode in a frenzied pack with a thin man in the lead.

Augustus adjusted the sights on the Sharps, rested the rifle on a flat rock, and leaned into the stock. He squeezed the trigger, felt the kick of the Big Fifty, and looked quickly through the cloud of smoke to see a comanchero pitch from his saddle.

He loaded, took aim, and fired again. Through the smoke he could see another comanchero roll off the back of his horse.

Ernst was amazed and stared at this Colored stranger. "We must be three hundred yards from them."

Augustus took aim. "More like two-fifty." He squeezed the trigger and another comanchero spilled from the saddle. He raised the binoculars and scanned the band of comancheros, which he estimated at more than two dozen. "Get ready. They're coming into your range."

Seconds passed like hours as Ernst took aim at a comanchero.

"Not yet," said Augustus. "Let's give them a chance to get closer. Then'll we surprise the hell out of them." He grinned. "So far they think there's only one of us."

The band of renegades were riding in a tight pack when Augustus said, "Fire!"

Their rifles barked in unison, and two comancheros fell from their horses.

"Good shooting." Augustus slapped Ernst on the shoulder, then watched the comancheros break into two groups. "They're going to try to flank us."

"What does that mean?"

"They'll come at us from two sides." Augustus reloaded. Ernst was already shouldering the Spencer and fired at the thin comanchero in the lead. When the bullet struck, a demonic look of satisfaction came to the boy's face. "I saw him cut my mother . . . my mother's . . ." He reloaded and fired again.

Augustus fired. Ernst fired. Both were now in a near state of trance, two young men killing murderers and slavers with a concentration they had never known.

"They're going to ground!" Augustus shouted as a bullet struck dangerously close to him.

The comancheros leaped from their horses and then disappeared into the thick brush. There was a sudden look of fear on Ernst's face that Augustus understood.

"Now we just have to hold out. The cavalry will be here. I can feel them on the way." Augustus checked his cartridge belt; there were eight rounds left. "How you doing on ammunition?"

Ernst made a quick count. "Ten cartridges."

Augustus clamped his jaw tight, then said, "I suggest you save one for yourself. I plan to. If they take us alive they'll roast us over a fire."

Ernst took one cartridge and laid it separate from the rest of his ammunition, then reloaded the Spencer without a word.

The plains remained quiet for what seemed an eternity as the comancheros worked through the thick underbrush, trying for position on the two deadly marksmen.

Then the shooting started again. The renegades had closed the circle to within thirty yards.

Augustus and Ernst fired with deadly precision, hitting three more comancheros, but the fire coming from below was now withering as the remaining comancheros moved closer.

"I'm down to one cartridge," said Augustus.

"I've only got one left."

Augustus took his last cartridge and reloaded; Ernst did the same; and then Augustus saw the flash of a red shirt moving down below the knoll. He glanced to the front and saw a comanchero racing away. Then another.

"What is happening?" asked Ernst.

Augustus grinned and started to speak, but was cut short by the most beautiful sounds in the world: the pounding of heavy hooves and the rattle of sabres, and then the bark of a dozen Spencer rifles.

And the bugle blowing, "Charge!"

The two young men watched as the troopers of the 10th raced past the base of the rocky knoll and into the thick brush, flushing the comancheros like so many quail. Then they were on their feet cheering the charging cavalrymen.

The renegades' horses were now driven off by the troopers, making the comancheros easy prey for the mounted cavalrymen.

Trooper Williams flushed one comanchero, who fired, missing his head by inches. The renegade dropped his weapon and ran, with the angered Williams in pursuit. When he rode the comanchero down he wheeled his horse and raced back, his sabre drawn and to the ready. The comanchero had barely reached his feet when the steel of Williams' sabre slashed through his neck.

Augustus and Ernst raced down from the knoll and joined the battle, but there was no fight left in the comancheros.

An hour later, eight surviving renegades had been subdued, hog-tied and loaded into the wagons they had stolen.

As the caravan led out, vultures were already picking at the dead comancheros.

The caravan reached the Bruner ranch late that afternoon, where Ernst and his sisters had decided to remain instead of going to Fort Sill.

"This is our home, Augustus," said Ernst. "Our parents are buried here, and this land belongs to my family. We won't be driven off by Indians or outlaws." Ernst offered his hand to Augustus. "Thank you for taking the time to bury my family."

Augustus shook hands with Ernst, saying, "This is something to remember me by," and handed Ernst his last Sharps cartridge.

Ernst took the Spencer, jacked the last round out of the chamber, and handed it to Augustus. "And me."

13

★ ★ ★

May rolled into June. The soldiers and civilians at Fort Sill looked forward to the Fourth of July picnic and cotillion, but until the Fourth, there was still the usual hard work to be done. What made the work tolerable, especially for the few young girls, was the thought of the music, the dancing, and the young men who would be buzzing around them like flies.

Young Colored women were not plentiful on the plains, but the steady advance of the railroad to the west and southern plains was bringing Colored families into the Indian Territory. The eight years' service of the four Colored regiments on the western frontier had given the former slaves a focus of pride that brought young men into the army from all parts of the country.

With enlistment came a payday.

Soldiers' payday was also payday for Selona and Marie, who drew their meager salary from the paymaster, just like the soldiers.

Marie was now total companion to Selona, since Moss was rarely home except during the late hours of the night or early hours of the morning. He spent more time in the orderly room than with Selona, who was already attracting the eyes of many of the young soldiers at the fort.

With her corncob pipe clamped tight in her mouth, Marie practically dragged Selona through the line of troopers waiting to receive their pay.

"Get out the way. Go on, move now. Act like gentlemen. Let this tired old woman through!" she shouted, pushing her way to the table in front of regimental headquarters, where Sergeant Major Brassard, whose job was to confirm each man's pay from the ledger, sat beside O'Kelly, who was the acting paymaster.

Marie had not pushed too quickly. She had timed her move just right.

When Augustus stepped forward to report for his pay, he found himself being nudged by Marie. She smiled slightly, then pulled Selona in front of her, trapping Selona between her and Augustus.

Augustus couldn't help but notice the fresh smell of soap coming from Selona. The wind blew a wisp of her hair against his face, tickling his nose, and he noticed she had grown taller since he had last seen her. She was no longer a child. She had grown into a young woman. A beautiful young woman with eyes soft, despite the hardship she had known in her life, and a smile that was delicate and mysterious at once.

"How are you this morning, Miss Selona?"

Selona smiled and replied, "Just fine, Augustus." Before she could say another word Marie's voice boomed out.

"Marie, laundress, reporting for my pay, Roscoe"—Marie jerked her pipe toward Selona—"and my granddaughter's as well. No need both of us reporting."

Brassard chuckled, then examined the ledger and said to O'Kelly, "Forty-eight dollars, sir."

O'Kelly carefully counted out the gold coins, and as always Marie handed one to Brassard for inspection. There was a time when she'd had teeth good enough to bite into the coin, but now she was totally toothless. She watched as Brassard bit into the soft coin, leaving a slight mark on the edge.

"Now, Miss Marie, you don't think the army's going to cheat you, do you?" asked O'Kelly.

Marie held the coin up for O'Kelly to see the mark, and said, "Not today, it ain't."

Laughter rose from the ranks, and even O'Kelly chuckled. Many of the troopers bit the eagle, for they had learned through harsh experience: Many a Colored man had been cheated by imitations made of copper, lead, or wood.

Marie turned to leave and paused, saying to Augustus, "You're a big strong man. Could you help me with a chore?"

Augustus nodded. "I would be delighted."

Marie grinned. "Meet us at the sutler's when you get paid." She walked off, followed by Selona.

The sutler's, a combination grocery store for civilians, commissary for soldiers, and saloon where the whiskey was more expensive than that of the peddlers outside the fort, but certainly safer to drink, was a focal point of army post life.

Marie had had her eye on a rocking chair for some time and had decided that now was the time to give herself a present. She seldom spent money on herself, since there was little to start with and the end always came before the payday, which could be several months late. But today she had that rocking chair in mind, and something for her granddaughter.

She settled her account with the sutler, then paid one dollar for the rocking chair. Next, to Selona's surprise, she said, "I'd like three yards off that bolt of calico."

"What you up to, Grams?" asked Selona.

Marie said, as Augustus appeared, "Never you mind. Augustus, you take this rocking chair over to my tent. Selona, you go on along with him. I'll be along directly."

Augustus picked up the rocking chair and followed Selona down an aisle of the sutler's. Marie stood watching. How fine they looked together! That's when she turned and noticed Brassard standing in the back, looking at her with a huge, knowing grin.

Marie grinned in return.

14

The four riders approached from the south near sunset and rode into the fort covered with trail dust and carrying a powerful thirst. They tied off their horses in front of the sutler's and used their hats to slap dust off the long coats they wore over their gun belts, then walked inside, where piano music could be heard.

Haymes was sitting at the piano, as he did every night he wasn't on patrol, and though one of the men wore his blond hair to his shoulders and had a heavy beard, there was no mistaking John Armitage.

The music stopped as Armitage removed his coat, revealing a Texas Ranger badge.

"Whiskey," he demanded. The other three Rangers ordered the same and stood drinking in the silence, their eyes trained on the mirror, watching the sullen faces of the Colored soldiers sitting at tables behind them.

They drank two drinks each, fast, the way hard men drink after a long ride.

Augustus was sitting near the piano, watching Armitage's

eyes scan across the mirror until their eyes met. Armitage
smiled lightly, then turned, facing Augustus.

"You, boy." He pointed at Augustus. "Trot on over to
headquarters and fetch your officer of the day. Tell him Captain Armitage from the Ranger battalion at Fort Richardson
is here to collect them comancheros."

Augustus stood slowly, his eyes on Armitage. There was
movement as some of the troopers slipped on their drinking
jewelry, but Augustus spread his hands and the tension eased.
"The officer of the day is in the orderly room." He pointed
through the door. "You can't miss it, Captain."

Armitage poured another drink and swallowed it quickly,
placed the glass on the counter, and walked out without turning his head, followed by the other three Rangers.

Haymes rose from the piano and stood with Augustus. "I
sure wouldn't want to be those comancheros. Not with Armitage taking me to Texas."

Augustus said, "I don't care about those comancheros. Not
after what they did to the Bruners. Might save everyone time
and trouble if Armitage strings them up to the nearest tree. It'll
be the only thing me and that bastard will ever agree on."

It was past midnight when the barracks door slammed open
and Moss Liberty loped down the aisle between the line of
bunks, straight to Augustus' bed.

Augustus jerked from a deep sleep to find Liberty staring at
him, a lantern in his hand. Liberty's face was a twisted mask
of pain and anger.

"Get your clothes on and come with me. Bring two more
men," he ordered. Then, with an almost animal, guttural moan
he added, "And bring your pistols."

Augustus rousted Haymes and Williams. All three dressed
quickly and were out the door while strapping on their pistol
belts.

Liberty was plowing ahead of them, the lantern swinging

wildly as he hurried through the main gate and walked into the darkened plains.

"What's happening?" Haymes asked, yawning.

Augustus shook his head and kept following the lantern until it stopped at the Liberty tent.

Augustus' stomach tightened, and anger and fear welled up in his chest as he stooped and went inside.

Selona lay on a pallet, curled in the fetal position, her eyes blank, like the eyes of the buffalo he had shot in Kansas. She had a piece of calico covering her hair.

Moss was on his knees, moaning and weeping, the most pitiful sight Augustus had ever seen. He gently touched Selona's bruised cheek with a wet cloth; blood oozed from beneath the calico, and despite his repeated dabbing with the cloth the blood continued to come.

"Look what they done to my baby." Moss spoke in a wail so painful it made Augustus's skin crawl. "They done beat her . . . and took her!" Then with the most terrible shriek Augustus had ever heard, Moss removed the calico cloth covering her head.

The men all stood in shocked horror. Moss whispered, "Then they scalped her!"

Selona's hair was gone from just above the ears in a clean circle around her head.

"Who?" Augustus asked.

"Those goddamned Texas Rangers!"

Augustus thought he had known hatred for the Kiowa, but that was nothing in comparison with what he now felt.

Brassard entered the tent with O'Kelly, then said to him, "You best get on back to the fort, sir. This is an enlisted matter." His tone was more an order than a request.

O'Kelly's eyes hardened, then he turned and spoke through the tent flap to someone outside. "Come in here."

Armitage stepped through the flap. He was disheveled and appeared half asleep.

"I want you to take a real close look at what your men have done." O'Kelly's voice was as cold as the plains in winter.

Armitage spoke without emotion: "How do you know it

was my men? You've only got the word of a bunch of niggers."

Liberty rose wildly, drunkenly, as though out of control of his own body. His eyes were maniacal as his hand went for his pistol.

Augustus found himself drawing his pistol, only with a different purpose. His arm rose, then fell, laying the pistol against the side of Liberty's head. Moss fell unconscious as Armitage pulled two pistols and held them on the soldiers.

"Drop your guns. All of you." Armitage looked at O'Kelly. "That means you, too, O'Kelly."

The soldiers slowly unbuckled their pistol belts.

"Throw them over here."

The soldiers did so. One by one Armitage kicked the belts through the tent flap. "I ain't sure my men did this, and I ain't turning them over to a bunch of niggers. We're going to ride for Texas. If any of your brunets follow us, O'Kelly, we'll be waiting with more hell than you'll see in a lifetime."

Then he disappeared into the night.

Augustus started out but O'Kelly barked, "Private Sharps, remain where you are. That's an order."

"But, sir, you can't let them get away!"

O'Kelly flashed an evil grin. "They won't get far. We'll do this in a proper military fashion. We are soldiers. Not a lynch mob."

"He's right," Brassard said. "They camped in that gulley on the other side of the rifle range. We'll pick up their trail at first light and—"

Marie entered the tent, looking like a woman who had lost everything. She went straight to Selona and knelt by her and took her in her arms.

"I'm going to get the surgeon," O'Kelly said. He hurried from the tent.

Selona looked at Marie, and whispered, "Oh, Grams, why did they do this to me?"

In the pale light they saw Marie's hand softly rise to stroke Selona's cheek.

The soldiers froze. It was a hand covered with dark blood.

                                *   *   *

At first light O'Kelly and eight troopers, including Liberty, Augustus, Haymes, Williams, and Brassard, walked their horses through the thin mist to where they believed the Rangers had camped.

When they entered the camp they were surprised to see three horses still tethered to a picket line.

Then they found the three Rangers, lying as though asleep beneath blankets, their heads resting on their blood-soaked saddles.

Their throats had been cut from ear to ear. And they'd been scalped.

Augustus walked to the edge of the gulley. There, a single set of horse tracks led south.

Selona's screams were nearly more than Marie could endure, but she knew that the only way to survive pain was to use it as a driving force.

"Don't let those butchers win, baby," she whispered into Selona's ear. "If you die, they win. If you live, you got more than what they got right now."

Selona whimpered. "I'm going to be so ugly." The pain in her head was so great she couldn't feel the pain in the rest of her body.

"Your mama used to say, 'Pretty is as pretty does.' You do pretty and you'll always be pretty. Now, let's tend to you. How you look don't matter. It's living that matters."

Marie began once more to remove the calico rag and, once more Selona screamed. It was more than twelve hours since the scalping, and in places flesh had stuck to the rag, making removal an agony. But Marie had to clean the wound.

"Go on, baby, scream your heart out. Nobody cares."

Selona screamed with the removal of all the minutiae.

"Why would men do this to a person, Grams?" she panted.

"Why do men do the things they do? It's their nature, I reckon."

Marie washed her head tenderly, then put on a boiled-clean rag, dried in the good sun.

Selona was resting when the tent flap opened and Moss came in, followed by Surgeon Donaldson.

Donaldson hadn't learned his trade in schools, but at battles from Antietam to Vicksburg, and in the butcher shops that were field hospitals during the Union army's march to the sea. His fat fingers were soft and gentle; his eyes were blue and friendly.

"My apologies, Marie, I was away at the Anadarko Indian agency. When the dispatch rider arrived, and told me what had happened, I spoke with one of the Cheyenne medicine men. He gave me a poultice the Indians use to treat this sort of wound. Now, child, let me examine you."

Donaldson carefully removed the calico rag and looked with disgust at her head. "Dear God, she's been scalped clean to the bone."

Selona began crying again as he stared incredulously at the white of her skull, and the small bits of remaining tissue in the circular area surrounded by the severed edges of her skin.

"It's a medical fact that the scalp bleeds the most in the early stages of injury, but once the blood congeals, the tissue heals very quickly." He touched her skull and asked, "Does this cause you pain?"

"It hurts worse above my ears, and all around my head."

Moss just stood there, looking helpless.

Donaldson took out a leather pouch, containing a greasy poultice, which he gently applied to the edges of the scalpline. Marie handed him another triangle of calico. He carefully tied the rag on Selona's head, and for the first time since the girl had crawled into the tent the night before, Marie thought she recognized her granddaughter.

Worn out, Selona drifted off to sleep. Donaldson handed Marie the pouch. "Put on a new dressing with the poultice at sunrise and sunset. And be certain to use a boiled rag for a bandage."

Marie took the pouch. "What about her other hurts?"

Donaldson gently examined her face. "The swelling will go

down in a few days. There's no broken bones, and her teeth weren't broken."

"What about her place of womanhood?" Marie asked.

Donaldson smoothed his face roughly. "The only thing we can do about that is put her in a hot bath. If she's with child, you'll know that soon enough. If she has disease, we'll know that much sooner. I'll stop by and see her in a few days. But put her in a hot tub of water twice a day. As hot as she can stand it. That'll ease the pain and fight infection."

Moss looked at Marie. "What if she's with child?"

Marie's mouth tightened. "Then we'll have another young'un to raise."

Moss left without saying a word. Marie slipped out and watched him walk toward the fort, his shoulders slumped.

There was a knowing look in her face as she reentered, turned to Donaldson, and asked, "Will you stay with her for a bit? I've got some business to tend to."

Donaldson nodded and knelt beside Selona as Marie left the tent.

First Sergeant Liberty was saddling a horse in the stables when he felt the presence of others. He turned to see Brassard, Marie, Augustus, and five troopers.

Moss tightened the cinch on his saddle, then shoved his Spencer rifle into the boot.

"Where do you think you're going, First Sergeant?" asked Brassard.

Moss said nothing. He gripped the reins and started to lead the horse away, when Brassard blocked his path. The two men stood staring at each other, neither saying a word. Moss's fingers inched to the flap on his holster.

"I'm going for a ride, Sergeant Major."

Brassard's eyes narrowed, then he looked at Augustus and softly said, "Take the first sergeant to the barracks."

Moss's fists balled as Augustus stepped beside him and gripped his elbow. Augustus gently pulled Liberty away from his horse. "Come on, Sarge."

Liberty looked at Brassard, his face etched with the special pain of a man compelled to commit wrong for the right reasons.

"What would you do, Sergeant Major?"

"The same as you," he replied.

"Then leave me to my business."

Brassard shook his head. "You're a soldier with a family to think about, Sergeant. That's your business. That's all that matters at this time."

Moss curled forward, his fists pressed against his thighs, his body trembling with rage. "You know what that man did."

"There's no proof he had anything to do with the attack on Selona."

"I got my hurt child. That's enough for me."

"I won't let you destroy yourself. Enough harm's been done by that man." Brassard looked at Augustus. "Put this man in the guardhouse."

15

M oss was released from the guardhouse after two days, and life was returning to some semblance of normalcy at Fort Sill, except for Selona and Marie. For two weeks Selona stayed in the tent and refused to take visitors. The washing was handled solely by Marie, and the burden was beginning to take its toll, when Marie looked up from her rinsing kettle and saw Vina Gibbs approach.

"Mornin', Miss Marie."

Marie grunted and touched an ember to the bowl of her corncob pipe. Lord, she thought, I'm bone tired.

"How's Selona doin'?"

"She ain't doin' nothing.' That's the problem. She don' do nothin' but sit on that pallet and stare at the wall."

"I tried to see her yesterday, but she screamed at me."

"I know. She done the same to me, her daddy, and Augustus when he come over a few nights ago."

"That ain't good."

"Ain't good a'tall."

The old woman picked up a huge pile of clothes and started for the wash kettle.

Without another word, Vina took the clothes from Marie and started back to her tent.

Surprised, Marie asked, "Where you goin' with them clothes?"

Vina replied, "You need help, Miss Marie. Until Selona's on her feet, I'll be helpin' you with your wash."

"I can't let you do that. You got your own washin'."

"I ain't got that much that I can't handle some more."

There was relief in Marie's heart, but she warned, "I can't pay much."

Vina called over her shoulder, "You don' have to pay me, Miss Marie. You and Selona are my friends. Friends don' go along payin' for friendly help. Besides, you'll probably be doin' my wash when the baby comes."

Marie said nothing, but there was a soft smile on her leathery face as she went into the tent.

Selona was sitting on the edge of her pallet, staring emptily at the floor.

"How's my baby?"

Selona said nothing for a long moment, then she spoke in a low voice. "I'm not with child. My time of the month done come."

For the first time since the attack, Marie felt a great weight fly from her body. She knew something else as well, saying, "I expect it's time you got back to livin'."

Marie grabbed Selona by the wrist and jerked her off the pallet, and before she knew what was happening, Selona was standing in the sun for the first time since the attack.

"No! I don't want anyone to see me. I'd rather be dead." She started back inside but Marie was on her like a hawk.

"Come here, girl. You can't hide in that tent all your life. We got work to do."

"Yes, I can hide! Look at me!" She ripped the calico rag from her head and pushed Marie aside and went back inside the tent. Marie stood staring at the tent, listening to the whimpers coming from inside.

Marie began walking in circles, puffing her pipe wildly, her thoughts flashing through her head like bolts of lightning.

Suddenly, she stopped, and squinting for a moment at the tent, clamped down hard on the stem of the pipe and marched back.

Marie began by dragging her own pallet outside; when she returned she waved Selona off her pallet.

"What are you doing, Grams?"

"Doin' some house cleanin'."

Marie dragged the pallet outside and went back into the tent, where she furiously began sweeping up personal belongings, clothes, what few treasures they owned, and carried them outside.

In less than ten minutes Marie dragged her rocking chair to the pile, which lay some thirty yards from the tent. A devilish grin suddenly filled her face as she walked to the washing kettle and shouted, "You say you'd rather be dead, do you? Well then, child, let's go on and give you what you want."

Marie grabbed a burning piece of wood from the fire and tossed it to the edge of the canvas tent. The flame licked slowly at the canvas. For a moment Marie didn't think it would catch, when there was a sudden burst of fire.

Marie cackled, "Go on and die. Might as well. You been actin' like you already dead."

The tent began to burn, slow at first, then consuming an entire wall.

Marie heard Selona scream; black smoke rose into the air and the back wall was beginning to burn.

There was another scream from Selona, then shouts from others who lived along the Row.

"Miss Marie! Miss Marie!" Vina Gibbs was running toward her with a bucket of water and was starting to throw the water onto the burning tent when Marie stopped her.

Vina stared at her with a mixture of fear and astonishment.

At that moment the tent flap opened and Selona came running out, choking and coughing, her clothes smoking but not afire. Marie grabbed the bucket from Vina and threw the water on Selona.

Selona looked like a half-drowned rabbit as she saw the tent afire, and the faces of her neighbors. She stood there frozen, unable to speak; she wanted to run but the only place she could hide was now completely consumed in a ball of flame.

Marie eased beside Selona and whispered, "I knew you didn't want to die."

Selona looked at her incredulously and sputtered, "But where are we going to live?"

Marie shook her head philosophically. "We can always find a place to live, child. What's important is, we're alive."

16

The next day was the Fourth of July. After sleeping beneath a carpet of stars, and with no place to hide, Selona sat in Marie's rocking chair, listening to the commotion from the fort where preparations for the festivities had begun well before sunrise, when Moss appeared leading a horse loaded with a huge roll of canvas.

"What you got there?" she asked.

He untied a rope supporting the roll and let it fall to the ground. "Sergeant Major Brassard give me this old tent. It'll be up and ready directly."

She watched him lay out the canvas and begin erecting the tent. He talked while he worked, gradually leading the conversation to what he thought was important.

"Goin' to be a good day, Selona. Big parade. Good food. Good music. Dancin'. Folks laughin'. All kinds of carryin' on."

There was a twinkle in his eye, and she sensed he was up to mischief.

"You'll all have a wonderful celebration, Daddy."

"*We'll* all have a wonderful celebration. Selona, you're a

part of this celebration. You and every Colored in this country is a part of this celebration."

"But, Daddy . . . my head!" she wailed.

Liberty crawled through the tent flap, dragging a centerpole,
talking while he worked. "You're beautiful, Selona. Just like
before. Only, you look a little different." His head suddenly
popped out from inside the tent, and he said with a majestic
smile, "A beautiful kind of different."

She shook her head angrily. "I ain't going to the celebration, Daddy. Folks'll be staring at me."

Liberty raised the tent and set the pole into the ground. He
eased out, telling her, "Hold the pole while I set the stakes.
Show me you still got some life in you."

"I got life."

"You got life?"

"Yes. I got life."

He shook his head. "Naw. You ain't got life."

"Yes, I do."

He looked off to the distance, not to anything particular,
but it was clear he was looking at something on the horizon
as he rubbed at his face.

The sweat was running fast as he said, "Your mama . . .
now she had life."

There was a long, painful pause that couldn't be missed. He
said, in a quaking voice, "I done seen a lot of dyin' in my time,
but I ain't never seen nobody that thought every mornin' they
woke up . . . was a birthday." He wiped at his eyes, not knowing if it was sweat or tears, and continued, "Ain't never seen
no woman so weak with so much strong. She never had
nothin', never asked for nothin', never had . . . " His voice
trailed off into silence for a moment, then he said, "She
could've gone off somewhere else. But she come with me. She
come with me 'cause I told her I wanted to be proud. I wanted
to be a man. I had been a slave, treated like somethin' that
wasn't even human. Then I became a soldier. Not that that
means I was a man, but that I could be a part of somethin'.
Part of a country that didn't even know I was alive, but had

done so much dyin' so's I could be free. I never give her nuthin', but then, she never asked for anythin'."

"She had you. And me. And Grams." There was a pause. "Wasn't that enough?"

He gave her that big grin of his that had carried her through so many hard times, and said, "More than enough, I reckon." He reached out to her with the pole. "Come on, now. Time to be buildin' you another place to hide."

With a deep sense of shame, she held the pole while he attached rope to the canvas corners, then took a hammer and drove a stake into the ground. He tied the rope to the stake, then went to the next corner. He said nothing as he worked, glancing occasionally to Selona, who was obviously thinking about what he said.

Then, as though thinking aloud, she said, "Oh, I know, they'll all be polite, and fall all over themselves, but I'm still ugly."

Liberty ignored her as he stepped back, looking pleased at the newly erected tent. "I believe that'll do just fine. But you best remember, the army ain't got enough tents to supply a grown woman a place to hide from the world. 'Cause sure as there's a Good Lord in Heaven, Miss Marie'll burn this one to the ground if you go back to hidin'. "

Selona jumped from the chair and opened the tent flap, and before she disappeared inside, said angrily, "I ain't going hiding . . . and I ain't going to the celebration."

Augustus was in the barracks, polishing his plumed dress helmet when he saw Haymes approach.

"First Sergeant Liberty wants to see you in the orderly room."

Augustus went to the orderly room, where he found Liberty sitting at his desk.

"You're a smart young man, Augustus. I need your help."

"Selona?"

He nodded. "Selona's getting stronger in body, but it's her mind I'm worried about."

"That's only natural, Sarge. She's been through a rough time. It's a miracle she's doing as well as she is." He paused. "What about the baths? Are they helping?"

Moss chuckled, and Augustus realized it was the first time he had seen Moss laugh since the attack. "Marie's about boiled the hide right off her, Augustus. But she ain't with child, and she ain't infected. Burnin' that tent was the best thing that's happened. Now she's around neighbors, folks who know her. But she won't go to the fort, and she says she ain't goin' to the cotillion. She thinks she's some ugly critter nobody wants to look at."

"She's lucky her face wasn't ruined."

"Face ain't everything to a woman. A woman's face is important, but so's their hair. A woman thinks about her hair in a prideful way, like that Sharps is prideful to you."

"What do you want me to do?"

"I recollect you fixin' that Sharps when it was busted. I want you to think about fixin' Selona's hair."

Augustus considered that for a moment, recalling the night on the Kansas prairie when he had repaired the rifle using renderings from a buffalo. Then something came to mind.

"I'll meet you at your tent in one hour. I think I know what we can do."

Augustus disappeared toward the barracks, and Moss returned to the tent, where Selona was sitting in Marie's rocker.

An hour later Augustus appeared. Selona jumped from the rocker and started to retreat into the tent.

"Selona, I've got something you need to see," he shouted, but she was gone from sight.

She called through the canvas, "Go away, Augustus. I don't want to see you."

"I don't have to see you. Not just yet. I've got something for you to put on your head. Please, Selona, take this and put it on your head."

From a large leather pouch he pulled out a thick piece of fur and pushed it through the tent flap. When he felt her take the fur from his hand, he stepped beside Moss and waited. Minutes passed, then more; finally, after nearly half an hour,

the tent flap opened and Selona stepped into the bright sunlight. She wore a look of fear and excitement. But mostly fear.

Moss straightened suddenly, then beamed. "Needs washin',
and a little clippin' here and there, but I think it'll work."

Marie arrived at that moment carrying an armful of dirty
clothes and nearly fell over as she looked at Selona. "Lord, Augustus, what is that?"

"Bring a mirror," he said quickly. Marie went to the pile
that was still sitting on the ground, rummaged through their
belongings, and returned with the mirror.

Moss held the mirror for Selona to see her image.

Selona stared at her image, and the light in her eyes began
to return. Then her fingers went to her head, and for the first
time since the attack she saw herself as being pretty.

Made pretty by a wig Augustus had fashioned from a buffalo robe.

17

✻ ✻ ✻

The celebration at Fort Sill began with a mounted parade of the troops not assigned to field duty. Four companies of 10th Cavalrymen passed in review of regimental commander Lieutenant Colonel J. W. Davidson, a Civil War brevet general who had recently assumed command from Colonel Benjamin Grierson.

The sun danced off highly polished dress helmets and steel sabres, which rattled in cadence from the saddled horses; young and old soldiers sat ramrod straight in their saddles, their eyes unmoving as they passed in review. The regimental band, in formal uniforms, played near the reviewing stand, thrilling the crowd with prancing music.

The afternoon was filled with riding competitions between the cavalry companies, and was highlighted by a baseball game. The cooks had set up a large barbeque area where four spitted steers turned slowly over the glowing coals in the hot afternoon sun.

Then the cotillion began.

Later that evening Selona was sitting in the rocking chair

watching from a distance when Marie appeared carrying what seemed to be some folded blue calico.

"What's that, Grams?"

Marie said, "Come inside." Selona did so just as Augustus and Moss appeared, both dressed in their formal uniforms, including the brightly plumed helmets with regimental insignia of the 10th Cavalry.

Moss paced about, waiting, as did Augustus. It was when the two collided that Selona appeared through the flap, followed by a grinning Marie.

"Ain't she beautiful?" said Marie.

Augustus stared at Selona and couldn't take his eyes off her. The wig had been washed and trimmed. There were enough curls in the fur to give it the look of real hair. Adding to her beauty was the calico dress Marie and Vina had hurriedly sewn that day.

Augustus put out his hand, and realized it was the first time he had touched her since she was a child on the mud-covered streets of Fort Wallace.

What he saw now was a woman who had the strength to overcome pain and hardship; a woman of great inner beauty. A woman of incredible outer beauty.

"May I escort you?" Augustus asked.

He guided her into the rocking chair, and when she was comfortably seated, Augustus and Moss looked at each other, nodded sharply, then knelt.

From each side they hoisted the rocker onto their shoulders and started walking, despite her giggling protests.

"Where are you taking me?"

Augustus looked up and said loudly, "To the cotillion!"

Selona Liberty entered the area roped off for the cotillion through a parting wave of Colored soldiers, carried like a Nubian queen on the shoulders of slaves. But these were not slaves, they were free men who stood ready to die for those who had once enslaved them.

"Put me down," she squealed.

Augustus and Moss lowered the rocking chair to the ground as the band struck up a waltz.

Augustus bowed to Selona, asking politely, "May I have this waltz?"

Selona's eyes filled with fear and then tears. "I'm not strong enough to dance. Besides, I don't know how."

He leaned over and picked her up in his arms, and whispered, "Me neither. But I'm willing to try."

Augustus carried her into the center and, sometimes stumbling awkwardly, whirled and twirled Selona around the dance arena in his big arms beneath a carpet of flashing stars.

As she looked on, her pipe clamped in her mouth, Marie dabbed at her eyes with her sleeve. While life could be hard for her granddaughter in the future, and probably would, tonight her life had paused for a precious moment of magic.

18

L ate in the evening of August 21, Fort Sill came alive with the rattle of sabres and the mounting of horses.

Lieutenant Colonel Davidson had ordered companies C, E, H, and L to proceed to the Indian agency at Anadarko, thirty miles north of the fort, where Lone Wolf and other Indians were on a rampage.

Augustus swung into the saddle behind Captain Louis Carpenter as Carpenter wheeled his horse in front of the company and ordered Liberty, "Move them out, First Sergeant. At the gallop."

The Buffalo Soldiers rode through the night, crossed the Washita River around noon, and entered the Anadarko Indian agency. The agency sat beneath tall bluffs to the north that overlooked the Washita River, which flowed near the main office and commissary. Upon entering the grounds the soldiers could see small camps of Wichita, Caddo, Pawnee, Delaware, and Penateka Comanche. The Kiowa were camped up on the bluffs. The Indians had "come in" for their rations of food and blankets from the commissary; they had properly "enrolled" and had submitted to the government demand to stay on the reservation.

Big Red Food, chief of the Nokoni, was the only holdout, refusing to turn over his weapons, and was not allowed rations.

The acting Indian agent was a man named Connell, who approached Carpenter from the commissary, explaining the situation.

"All the Indians had their chance to come in, Captain. Only Big Red Food and his warriors refused. Now they want rations, and we both know what that means."

Carpenter understood. "They'll scatter to the plains as soon as they get their rations."

"Join up with the Kiowa, I expect."

Carpenter nodded. "How many warriors are with him?"

"Thirty, maybe forty. All of them painted up like hounds from hell."

Carpenter thought for a moment, then told Connell, "Send a man to Big Red Food. Tell him his people can't enroll because they refused to come in voluntarily, and my orders from Colonel Davidson are clear: I'm to bring him and his people to Fort Sill, either peaceably or with force. Tell him there may be a way out of this situation that will save many of his warriors and get his people fed."

"What do you suggest?"

"Tell Big Red Food if he and his people surrender their weapons and agree to return to Fort Sill as prisoners of war, the government will enroll them and return them to the reservation at a later date. But they have to surrender and go to Fort Sill."

Connell sent a Penateka named Tosh-a-way to speak with Big Red Food. The chief agreed to the terms, and Davidson sent Lieutenant Samuel Woodward and forty troopers to collect the weapons, but a group of Kiowa braves began taunting Big Red Food, shouts filling the air about the chief's cowardice in front of a few Buffalo Soldiers. Big Red Food jumped onto his horse, with a war whoop, and rode off in a hail of bullets from the troopers.

Indians began firing from all directions and the Buffalo Soldiers quickly returned fire, killing many Indian bystanders caught in the crossfire.

Sergeant Moss Liberty reared up on his horse, a bullet wound in his back, but ignored his injury and rode quickly to Carpenter, as bullets kicked at the ground around his horse. He spoke with the captain, then galloped back to his squad. "Get to the trees. Dismount and take cover."

H Company raced to the thick trees.

Augustus had pulled his Sharps from his saddle and was dismounting when he saw Liberty fall from his horse. Augustus raced through the trees and dropped beside Liberty. There was a pained look on the first sergeant's face as he struggled to speak, but the words couldn't come, not even a whisper.

Augustus raised him to a sitting position, then looked at his hand. From the darkness of the blood he figured Liberty was liver shot.

"We can't sit here, Sarge."

"Take some men and move forward to the edge of the tree-line. Don't stop firing until the captain orders the charge."

Augustus looked through the trees and could see that the Indians were now firing from the corral and commissary. "You think he'll order a charge?"

Liberty forced a smile. "If I know the captain . . . he'll order a charge."

Augustus nodded and started away; Liberty pulled him back. "You got to do something for me."

"Anything, Sarge. Anything."

"Look after the old woman and my little girl."

Augustus shook his head. "You'll do that yourself."

Liberty forced a smile. "You'll come by afterward?"

Augustus nodded. "I'll come by." Then he was moving through the trees until he found Gibbs and four other troopers shooting from behind trees.

"How's Liberty?" Gibbs asked.

"Liberty thinks the captain'll order a charge."

"He better do something. Them Injuns have got us in a pickle."

That was when a trooper rode up to Augustus, leading a string of horses. "Mount up! The captain says we're going to charge."

"What about Liberty?" Augustus asked.

"Lieutenant Woodward's going to stay with his platoon and cover the rear."

Augustus swung into his saddle and rode toward Carpenter, who had H Company assembled and mounted. Carpenter pointed his sabre toward the corral, where the Indians were now mounting their ponies.

Carpenter shouted, "Charge!"

The troopers charged, pistols in hand, as Big Red Food's warriors thundered out of the agency and raced along the edge of the Washita.

It took Augustus only moments to realize that the Indians, with their swift ponies, had the advantage over the troopers' horses. Their horses were in poor condition to begin with, heavily laden with equipment, and still tired from the long night's march from Fort Sill.

The cavalry had pursued for a mile when the Indians entered a hay field; then, there was the sound of gunshots. Moments later, the soldiers saw the dead bodies of four farmers who had been cutting hay.

Seeing that Big Red Food was escaping, Carpenter raised his hand in the air and brought the column to a sudden halt.

Carpenter's face was etched with the frustration the 10th troopers had often known when pursuing Indians riding fast ponies, while they rode broken-down mounts passed down from white cavalry regiments.

Carpenter turned to his soldiers, released a long sigh and started to say something, but stopped suddenly as his eyes stared to the west, where he saw a black pillar of smoke rising from the agency.

"Back to the agency!" he ordered.

Minutes later the soldiers had returned. The Kiowa had left the bluffs and attacked Woodward's platoon. The commissary was burning, and the bodies of Indians lay all around the agency.

The Kiowa, seeing the charging Buffalo Soldiers, retreated across the Washita and rode hard, knowing their ponies could climb the steep bluff trails better than the cavalry horses.

During Carpenter's pursuit of Big Red Food, Woodward's troopers had been forced into a defensive position at the corral; Woodward approached now, his left arm in a sling from a Kiowa bullet. Three Indians lay dead inside the corral; beyond the corral dozens of Kiowa lay dead.

Carpenter's face darkened. In a low but commanding voice, he ordered his men, "Cross the river, then dismount. We'll take the bluffs on foot!"

The Buffalo Soldiers spurred their horses and crossed the Washita, where they quickly dismounted inside the trees lining the river, and began the assault on the bluffs, where the Kiowa were now dismounting.

The sound of a bugle caught all the soldiers' attention.

"It's Captain Viele and C Company!" Gibbs shouted.

At the east entrance onto the agency the troopers of C Company were riding hard, bugle blowing, their guidon distinct at the head of the column.

Augustus looked up to the bluffs. The Kiowa were retreating to the north.

Later that day, Lieutenant Colonel Donaldson ordered the 10th to take up positions along the bluffs. Trenches were dug for protection, sentries placed as dusk began to settle. The wounded were brought to the center of the bluffs, where Davidson met with the commanders and issued orders for the night. On this August day the three hundred men of the 10th Cavalry had fought well, suffering only four wounded against overwhelming numbers.

Liberty had lost a lot of blood and was weak, but conscious and in good spirits. Brassard and Augustus were with Liberty when a scout rode in and handed the sergeant major a report for Davidson.

Brassard read the report aloud. "More Injuns moving onto the agency, and they ain't carrying peace pipes."

"Going to be hell to pay come morning," Liberty said softly.

"More hell than them Injuns ever thought existed," Brassard growled emphatically. He stood, telling Augustus, "Stay with him, son. I got to report to the colonel." Brassard reached into his pocket for a plug of tobacco and cut off a chew. He put the chew in Liberty's mouth. "You rest easy." Then he walked off toward the command center.

Augustus and Moss talked about many things through the night, with Liberty drifting in and out of sleep. His pain began to fade, but Augustus knew the end was close when Liberty sat up as though there was nothing wrong. As if he were using his last bit of strength. His words were strong and clear as he said, "I got to know something before morning comes."

"What's that, Sarge?"

"I got to know what's going to happen to my baby."

"She'll be fine. She'll be looked after, I promise."

Liberty smiled and extended his hand. "You promise?"

"I promise."

"That's what I wanted to hear. You a good man. A good man keeps his promise." Augustus felt Liberty's hand go limp and watched him fall back as his eyes closed.

The next morning the Indians gathered, nearly three hundred strong, and began the ascent to retake the bluff. The Buffalo Soldiers responded with withering fire from their Spencers, repulsing the attack. The Indians set fire to the dry grass around the agency, but the soldiers descended, pushing back the warriors, building counterfires and cutting trenches until the fire was extinguished and the agency made safe.

On August 23, when the Battle of Anadarko ended, the victorious Buffalo Soldiers returned to Fort Sill. They had proven their mettle.

Two days later, still in a coma in the post infirmary, First Sergeant Moss Liberty, H Company, 10th Regiment of the U.S. Cavalry, died without regaining consciousness.

19

The moment the bugler completed "Taps," Marie grabbed the hand of Selona Liberty and led the girl toward Sergeant Major Brassard, where Augustus stood beside Brassard, watching the two approach. Selona now wore her wig with distinction and dignity, and in her own way had become legendary in the eyes of the 10th Cavalry.

Marie came directly to the point. "What we going to do now that Moss is dead? How's this child going to survive?"

Selona stood behind her grandmother, peering past a floppy bonnet that was betrayed at the edges by curls from the buffalo wig. Her eyes were on Augustus, watchful and obedient.

Brassard put his hands out as though to defend himself. "Hold on, now, Miss Marie. You know we're all sad about Moss. But I don't know what you mean."

"What I mean is, what's me and this child going to do now that her daddy's dead? The money coming in off the laundry ain't enough for a bird to live on. Now that Moss's dead and we ain't got his army pay, we can't stretch a living."

"The regiment's going to take up a collection. You'll get a nice piece of money." Brassard was starting to sweat in the hot sun. Or, wondered Augustus, was it the hot wrath of this woman?

"That ain't good enough. Last trooper to go down, his wife got eighteen dollars. Eighteen dollars! And I heard talk the army's going to start using different laundresses."

"There's some talk about that, Miss Marie."

"Say they going to have to be married to soldiers."

"I believe that will come, Miss Marie."

Marie grabbed Brassard by the sleeve. "Come on, I want to talk with you."

Brassard followed, leaving Augustus standing with Selona.

"I'm sorry about your father. He was a good man." Augustus remembered the promise. "If there's anything you need, I'm at your service. I promised your father I would look after you."

"Did you, now? And how you going to look after me?"

Augustus flushed. He was schooled as a soldier, but not in the ways of handling a woman, even if she was a girl of seventeen. "Like I said, if you need anything, you just have to ask."

A grin curved her mouth. "Would you take supper with us tonight, Augustus?"

Augustus was quick to answer. Word had it that she was the best cook on the fort. "I'd be delighted."

She giggled. "You're so polite." She walked off toward her grandmother, who was talking a storm to Brassard.

Brassard came back to Augustus. "Come on, boy." His voice was serious.

"What's wrong?"

"Never you mind. I'll tell you."

They went to the Evan and Fisher trading post and found a table near the bar. Brassard poured a drink for each of them and lifted the glass, saying, "To the regiment."

"To the regiment." Augustus had drunk whiskey only a few times in his life, and found the taste too bitter for his liking. He had stayed away from the whiskey and hog ranches near the forts, where a dollar could buy a bottle of mean whiskey and an hour with an even meaner prostitute.

Brassard poured another glass for himself and one for Augustus. "What do you know about women?"

Augustus looked at him. "Women? Why do I need to know about women?"

Brassard downed the whiskey and poured another. "You best learn something about women right now. When they come after you, there ain't but two things you can do: step or fetch."

Augustus laughed. "What does that mean?"

"That, young soldier, means you better step quickly out of sight, or fetch up the broom."

"The broom?"

"You were a slave. Get ready to jump the broom."

Augustus understood. It was the way slaves wedded in the south because they were forbidden legal marriage. The bride and groom would hold hands and jump over a broom. That was the wedding ceremony.

Augustus was flustered. "What are you talking about, Sergeant Major?" He gulped down the drink in front of him.

"I mean Miss Marie's got plans. Matrimonial plans that include you and her granddaughter. And, unless I don't know Miss Marie, those plans include her as well." Brassard took a deep breath. "Boy, you only got two choices: you going to get married . . . or do you want a transfer to another post?"

Brassard poured Augustus another drink. Augustus stared at it and sat there, wondering.

The sergeant major had personally helped Augustus dress for dinner that night, to the hoots and jeers of his comrades in the barracks. The word had spread quickly, as news generally traveled on an army post.

Augustus made the long walk to the tent where Selona and Marie lived wearing his ceremonial dress uniform, pistol belt, sabre, and highly polished parade helmet with plume. He carried the fistful of flowers Brassard handed him as he shuffled through the door of the barracks to the raucous laughter of his comrades.

Augustus was in a terrible sweat by the time he reached the tent. He knocked lightly at the flap and waited until Marie appeared. She was smoking her corncob pipe and was holding a freshly beheaded chicken in her hand.

Private Augustus Sharps stepped inside the tent, where he felt his head begin to spin, and he would never know if it was the whiskey, the tight collar, the smell of Marie's tobacco, the pressure of the moment, or all those factors combined.

The moment he saw Selona he fainted dead away to the floor.

Augustus and Selona were wed the following week by the regimental chaplain.

The bride and groom didn't jump the broom; they recited the marital vows from the Book of Common Prayer and walked from the church beneath an arc of poised cavalry sabres. Sergeant Major Brassard gave away the bride, and that night there was a party in honor of the new couple.

They began their life on the prairie together in the tent where Selona and Marie lived. That first night, they slept alone in the tent, but the next night they shared the tent with Marie, who laughed at the giggles coming from behind the blanket that divided the tent into two rooms.

Marie was awakened later in the night as the two newlyweds slipped from the tent, Augustus carrying a heavy buffalo robe.

She lit her pipe in the darkness of the tent, and rose, watching over the two as they settled into the soft earth of Indian Territory, becoming lost beneath the heavy robe, oblivious to the stars above, the dangers not far in the distance.

PART 3

1880-1882: FORT DAVIS

20

✫ ✫ ✫

The night her second child arrived, Selona Sharps jerked awake to a brilliant flash of light; when she tried to rise from the straw-filled mattress in her adobe house at Fort Davis, Texas, she found she could not move. But her eyes could move, and she could see the cloud of light begin to move toward her from near the hearth.

A man suddenly appeared from the cloud, his features growing more distinct with each advancing step.

When he pressed the point of the blade against her temple she tried again to rise, but to no avail. Then there was the sting of the knife slicing through her flesh, cutting evenly above her ear, around the circumference of her head. Smoothly. Well practiced.

Selona screamed as she felt his fingers slip into the incision above her ears. Then there was a sucking sound, like a foot pulling from deep mud. Her head felt as though it would pull from her shoulders—when suddenly the man straightened up above her and began laughing.

In his hand dangled her scalp!

His laughter pierced higher until it turned into a shriek, then a howling, like the wind . . . howling . . . howling . . .

Selona thrashed violently to the floor and tore herself from the nightmare that had tormented her for years. She was soaked with perspiration, and the sound of thunder crashed through her head as she instinctively reached to her hair. When she felt her smooth scalp, and saw no blood on her hands, the shock began to wear off and she could distinguish between the howling in her nightmare and the howling that persisted outside her house.

She opened the door and found Vina Gibbs standing veiled in light from the lantern she held.

"Selona? You all right? I could hear you screaming from the other end of the Row."

The Fort Davis Suds Row was nestled at the base of Sleeping Lion Mountain, near the fort hospital. In 1876, the army had decided the traveling troupes of laundresses had caused too many problems. Now the laundresses had to be married to soldiers, so that the army had a means of controlling the women through their husbands.

Selona rubbed her face roughly, trying to push away the remnants of the nightmare, and motioned Vina inside.

Vina handed her the lantern, and in the swinging light Selona could see that Vina was carrying a bundle pressed against her breast. The bundle moved; then there was the howling of a child.

"What do you have there, Vina?"

"A bundle full of trouble." Vina paused, taking in Selona's disheveled appearance. "You had that nightmare again?"

Selona didn't answer. "Never mind. What trouble?"

Vina thrust the child into her arms. "This baby boy was born this afternoon to one of the young Mexican girls at Adams' hog ranch. One of our Colored troopers is the father. Don't know which. Guess she didn't neither. Old Man Adams brought the baby to the fort. He said, 'Coloreds are the father . . . Coloreds can look after him.' One of the troopers brought him to me."

Selona slowly unfolded the bundle and stared at a dark-skinned newborn baby. He was beautiful.

"Why did you bring this baby here, Vina?"

Vina's face tightened. "The Mexican girl died just after sun-set. That child's hungry, and you're the only woman I know that's got mama's milk."

Selona looked to the straw bed, where three-month-old Adrian lay beneath a shawl. Then she suddenly realized—

"You mean to say you want me to feed this child?"

Vina smiled softly. "You're the only one I know." She had the look of someone waiting for a blessing. "This baby ain't been fed since it drew first breath."

Adrian suddenly chimed in with his own scream of hunger; the two babies formed a chorus that Selona might have thought comical were it not tragic.

Then she motioned for Vina to take the newborn while she opened the top of her nightshirt. Vina helped her, guiding the newborn to her left nipple while Selona guided Adrian to the right.

She sat on the edge of the bed in the flickering lantern light, feeding two children, wondering what would become of both of them.

"What am I going to tell Augustus?"

Vina's eyes glistened. "Tell him the Good Lord called on you with another child lost in the wilderness."

That was the last night she ever had the nightmare.

That was four years ago, thought Selona, who was now twenty-six and already stooped like a woman of fifty.

She wore her buffalo wig beneath a scarf, which gradually worked loose from the wind, and the heat of the laundry fires, and the sweat running from her forehead, until the wig came to rest just above her eyebrows. She would pull the scarf back, resetting the wig, then hitch up her skirt and throw another piece of wood onto the fire burning on the dry, sun-baked west Texas ground.

The morning wind blew hot and dusty around her tired legs and back as she stirred at the layer of white, gurgling lye soap foaming above the dirty clothes in the large iron kettle. She would pause from time to time and wipe at her forehead, then throw on more wood and step back as the froth hissed, then bubbled and popped against the heat of the day, which was nearly as punishing as the heat from the fire. Her long stick fished around the bottom to raise up a pair of sky blue trousers as another blast of hot dust swirled around the fire.

Looking down the line of boiling kettles on Suds Row, Selona could see the other laundresses buzzing about their kettles. At each of the eight boiling cauldrons, the women held children, except Selona.

Nearby Adrian and David—the name she and Augustus chose for the child brought to her by Vina Gibbs—were playing beneath a pinion tree in a swing fashioned from rope and an old McClellan saddle.

Adrian was tall, with deep ebony skin, like his father. He was a quiet lad, prone to sit for long spells on the back porch, his eyes scanning the desert in search of the many types of animals that lived not far from their house.

David was short, with cinnamon-colored skin, a mixture of Negro and Mexican. During the summer the boys lived in a small tent in back of the house on Suds Row, near the rabbit pens, scampering about half-naked like a pair of Apaches. They knew no fear, which terrified Selona.

She looked up as Vina Gibbs approached, pregnant with her fourth child. She had an armful of wet clothes and was wringing out the water with her powerful hands.

That was when Selona, out of the corner of her eye, caught movement in a thick patch of sage twenty feet away, ten feet from the boys' swing. She eased to a wooden box stationed near one of the kettles, all the while talking, but not to Vina.

"David . . . jump up in that saddle with your brother."

David knew what that meant and was in the saddle as fast as her hand went beneath a white cloth lying on the box.

"Lord have mercy!" Vina moaned. She, too, had seen the movement.

Selona's hand whipped straight out, steady, and with a smooth move she cocked the Colt revolver and fired.

The boom shook along Suds Row, raced through the air and

ricocheted with dramatic echo against the caverns and crags of nearby Sleeping Lion Mountain, bringing the Row to a sudden silence.

The laundresses looked up and saw Selona step beyond the piñons, knew everything was all right, and went back to work.

The boys watched as she hiked up her dress, Colt horse pistol still in hand, and walked cautiously from clear ground into the thick sage. She bent, looked, then stepped again, all the while watching. There was nothing but silence as she squatted, adjusting her eyes to the brown sage, then suddenly hurried a few feet forward and reached with her free hand into a thick patch of sage.

The rattlesnake was four feet long, and would have been longer had the bullet not blown the head clean away. She raised up the rattler, smiled, and stepped back, walking as though she were stepping on stones to cross a brook, careful should there be more rattlers.

"Good shot, Mama," David said.

Selona grinned as she handed the snake to Adrian, telling him, "Put this in the root cellar. Later on I'll skin it, clean it, then wrap it in a wet rag." Then she whispered as though conspiring, "We'll have it for breakfast in the morning."

David snatched the snake before Adrian's fingers could take it and ran off toward the house with Adrian in hot pursuit. Selona called to them, "Don't tear up that snake . . . I'm going to make your daddy a hat band."

That was when she realized it was the first time she had thought about Augustus since waking that morning in her empty bed.

The sky was purple to the west as Selona sat waiting on the back step of their small house. Smoke from cook fires rose from the chimneys, then settled, moving casually across the ground with the wind. From other quarters came murmurs, and some shouts. A few children cried, and then there would be silence.

Her eyes went again to the west.

Augustus will come riding in soon, she thought. He would be tired, dirty, and a little more ancient after the long scout that she knew was supposed to cover nearly three hundred miles. She went over it now, for the routine was a permanent part of her memory, as so many things concerning the army were now forever a part of her.

Augustus and three troopers would ride toward the Rio Grande, then follow the river south, watching for signs of Injuns or Mexican raiding parties crossing into the United States. They would sleep at night on low ground, in an arroyo, the campfire probably small and set a foot into the ground. They would eat hardtack and drink brackish water and sleep fully dressed; even their boots would remain on. Their horses would be hobbled, but saddled. There was no truth to the rumor that Indians wouldn't attack at night. And the Mexican bandits preferred to fight at night.

The next morning the four Buffalo Soldiers would rise and try to stretch the soreness from their muscles. After watering and feeding their horses oats from the saddlebags, the troopers would move out, with a point rider scouting the front, then reporting back, replaced by another scout in a continuous back-and-forth process designed to give them early warning of ambush. They would stop and talk with ranchers; white ranchers who held their guns lowered, but to the ready. Augustus had always said he wasn't certain who the ranchers hated most: the Injuns, the Mexicans, or the Buffalo Soldiers.

When they turned east toward Fort Davis and home, they would move less cautiously. The thought of home would excite their spurs against the horses' flanks, making them a little more careless, a little more vulnerable.

She stayed outside until well after sunset. Finally, she started in, knowing Augustus wouldn't be riding in tonight.

21

Marcia O'Kelly felt both anger and sympathy streak through her, as though two lightning bolts had entangled and found the same ground at precisely the same moment.

It was noon in Del Rio, Texas, a sweltering border town between El Paso and Brownsville on the Rio Grande, far from Marcia's home in Dayton, Ohio, which she had left only three weeks before, sailing from New York to Brownsville en route to the west Texas frontier to join Lieutenant Jonathan Bernard O'Kelly, her husband of two months.

Marcia and Jonathan had met while Jonathan was in Ohio for one of the rare trips he made back east. After a whirlwind romance of merely a week, they were married. Lieutenant O'Kelly had to return to Fort Davis ahead of Marcia, who had to get her affairs in order before going to what her family considered "the edge of the world."

The journey by ship had been exciting and enjoyable, but at Brownsville she started the last leg of the trip to Fort Davis by stagecoach.

Now she sat on a wooden porch, caught in the whirling devil tails skipping from the dusty street, the stench of a dog urinating on a nearby hitching post, and the storm of angry shouts that had erupted moments before in front of the stage depot.

"I don't give a good goddamn what some Yankee colonel has to say!" shouted Three-fingers Johnny Braxton, the stage driver. "There ain't no nigger-Injun riding in my stagecoach."

Braxton was short, leather brown from the sun, and quick to use his long flowing beard to wipe at sweat flowing into his angry eyes. From what depot manager Frank McKay could see, Braxton wasn't backing off despite the order sent him by Colonel Benjamin Grierson, who had returned as commander of the 10th Cavalry, now headquartered at Fort Davis, and responsible for maintaining the safety of west Texas against Indian raids, forages by Mexican bandits from across the Rio Grande, and white hooligans rampaging from El Paso to Brownsville.

"It just ain't proper," shouted Braxton. "My God, what would the passengers say?"

"Why don't you ask us?" Marcia stood quickly, her eyes flaming. She adjusted the bonnet covering her long dark hair and for the first time in three weeks wished she had stayed in Dayton. In her hand she carried a parasol as though it were a sabre.

Braxton spat a stream of tobacco juice and hitched up his pants. "Sit down, lady. I ain't talking to you."

McKay held up his hand. "Yes, ma'am. Please stay out of this. This is a stagecoach matter."

Marcia walked quickly over to the young woman sitting in a nearby chair. The young woman who was the focus of discussion.

The moment Marcia had seen her she was immediately intrigued, for she had never seen such a magnificent face; a face that was brown but not ebony; features that were narrow and delicate; black-diamond eyes that stared straight ahead as though oblivious to the fury about her.

McKay, a short, balding man with pale blue eyes that seemed to have turned cerulean from frustration, flashed the letter again to Braxton. "This here girl is Juanita Calderon.

She's John Horse's niece from over at Piedras Negras and her fare is paid through to Fort Davis by the army. You best listen to what I'm saying. Good God, man, do you want all them Seminole niggers coming over here and burning this whole damn town? This girl's practically royalty in her family!"

Juanita Calderon's facial expression changed only momentarily as a thin smile drifted across her mouth; then she again became stoic. She was certainly special, thought Marcia. She wore a calico dress, a flaming red bandanna around her forehead, and high leather moccasins, and her long black braided hair hung to her waist.

Marcia knew nothing of the Seminole Negroes, except what she had heard along the stage trail. The children of runaway slaves and Seminole tribespeople, thousands had been shipped from the Florida Everglades to the Indian Territory before the Civil War, where they became prime targets for Arkansas slave traders. Under the leadership of John Horse, a former slave who had married a Seminole woman, and Blue Cat, a nephew of Osceola, hundreds had crossed Texas to Mexico, where they provided border security for the Mexican government in exchange for diplomatic immunity from slavery. After the Civil War dozens had joined the American army in west Texas and had become known along the border as Seminole Negro Scouts. The Scouts were ferocious fighters, but known best for their tracking ability.

"This girl's going to Fort Davis to marry one of them young Colored soldiers," McKay said. "And she's going to ride on this stagecoach if I have to drive the team myself."

Braxton spit again. "She can ride in the boot. Or you can damn well drive the team."

"That's inhuman," Marcia said, stepping into the street while opening her parasol with such fury that Braxton stepped back and suddenly looked defensive. "This woman can't ride in the boot. She'll choke to death from the dust."

"That's my final word on it." Braxton snapped a quirt against his leg and walked to the stagecoach, angrily kicking at the dog and the dust devils.

Without a word, Juanita stepped from the porch carrying her valise and walked to the rear of the stagecoach. Looking as though she had somehow anticipated such a situation, she pulled her bandanna down, covering her mouth and nose, and climbed onto the baggage lashed into the boot.

Marcia, defeated, started to close the parasol, then paused, stepped to the rear of the stagecoach, and handed the parasol to Juanita, saying softly, "I wish I could do more."

Juanita took the parasol slowly, and Marcia thought she saw her dark eyes smiling over the bandanna.

Then Marcia realized the eyes weren't smiling, they were shining with tears.

Two hundred and fifty miles north of Del Rio, the sun beat down mercilessly; relentlessly. There wasn't the slightest sign of life west of Fort Davis, beyond the Alamita River, which was nothing more than a small stream that time of year. The land was arid and desolate.

Nothing could live out here except hard men used to hard times, thought Corporal Augustus Sharps, 1st Troop, H Company, 10th Regiment of Cavalry, as he led his horse at a walk. Now thirty years old, he was a tall man, his facial features looking fuller within a ten-day growth of beard, the number of days he and his men had been on patrol.

Following in close trail were Private Darcy Gibbs and Trooper David Bane, a short, muscular young man who had been in the 10th for two months; a "young soldier," as new recruits were called until they finished their first year of service. A third trooper was out front, scouting for sign of ambush.

Augustus took his canteen and halted his horse, removed his Kossuth hat, and poked the top inward, forming a depression. He poured water into the depression, then held the hat to the horse. The horse sloshed the water, which Augustus tried to catch with his fingers. He licked the wetness, ignoring the horse saliva that mixed with the water. Water was more important than any thought of germs. A man might die from germs; the same man would surely die without water. The horse as well, and all soldiers knew it was better to be thirsty and riding than to be sated and walking through the desert of west Texas. Then he took some buckshot from his pocket, shoved the lead pellets in his mouth, a trick he had learned to stave off thirst, and took a small sip of water.

"Tighten up," he ordered. The troopers tightened the cinches on their horses.

"Mount up." They threw their legs over the McClellans and settled their weary bodies into the saddles. Augustus led them out at a canter; sitting tall in the saddle he could see a rising cloud of dust to the front. Beyond that he could see the Davis Mountains.

The trail of dust grew closer, and through the rising waves of heat he saw the familiar figure of Trooper Gabriel Jones approaching. Augustus pulled up as Jones drew to a halt.

Jones wiped the sweat from his forehead. He pointed toward the mountains. "Nuthin' ahead. Just a sweet stroll into the fort."

"We'll water the horses at the Alamita, then push hard for Fort Davis." Augustus started to say something else but his mouth froze. To the east there rose such a storm of dust that the very size of the cloud suggested a number of riders.

"Patrol?" asked Bane. He was eighteen years old and had not yet developed the ability to mask his fear. That took more than two months; more than two years. Sometimes, it never came at all.

"Don't rightly know," Augustus muttered.

"Could be Mexicans. Or Injuns," said Gibbs.

"We'll sit a spell," said Augustus. He motioned toward an outcropping of rocks some twenty yards away. To Bane he said, "Take the horses at a walk. Nice and slow. Don't throw up any dust."

Bane took the link attached to the left side of his horse and snapped it to the halter ring of the horse to his left; the others did the same, then removed their Springfield carbines from their saddle boots. This joined the horses, and Bane walked them behind the rocks and waited while the others selected a position in the rocks.

The boiling heat of the desert chapped their dry lips further as the dust drew closer; soon, they were able to make out the shapes of twelve riders.

"Ain't nothin' from a cavalry troop," said Augustus matter-of-factly. "The horses are many colored." All the horses in a troop were the same color, giving the troopers a means of quick identification.

Augustus eared back the hammer on his Sharps. The others quietly removed their pistols and laid them at their sides. Augustus took fresh rounds from the cartridge case and put them on a rock. He adjusted the rear sight. "We'll take them at fifty yards . . . if they be Mexicans or Injuns."

The riders approached in a group and Augustus immediately eliminated the possibility that the riders were Indians. Indians generally rode in single file to deceive trackers about their numbers. That still left Mexicans, and any number of gangs of horse thieves and outlaws in Texas.

"Jason Talbot." Augustus breathed heavily, wishing the riders had been a threat. A physical threat. Jason Talbot, a local rancher, was more a mental threat than physical.

Jason Talbot was the brother of the man who had once owned Augustus and his family.

The Buffalo Soldiers stood, their Springfields resting on their hips, fingers lightly on the triggers.

Talbot, a tall man, slowed his horse to a walk and approached warily. His face was covered with dust; his gray mustache hung to his chin. His black diamond eyes were like banked coals; fiery, gleaming, even in the heat.

Talbot reined in his horse; the others, all white men except for one Mexican, sat quietly in their saddles while Augustus and Talbot talked.

"You niggers seen any men running a string of horses through these parts?"

Augustus felt the chill streak along his spine as he had many times before. He spoke calmly. "I'm Corporal Augustus

Sharps. My last name used to be Talbot. Do you remember me, Mr. Talbot?"

Talbot's voice was chilly. "I know who you are. I remember when you was a pickaninny over to my brother's ranch." Talbot spat. "I heard you was wearing Yankee blue."

The Buffalo Soldiers looked uneasily at one another; then to Talbot, who spat again. "I asked you if you've seen any men with horses."

Augustus lofted the Sharps onto his shoulder. He shook his head. The hell with this man, he told himself. Then he laughed. "Lost the trail?"

Talbot's face hardened. "You boys are suppose to protect us ranchers from horse thieves and Injuns. Not doin' much of a job, are you?"

"We do just fine, so long as you folks stay out of the way and let us do our job." Augustus spat, which took all the moisture left in his mouth. But it was worth the dryness to see the look on Talbot's face.

Talbot wasn't a man to leave without the last word. "I'm buyin' my brother's place. The crazy old fool has been evicted by the bank. I want you to know I'm goin' to plow the whole place under and plant cotton."

Talbot wheeled his horse and rode off without another word.

Augustus stood stunned; he thought he heard Gibbs cursing, but wasn't sure if he could hear anything except the great anger resounding from his very soul. His legs weakened for a moment, then he righted himself, squared his shoulders, and wiped away the perspiration clouding his eyes.

Or was it perspiration?

He took several deep breaths, then slowly walked to his horse, feeling the heat of the anger from his men. They still had a long way to go, and there was nothing that could stop him from reaching his destination.

"Mount up. We've got a lot of riding," Augustus ordered.

"Hadn't we best move slower, Sarge?" asked Bane.

Augustus grinned. "Talbot and his men will have scared off anything that might be waiting for us."

*   *   *

The sun was setting when the patrol reached the Talbot ranch, but Augustus didn't ride directly down. He sat on a hill studying the large adobe ranchhouse, which was in sad disrepair, watching with particular interest the various cross-shaped gunports cut into the closed windows and door.

One port at the door was open; the barrel of a rifle jutted through.

When Augustus rode down, he rode slow, making certain they were seen in clear sight. Stopping at the front door, he spoke to the man he knew was holding a rifle trained on his heart.

"Mr. Talbot. This is Augustus. Do you remember me?" He always said that when he rode over to visit the graves of his mother and father, knowing old man Talbot's mind now worked on a moment-to-moment basis.

The door opened and Talbot stepped out, wearing a tattered Confederate uniform. His left arm was off at the shoulder but Augustus knew he could still shoot.

Talbot eyed him for a moment, then in a wild, crazy voice that sounded like the wind, he shouted, "The bank took my ranch! I ain't got nothing no more. Now you git! Git, I tell you."

Augustus spoke slowly, saying with a steady voice, "It's me, Mr. Talbot, Augustus."

Talbot merely stared long and hard, then turned for the house, but paused at the door. "You was one of my nigras, weren't you?"

"Yes," replied Augustus.

Talbot's cruel voice barked, "I used to have a lot of nigras. Now the bank owns them." He opened the door, then called as he stepped into the darkness of the house, "Take them and be gone."

Augustus stepped down from his horse and took the blanket from his saddle and walked to the rear of the house. A small cemetery sat in hard, open ground. Wagon wheels half buried there marked the graves of his mother and father.

Gibbs spread a blanket on the ground while Augustus and the others took off their blouses.

Then, beneath the scalding sun, the Buffalo Soldiers took their sabres and dug into the hard, bitter ground, performing an act no human being should have to perform. But Augustus couldn't leave them to be plowed up.

22

The following day the small patrol rode into Fort Davis, and after reporting to the orderly room, Augustus dismissed his men and went to his quarters on Suds Row.

When she saw him approach, Selona dropped the stick she was using to stir one of the washing kettles and raced toward him. As she neared she suddenly stopped, and looked at the blanket and blouses tied to his saddle in two bundles.

He dismounted and she slowly stepped into his open arms and kissed him on the cheek. There was something in his eyes that was different, not like the times before when he returned wearing a big grin and swept her off her feet.

"I thought you would be here yesterday."

Augustus replied solemnly, "I had to go over to the Talbot ranch. Old man Talbot lost his land to the bank. His brother bought the land and said he was going to plow and plant cotton."

It took a moment before the reality made her eyes widen, and she could only stand there and feel the depths of human shame. And the anger.

Augustus picked up the bundles and walked into the house.

Selona stood stone solid for a moment, then walked into the piñons and sat beneath a tall cactus and wept.

That afternoon the heat was almost unbearable, but Augustus dug the two graves, small, like graves for children. He took Gibbs' hand and was pulled out, facing the group of Buffalo Soldiers, the wives from Suds Row, and several officers from the regiment.

Chaplain O'Donnell stepped forward and read a brief prayer. Then the remains were interred alongside the remains of scores of Negroes, many of whom had died fighting to protect the white settlers and former slaveowners of the Texas frontier.

Colonel Grierson took his violin and began playing "The Old Rugged Cross," joined by a few troopers of the regimental band. The voices of the gathering joined the music and for a long moment, on the edge of the violent frontier, the dead were given a decency they had not known in life.

Slowly the group broke up, leaving only Augustus, Selona, and the children to their private moments.

"I never knew them, Augustus. They never knew their grandchildren. Never knew they would even have grandchildren. But you know what's the most hurtful?"

"What?"

"They didn't even have a piece of ground where they could be buried and rest in peace."

Augustus walked off, stooped at the shoulders, followed by the boys.

Selona visited Marie's grave, as she did every day, and had brought along a gourd of water for the flowers she planted each spring. The grave was marked by a white board bearing Marie's name and the date of her death, March 7, 1876, two months before the birth of David. There was no year of birth since Marie hadn't known it.

"Well, Grams, you finally got your piece of land," she whispered.

Some piece of land! Six feet deep, two feet wide, and six feet long. A flood of memories rushed in as she thought of the craggy little woman.

"You got me that husband, and we've got children, but there's no piece of land in sight. I don't think I'll ever own any more land than what you've got, Grams."

How in the world could Colored people save enough money on army pay to buy land?

But it was her dream, one Selona felt gnawing at her with more intensity with each rising of the sun. As though Marie would never rest in peace until a part of the earth belonged to her.

"I'm going to own me a piece of land," she whispered. "Some day me and my family's going to have our own land. I don't want to be buried in some lonesome place like Mama, you, and Daddy. The children never knew any of you. Won't know what you looked like. How you sounded."

She sprinkled each of the flowers lightly, then stood and started back to her kettles on Suds Row.

The stagecoach boiled into Fort Davis the next afternoon, followed by a cloud of white alkaline dust that settled over the coach, driver, and horses as Three-fingers Johnny Braxton jerked the team to a halt in front of the sutler's.

Lieutenant O'Kelly waded through the cloud and pulled open the door to find his wife sitting in an inch of thick dust, her face and clothes white as silver, as was her dark hair. The only color was the fire in her eyes.

O'Kelly reached and helped her down. She moved slowly, the discomfort from the bone-jolting ride evident on her twisted face. He started to put his arms around her but she walked past him and went to the rear of the coach.

Juanita Calderon was tied to the boot; the parasol was nothing more than tattered cloth, and the frame twisted wires. Marcia untied the woman, then gently guided her to the ground. "Don't just stand there, John. Help this poor woman."

O'Kelly, stunned, moved automatically as he took Juanita's

hand and guided her to a chair on the porch of the sutler's.

Private Winston Jackson was tall and slim with narrow features, and holding a fistful of flowers as he stood transfixed
on the porch, his eyes bulging.

Lieutenant O'Kelly's quick glare seemed to pull Jackson
from the trance. He disappeared inside the sutler's and returned moments later with a ladle of water. Juanita sipped
slowly as the coach lurched off to the stables for a fresh team
of horses.

Selona had been walking to the sutler's when she saw the
coach arrive, and seeing Jackson tending the young woman,
she knew she was the Seminole Negro woman sent for by
Colonel Grierson. The colonel often arranged marriages
among the Coloreds and the Seminole Negroes, using the
matchmaking as a means to enlist the brothers of the brides
into the cavalry as scouts. That, and the offer of land on the
American side of the Rio Grande.

"Here, Missy. I'll tend to her," a voice called to Marcia.

Marcia turned and saw Selona, and her eyes went immediately to her head, for Selona had removed her calico rag, revealing the buffalo fur hairpiece. In all her life Marcia had
never seen anything quite so extraordinary. She stood dumbfounded as Selona dipped the calico in the water and gently
wiped at the dust crusted around Juanita's eyelids, then her
cheeks, all the while talking in a soothing voice.

"Got to find out what kind of pretty girl we got under all
this Texas dust," she whispered. "I know there's got to be
something pretty waiting for my eyes to behold." She looked
at Jackson, then said, "I know you going to be pretty enough
for Trooper Jackson no matter how you look, because he ain't
much to look at himself."

This brought a slight smile to Juanita's face. Her eyes went
to Winston Jackson.

For the first time in the three days since the stagecoach had
left Del Rio, Marcia heard Juanita speak: "He is a fine-looking man. We will have fine-looking children."

Trooper Winston Jackson stepped forward and gave her the
flowers. She accepted them with a smile.

"Come with me," said Selona. "We got your quarters all ready over on Suds Row. The chaplain's waiting to get you two hitched nice and proper."

Jackson and Juanita walked with Selona from the porch and started for Suds Row, as the wind whirled and dust flew around another couple starting their life on the west Texas frontier, not knowing that dark clouds were moving toward the Buffalo Soldiers from the harsh mountains of Mexico.

Late that night, on July 16, 1880, a dispatch rider from a patrol rode into the fort with an urgent message for Colonel Grierson: a Mescalero Apache war chief had crossed the Rio Grande and was moving toward New Mexico with several hundred warriors.

The war chief's name was Victorio.

23

The orderly room at regimental headquarters was buzzing when Lieutenant O'Kelly entered. It was packed with the company commanders of the four cavalry companies, along with the commander of a company from the Colored 24th Infantry now stationed at Fort Davis, and Grierson's son Robert, visiting from his college in the east. O'Kelly, a troop leader, stood quietly in the back as Grierson laid out his plan to destroy Victorio.

"Gentlemen, there's no doubt Victorio has crossed for winter supplies and will forage along this route." He ran his finger along the Rio Grande north into New Mexico. "Reports have already come in that he has attacked several small ranches, killed settlers, and driven off their stock. What we are going to do is quite simple: We're going to deny him access to the most precious supply of all—that being water."

Grierson pointed at the various wells along the Trans-Pecos area of west Texas, then continued, "We'll concentrate our main elements at Tinaja de las Palmas, Eagle Springs, and Van Horn Springs, where he's more than likely heading."

"From these concentrations we can patrol the area and maintain constant pressure."

Captain Carpenter spoke, "You intend to split his forces?"

Grierson shook his head. "I don't think he will do that. I believe he will arrive at one of these locations with his entire force."

There was apprehension on the faces of the officers. "That will give Victorio a decisive advantage, sir," warned Carpenter.

"That's precisely what I want him to think. But we will use scouts and pickets to determine his direction. Once we know, we'll converge all our strength on that location."

Again Carpenter spoke, saying, "Each concentration will be the bait in the trap."

Grierson nodded solemnly. "That's precisely what you will be."

Augustus stood at the open back door watching the sun as it approached dawn, not knowing that Selona lay in the thin light staring at his back. The word had started to spread late the night before, and by midnight all of Fort Davis was gearing up for war.

Including the wives and children, who, of course, along with a protective company left to defend the fort, would stay behind and endure the worst hardship of war: the wait.

Selona slipped quietly out of bed and went to the hearth and started a fire, then hung the coffeepot over the flame and started cutting fatback. Augustus didn't turn and face her; he knew what she would be thinking.

It was no secret along the Trans-Pecos—the west Texas frontier—that Victorio was bold, brutal, elusive, and a military genius, thwarting all efforts of capture over the years. From the mountains in Mexico his warriors had plundered the frontier with impunity, leaving in their wake hundreds of dead settlers and taking an equal number of captives to be sold in Mexico for guns and ammunition.

The fatback started sizzling. Augustus couldn't ignore her

any longer. He turned and saw her cracking an egg into a pan. She set the pan on a grate over the fire, and went to a chair by the table, and stared into his dark eyes.

This time he could be gone forever.

"I wish we'd never stayed in this army, Augustus," she said flatly.

"It's given us a home," he said, repeating the words he had used over the years when going on patrol.

She rose, saying softly, "I'll wake the children."

"No. Let them sleep."

She shook her head, saying, "I want them to see you, in case you—"

She stopped suddenly, then hurried past him through the door.

Except during the winter, and when Augustus was on patrol, Adrian and David slept in a small tent near the side of the house, giving Augustus and Selona some privacy, and them a place to call their own. She opened the small tent flap and looked inside. They were curled on their small straw mattresses.

She nudged them, saying, "Wake up, now. Come on inside. Your daddy's going to be leaving soon."

Adrian looked up, wiping at his eyes, then asked, "Where's Daddy going?"

That was the hardest question to answer. They could ask about how rattlesnakes live in rocks and she could give an answer. They could ask how come the sun comes up in the east and sets in the west and she could answer. She could answer questions about many things.

But she could never tell them properly that their father was riding into harm's way, and that he might never return.

Augustus was eating when the boys and Selona came inside. He laid down his fork and opened his arms to them. They raced into them and he hoisted each one onto his knee. "You boys be good while daddy's gone. Mind your mama, and don't be wandering off into the brush by yourself."

A question from Adrian: "Daddy, why do you have to leave again?"

"I'm a soldier, baby. I got some soldier duty to do. But don't you worry. I'll be back soon."

Selona looked at him, and saw that his eyes couldn't hide the lie.

Augustus stood them on the floor, then rose and went to the mantel. On the wall, perched on two wooden pegs driven into the adobe, was his Sharps rifle. He took down the rifle, then reached to another set of pegs for the sabre issued to him at Fort Wallace more than a decade before. The hilt was worn, and the scabbard dented, but the blade was razor sharp and polished to a gleam.

Corporal Augustus Sharps leaned and kissed the boys, then took Selona in his arms and kissed her long and gently.

Then, without a word, he pulled himself away and disappeared through the door.

Lieutenant Jonathan O'Kelly stepped down from the porch of his quarters, his arm linked with Marcia's, and placed his hat on his head. He turned and looked at her while in the background the sound of horses filled the air, the bugle blew assembly, and men filed onto the parade ground.

"I'm sorry we didn't get to spend more time together, my dear."

She squeezed his arm and laid her head on his shoulder. "You warned me that the life of an army wife meant that you lived in the present, and that the future was uncertain at best."

He chuckled. "Did I really say something like that?"

She nodded. "Yes, just before you asked me to marry you. So I was forewarned."

"I didn't realize it would come about this quickly."

Then she stopped, as though realizing that an army wife sending her husband to war must draw a line on the ground where she would stay and he would leave. A physical reference where she had to stay while he went forward.

A line of rose bushes grew twenty feet from their front door. She stopped at the line, picked a rose, and handed it to him, saying, "I'll be waiting for you here, when you return. And you will return, Jonathan. I know you will."

They kissed, then he walked past the rose bushes, his eyes straight ahead until he reached the stables.

The sun was high and the temperature rising as the 10th Cavalry made a broad formation, troopers sitting at attention as Colonel Benjamin H. Grierson rode forward and took the salute from Captain Louis H. Carpenter, designated as the battalion commander for the upcoming campaign against Victorio.

The battalion was right-turned, and with the sound of sabres and cavalry accoutrement competing with the strains of "When Johnny Comes Marching Home Again," played by the 10th Cavalry regimental band, the long blue line rode from the fort under the proud but worried eyes of wives, children, and soldiers left behind to defend the fort.

Selona had walked from Suds Row with the boys and stood at the edge of the parade field, watching the battalion slowly pass Colonel Grierson, who returned the salute of each company commander as the troops paraded past.

Marcia was standing just behind the rose bushes, her arms folded, watching Lieutenant Jonathan O'Kelly lead his troops toward battle. She too felt the mixture of both pride and fear. She turned and looked along the parade ground to where the wives of the officers and Colored troops stood watching, and realized that despite the difference in race, they shared a common bond that was profoundly obvious and joined them as one:

Their men were going to war.

24

The forced march to Eagle Springs, where H Company was assigned, covered the most difficult terrain in west Texas. The company moved at a gallop, followed by H Company of the 24th Infantry, who traveled by wagon and were miles behind the cavalry troopers. By four o'clock that afternoon, the horses nearly broken, H Company had covered more than twenty miles.

Augustus and Gibbs rode the point relay, each riding a half mile ahead of the company, scouting for sign of ambush or Apache movement, then waiting for the column to reach their position. Bane and Williams rode the right flank while Jackson and Haymes rode the left flank, keeping the company in sight while riding similar relays.

With the exception of Captain Nicholas Nolan and A Troop's scout through the Illano Estacado—the "Staked Plains"—the march was the most grueling for man or horse in the history of the 10th Cavalry.

The troopers had been raised to believe that God created the earth; but they knew that this part of the world had been created by the Devil.

The hard, bitter ground was laced with sharp rocks, thick brush, and dry ravines that seemed to be made of iron. Heat shimmered in the distance, wrapping the troopers in a blanket that made their ride an inferno.

By five o'clock, Gibbs was sitting on a small rise northeast of Mount Livermore, watching the column reach his position.

Augustus was riding beside O'Kelly, who raised his hand when he reached Gibbs' position.

Augustus studied the sky to the north, where black specks could be seen circling no more than two miles away.

"Corporal Sharps, you and Private Gibbs take six men and ride ahead and see what the buzzards are circling. It could be nothing more than a dead animal on the ground, but exercise caution."

Augustus pointed to his squad, motioned them to follow, then spurred his horse.

The men reached a dry riverbed and reined in their horses and dismounted. What they found was not a dead animal.

"Darcy, set up a defensive perimeter. Make sure the men's weapons are loaded and ready to fire." Augustus removed his pistol from his holster, fired into the air, then made his way down the dry bank to the riverbed.

A white man lay spread-eagled, his hands and feet staked to the ground. His throat had been cut beneath the chin and his tongue pulled through the slit. His eyelids had been cut off, and he lay naked, his private parts burned away by a fire built between his legs.

Augustus knelt, noticing something odd spread around the body. He picked up a piece of animal bone that had been cleaned of all the meat. Just then Gibbs walked up, saw the bones, and said, "What you figure they did?"

Augustus shook his head, then said, "Looks like the Apaches cooked some dog meat over the fire while he was being tortured."

Gibbs had a look of sheer disgust on his face. "That ain't no way for a man to die. No way a'tall."

"The Mescalero know how to keep a man alive for a long time when they're torturing him."

Gibbs shook his head. "I ain't ever goin' to let no Apache take me alive, Augustus."

The company reached the bank of the riverbed, where O'Kelly dismounted and ordered the troops to rest their horses. He posted pickets, then walked down the bank to where Augustus stood over the body.

These were men hardened by the brutality of the frontier, who had seen as much as they were looking at now, but it never became easier to see how vile one human being could be to another.

"Form a burial detail, Private Gibbs," O'Kelly ordered. Gibbs walked off, and O'Kelly squatted by the body. He took a piece of bone from the ground and looked at it curiously. "Any idea who this man is, Corporal Sharps?"

Augustus nodded. "Jason Talbot. His brother owned me and my family when we were slaves." Augustus stared at Talbot's face; his eyes were gone, burned out by the Apaches. "I reckon you won't be planting cotton this year, Mr. Talbot," he whispered softly.

Talbot was buried an hour later, near sundown, and realizing the poor condition of the horses, O'Kelly ordered the men to make camp. "We'll rest the horses and give the infantry time to catch up with our column." O'Kelly summoned Augustus. "Why would the Apaches take the time to torture this man to death, Corporal Sharps?"

Augustus had thought about that. The Apaches would want to conceal their presence from the cavalry, knowing they were being sought by the soldiers.

"Victorio is the smartest Apache alive, and he don't make mistakes, Lieutenant."

"My thoughts exactly. Which makes me wonder why one of his advance parties would deliberately make their presence known in this area."

Augustus pointed to the northwest. "The sign we found wasn't from a large band, no more than a dozen, and their trail is moving northwest, directly for Sierra Blanca Mountain."

O'Kelly mulled this over for a moment. "Pick four men

whose horses are in good shape. I'm going to send a dispatch to Colonel Grierson and report this."

Augustus understood what O'Kelly was thinking. "You don't think this was an advance party, sent ahead by Victorio, do you, Lieutenant?"

O'Kelly shook his head. "No, I don't. I think Victorio wants us to think he's crossed to the west . . . while he's actually planning to cross to the south."

"I'll take three men and ride for the colonel."

"No. I want you to stay with the column and scout on ahead. If the Indians who killed Talbot are leading us on a wild goose chase, I'll need your scouting skills. We'll play his game until we hear from Colonel Grierson, and press on for Eagle Springs."

Augustus saluted and started away, when O'Kelly said, "Make sure the men you pick are seasoned soldiers, Corporal. I don't want any young soldiers on this mission."

Augustus hurried away and selected the best troopers he could find. The four troopers rode out of camp a half hour later, traveling southwest toward Tinaja de las Palmas, where Grierson's command was located.

O'Kelly ordered the horses unsaddled, fed a ration of oats, watered, and picketed near the center of the riverbed, in case of Indian attack.

On the third day the column reached Eagle Springs, which lay between the Sierra Diablo Mountains to the east and the Rio Grande to the west. The men were tired and the horses were near collapse, but there was no respite. Scouts and pickets were dispatched to scour the area looking for sign of Victorio.

None was found.

On August 1, 1880, a dispatch rider rode into Eagle Springs with word that Grierson was en route with three companies of cavalry after engaging Victorio near Tinaja de las Palmas.

The engagement was nothing more than a skirmish, and Victorio slipped back into Mexico, beyond Grierson's reach.

Grierson knew Victorio had to go north to forage for the winter, and suspected that the Mescalero chief would have to return to Texas to make his northern march. The most likely trail, he concluded, would be to cross the Rio Grande to the south, slipping in behind the cavalry, then move north on the east side of the Van Horn Mountains. Grierson took part of H Company with him from Eagle Springs to Van Horn Springs, where he set up his headquarters and waited for Victorio.

On August 4, 1880, Augustus' small patrol approached Alamo Springs, a small trickle of water that lay between the Eagle Mountains and Van Horn Mountains, forty miles southeast of Eagle Springs.

The ten men in his patrol were moving cautiously, having slept the night before on the hard ground, fully clothed and their horses saddled. They rose before sunrise and continued the circular scout that would bring them to Alamo Springs later that day.

It was noon, and the sun, which seemed a greater threat to the soldiers than the elusive Apaches, had turned the flat plain into an inferno.

Augustus was studying the rocky terrain north of Alamo Springs through his telescope, when he suddenly ordered his men, "Draw your rifles."

Gibbs took the telescope and looked to where Augustus pointed. "Apaches!"

A party of twenty Indians could be seen moving along a ravine that wound toward the Van Horn Mountains.

"Colonel Grierson was right," said Augustus. He was carrying his Springfield, not the Sharps, for he wanted quicker reloading capability.

With a certain excitement Augustus and the other troopers prepared to move forward. The long marches, the harsh scouts that had always turned up empty, had finally paid off.

Augustus spurred his horse to the gallop, as did the others, and the ten cavalry soldiers raced in the direction of the rising dust.

The first shot was fired by an Apache outrider between the troopers and the main body. That warning shot put the Apaches to flight as they came out of the ravine and raced into open country.

Augustus raised his rifle, took aim, and fired, but the bullet missed the mark. In the next moment ten more Springfields fired, all missing their mark as the troopers shot from the saddles of their charging horses.

Augustus was the first trooper to reach the ravine, where he drove his horse down, then up the far wall. At the top he could see the Apaches were opening their lead on the troopers.

Frustration boiled to the surface as he realized their horses, driven to the point of breaking in the past weeks, were no match for the Indian ponies. Just as at Anadarko, he thought to himself, when the 10th had pursued the Kiowa from the agency.

Augustus quickly jumped from his horse, shouting, "Dismount and prepare to fire."

The troopers dismounted and knelt, their hearts pounding as they tried to take aim, but the Apaches rode through tall cactus and heavy brush, pushing north and out of range.

The Springfields fired in unison, but again, they did not find the mark.

That was when Augustus heard Gibbs shout, "There's more coming from the south!"

Augustus could see the dust rising from the south and realized more than one band was approaching. Now they were heavily outnumbered.

"Mount up!" he ordered.

The troopers spurred their horses and raced to the northwest, but the Apaches were closing the distance. Then he glanced to the east, toward the mountains, and a chill ran along his spine as he realized the first band had turned and was joining the second band.

Bullets whined past the soldiers, but what worried Augustus most was that his horse was losing strength, as were the other mounts, all lathered heavily and foaming at the mouth. The pounding of the hooves on the hard ground, and the rattle of their sabres against the saddles, could not mask the pounding in their hearts as the troopers veered toward the mountains.

If they could reach the mountains they might have a chance, thought Augustus. He pointed ahead to where the Eagle Mountains rose like a fortress.

A quick glance back and Augustus could see the Apaches had now formed one group of what he estimated to be forty warriors, and were less than five hundred yards behind the troopers.

Closer they came to the mountains, closer to some hope of making a stand, for it would be certain death to fight in the open, where the Apaches would simply overwhelm the smaller force.

The bullets began hitting closer, kicking up the ground around the troopers, but no one was hit; several Indians stopped their horses to take careful aim, but now the cactus and rock were giving the Buffalo Soldiers a measure of protection.

The horses were nearly broken when the troopers reached a finger of rocks that jutted from the mountains.

The eleven troopers dismounted and took cover, hearts pounding, as the Apaches drew closer, their yells filling the air.

Augustus first grabbed his Sharps and his Springfield from his saddle, then raced to where Gibbs was already taking aim.

"Prepare for volley fire on my command," Augustus ordered.

The troopers took aim, waiting for the Apaches to come within accurate range. Sweat poured down their faces as they saw the Indians approach cautiously, their horses slowing to a walk.

"What are they doin'?" asked Gibbs.

Augustus wiped the sweat from his eyes and shook his head. "I don't know."

From his position in the rocks, which was the high ground, Augustus could see two of the Indians in a heated discussion some three hundred yards away, where the band of Apaches were now stopped.

Then, as quickly as it had begun, it was over.

The eleven troopers of the 10th Cavalry sat and watched in total disbelief as the Apaches began riding north toward the Sierra Diablo Mountains, not east toward the Van Horns, the route Grierson had predicted would be Victorio's line of march.

25

The patrol arrived at Van Horn Wells, where Grierson was now headquartered with part of H Company, the remainder being at Eagle Springs. It was after midnight when they rode into the camp, totally exhausted on horses that could barely walk. Augustus went with Lieutenant O'Kelly to Colonel Grierson, to file his report of the encounter.

Grierson had been right, thinking Victorio would cross to the south, but now he was bothered by the obvious. "I'm afraid I've made a grave miscalculation in estimating Victorio's intentions, Lieutenant."

"How's that, sir?"

Grierson looked hard at Augustus. "You're certain the Apaches were moving along the Sierra Diablo Mountains, Corporal Sharps?"

"Yes, sir. We could see their trail dust for miles. They didn't turn back toward the Van Horns."

Grierson went to his maps. "If Victorio is traveling along the Sierra Diablos, he must be making for the Salt Flat Valley."

"If that's true, he couldn't have taken a more treacherous

route to New Mexico. That's the most Godforsaken land in west Texas."

Grierson nodded, then said softly, "It's the Devil's own country, with only one place to find water. From there he'll be able to move fresh into New Mexico. Do you know where he's going, Lieutenant O'Kelly?"

"I suspect he's going to Rattlesnake Springs, sir."

"I suspect you're right, and we have most of our people stretched along the east side of the Van Horns—more than sixty miles from where he's going."

They all understood the implication: Victorio would slip through the defenses and reach New Mexico, where he would plunder and pillage the territory, then make a full circle back to his stronghold in Mexico.

Grierson studied the map again. Rattlesnake Springs sat between the Sierra Diablos to the west, the Guadalupe range of New Mexico to the north, and the Delaware and Apache mountains to the east. Penetrating the center of the Salt Flats from the south was a small spur of hills known as the Baylor Mountains.

Grierson then made a decision that would test both man and horse. He tapped the map at the spur of the Baylors, telling O'Kelly, "Get your troops ready, Lieutenant. We'll move out at dawn. If Victorio is traveling along the eastern side of the Sierra Diablos, we'll travel the east side of the Baylors, to avoid detection. It's down to a horse race to the springs."

"I doubt our horses will make it, Colonel," O'Kelly said flatly.

Grierson's eyes hardened. "There's no choice in the matter, Lieutenant."

O'Kelly knew that Victorio had outwitted Grierson. If the Apache chief succeeded in reaching New Mexico, Grierson's career would end in disgrace.

The column left Van Horn Wells at dawn, with Grierson in command. Grierson and his son Robert rode in one of the two hospital ambulances, which were followed by the freight wagons that carried the supplies needed when the entire battalion converged around Rattlesnake Springs.

The pace was grueling, the country desolate. When a trooper's horse broke down, the soldier would take his rifle from his saddle, shoot the horse, then throw the saddle in one of the freight wagons and walk alongside the wagon, going from cavalry to infantry.

By sundown it was obvious they would lose the race. Still, Grierson ordered O'Kelly to make for Rattlesnake Springs as fast as possible.

H Company moved out at a gallop, riding hard through the night, stopping only to water the horses from their canteens.

Augustus and Gibbs rode the point, over ground that was coal black in the moonless night. They galloped down ravines, stopped, listened, then rode a few hundred yards more, dismounted, and walked their horses until the column caught up. Augustus and Gibbs each had two horses; they changed mounts after each hard dash a quarter mile to the front, but by the time they reached Rattlesnake Springs at midnight, the horses were nearly dead from exhaustion.

The company had covered the sixty-five miles from Van Horn Wells in the incredible time of twenty-one hours.

Grierson and the freight column arrived at three-thirty the next morning, August 6, 1880.

Victorio was nowhere to be seen. The Buffalo Soldiers had beaten the great Mescalero war chief to the springs, and now prepared to give the Apaches a proper welcome.

The sun rose over the eastern Delaware Mountains, running fast across the hard ground, turning the sand a deep red, then purple, then white as the starkness of the Salt Flat Valley made itself clear.

Grierson now commanded the largest military force ever assembled on the Trans-Pecos, composed of six companies of cavalry and one company of infantry from the 24th, which was slowly moving up from the south, guarding the vital supply train. He ordered scouts to scour the area south of the springs, specifically a deep arroyo named Rattlesnake Canyon.

As battalion commander, Captain Carpenter decided to place C Company under the command of Captain Charles Viele, and G Company under command of Lieutenant Ayers, in carefully selected positions along the arroyo, holding B Company and H Company in reserve, while Grierson remained at the springs to direct the battle.

It was just before noon when C and G companies moved out, with B and H companies mounted and ready.

At two P.M., the Mescaleros moved along the arroyo seemingly confident they would reach the springs without being detected, when one of their scouts spotted the Buffalo Soldiers of C Company.

Victorio, seeing only two companies of the Buffalo Soldiers, and in desperate need of the water at the springs, ordered his warriors to attack.

Volley after volley of gunfire erupted as the Apaches darted on horseback toward the Buffalo Soldiers.

Nearby, Carpenter, having heard the volley, knew the trap had been sprung.

Carpenter pulled his sword and ordered, "Charge!"

H Company boiled onto the battle scene, where the two cavalry companies were being hard pressed by the Mescaleros, who were attacking in force of over two hundred.

The arrival of H Company caught the Apaches off-guard as the Buffalo Soldiers charged into the Indians.

One Apache on horseback aimed his rifle and fired at Augustus, but the bullet struck empty air. Augustus raised his pistol and fired, but he missed as well.

The Apache pulled a spear from around his shoulder and charged Augustus, while around them other Apaches were starting to retreat for the hills.

The two spurred their horses toward each other as Augustus's hand went to his sabre. He withdrew the blade with one easy motion as the Apache's spear neared his throat, and with a smooth move parried the spear to the outside as the warrior raced past. Augustus wheeled his horse, turning directly onto the Indian, who was giving none of his ground.

They met on the hard earth of the arroyo, two men sworn to fight for their nations. As the war lance thrust at Augustus, he ducked, leaned, then rose and slashed the sabre across the back of the warrior's neck.

The Mescalero fell from his horse and lay still. The fighting quickly ended, the warriors of Victorio now in full flight.

The entire battle had been a bitter disappointment for Colonel Benjamin H. Grierson; though his beloved 10th Cavalry had defeated Victorio, the Apaches had retreated safely to the mountains and were now again moving south toward Mexico, losing only eight Indians, two of them women, and two of them children.

There was another skirmish that afternoon with the 24th Infantry approaching from the south, but the Apaches were driven off by withering rifle fire. Despite riding horses so poor they could barely walk, Captain Nicholas Nolan and A Company pursued the Apaches until nightfall, then returned to camp.

The forward advance of Victorio into New Mexico had been stopped, and the fact that the Buffalo Soldiers had accomplished a military miracle over the past few weeks, covering more than six hundred miles of territory, made Grierson proud. During the two battles at Tinaja de las Palmas and Rattlesnake Springs, and a few minor skirmishes that followed, more than thirty Apaches were counted dead, their supplies destroyed, and over a hundred animals captured.

26

Five days after the battle at Rattlesnake Springs, Selona watched Augustus approach, filthy and tired. She didn't mind the smell as he took her in his arms. His strength had been what she needed; his smell would be gone with water and lye soap.

The boys rushed out, yelping with glee, and jumped straight into his arms.

He was gaunt and haggard and had lost a lot of weight, but there was a shine in his eyes as he hugged the boys, saying, "It's good to be home."

Then they went inside, and as Selona watched him hang up his Sharps, then his sabre, it was as though they had passed through an invisible doorway into another phase of life.

Then she shivered, thinking to herself, Until the next time . . .

Selona had a rope and blanket stretched across the room and he bathed in her washing tub; soap splashed over the floor and she laughed at the ridiculous sight.

She peeped over the blanket. "Never thought a man six foot two inches could fit into my washtub." She clapped her hands, giggling as he tried to lower himself into the hot water. Then she turned to the boys and shooed them away, telling them, "Y'all go on out to your tent, now." There was a hunger in her eyes and firmness in her voice.

They grabbed their slingshots and went through the front door.

Augustus laughed. "I never have fit into this thing. But at least my feet'll get clean."

She washed his shoulders with a cloth, scrubbing him slowly, making certain each stroke soothed the muscles. How those muscles must be tired, she thought. Nearly a month in the saddle or sleeping on hard ground, if he did sleep.

Augustus sighed. "I've been trying to figure out a puzzle."

"What puzzle?"

"Why I married you, Selona."

"I'd say you didn't have much choice. Not once Grams had you in her sights."

Augustus roared with laughter. "That's a fact."

She slowly washed his back. "You got the puzzle figured out?"

He laughed. A knowing laugh. "You're the best cook and wash woman in the west."

"You know I can do other things too," she whispered in his ear.

Selona and Augustus carried a buffalo robe to the piñon trees near where she had killed the rattlesnake and lay beneath the moon, making love as the stars streaked across the heavens.

Later, she prodded him about the battle, but he said little, except, "The regiment did itself proud, Selona. Colonel Grierson wanted to go after Victorio in Mexico, but the government told him American soldiers couldn't cross the Rio Grande without permission from the Mexican government. So Victorio got clean away."

Selona shook her head in disgust. "Does that mean he'll come back?"

"Not for some time to come. He's chewed up pretty good,

and he'll have to lick his wounds before crossing back into Texas."

"That means you'll have to fight again."

"That's what I get paid to do, Selona."

"I wish you would find something else to do," she said, without realizing the words had come out.

"What would I do? The army's the only thing I know, excepting shooting buffalo, and there ain't no buffalo left. The army is where I belong."

"Even if it means getting killed?"

He didn't answer. He just stared at the stars.

Selona had noticed over the years that Augustus had changed his views on the army considerably. He was no longer just a soldier; he had become a leader. Which meant he had to set an example for the younger men. Examples sometimes hard to swallow, even by a disciplined soldier. A discipline tested to its extreme when confronted by the white people of west Texas.

He took the abuse from the whites with his eyes steady to the front. He would merely turn away and instead of venting anger would forge that energy into encouragement for his men.

"We have ourselves a home in this man's army, Selona. The army's where we have the most chance."

"Chance for what?" she snapped back. "Chance to live in this desert? Chance for you to get killed and scalped by Injuns?"

He laughed. There seemed to him something more important than his comfort or mortality. "There's a lot of Colored people that have nothing. And you can bet the Colored people won't get anything until the white folks gets theirs first. Jobs everywhere going to the white man. In the army, we have a little money coming in, and most important, we're staying together."

She knew he was right about one thing: There wasn't much opportunity for the Colored man.

"The army gives us something we couldn't have back east or down south."

"What's that?"

"The chance to keep our family together. To hold on and hope for tomorrow. To be steady."

"There you go again," she said. "Talking about tomorrow. I just live for today. That's all I need. That and you and my children."

Augustus grew quiet. "A man's got to have hope, Selona."

Hope. That was something she had never given much thought to in her life.

"Maybe the army isn't much in your eyes, but the army gives us a place. A steady place. Maybe it isn't much, but it's a start."

She sat up, looking at him. "What are you talking about?"

He spoke, low and soft, as though revealing some secret only he knew. "We're part of something new in this country. A Colored military family. There's going to be a lot more as time passes. Colored people serving the country, fighting the wars, keeping the peace, raising their children. The men in this regiment are leading the way for better things to come. Who knows . . . maybe Adrian and David will be soldiers. Maybe officers like Lieutenant Flipper over at Fort Concho."

Selona had heard about the first Colored officer in the army. Lieutenant Henry Ossian Flipper was the first Colored man to graduate from West Point and was assigned to the 10th Cavalry at Fort Concho.

"It can happen. The day'll come. You wait and see."

Selona thought about that for a long moment, then said softly, "Not my children. My children are going to get an education and be respectable. They ain't going to get killed for white folks that don't care nothing about Colored people. They ain't going to fight Injuns who ain't done nothing but want to hold on to their land. No, sir, Corporal Sharps. You best get that out of your thoughts right this second. My boys are going to have book learning and writing. Not shooting and killing."

But Augustus hadn't heard her; he was snoring softly, softly as the breeze that drifted in from the north.

*   *   *

It was the prettiest red dress Selona had ever seen, and she could only dream that it might one day be hers.

Selona had come to talk with Frank Conniger, the sutler. She had walked slowly around the wire mannequin draped with the dress, closing her eyes and trying to imagine herself in such a rich design. But she was pulled back to reality by the movement coming from her basket.

"You'd sure look mighty pretty in that dress, Mrs. Sharps," a voice called from nearby.

Frank Conniger was in his sixties, with a long beard and gentle eyes that were as green as the hills of Scotland, which he had left as a boy to come to America. He had a government contract to provide a combination of grocery store, dry goods shop, saloon, and stage depot.

"Uh-huh, Mr. Conniger. Not on a corporal's pay and two hungry children." She felt the bag shake inside her basket and said to him shyly, "Can I talk a piece of business with you?"

"Business?" Conniger's eyebrows raised into a single ridge of suspicion.

She reached into the basket and pulled out a croaker sack that jerked wildly in her hand. Deftly, she opened the sack and pulled out one of the rabbits from her pen. "This here rabbit's fat and plump, not stringy like them jackrabbits that run wild on the desert. It sure would make a fine stew for some officer."

Conniger eyed the rabbit warily, then said, "It would make me a fine stew. I'll give you five cents for that rabbit."

Her eyes widened. "You have a deal."

He continued, saying, "And for as many more as you can bring. I think they'll sell mighty fine."

"How you want them, skinned or alive?"

"Skinned. But leave a foot on one of the legs."

"Why a foot?"

"It's an old butcher's trick. That way folks know they're getting a rabbit and not a cat."

She gasped. "A *cat?*"

"Yes, ma'am. There's been more cats eaten in the name of good rabbit than you could count."

They shook hands and she left with her five cents, shaking her head while laughing. "A cat."

What she didn't see as she passed through the door was Augustus standing there, a thoughtful look on his face as he watched her leave.

Selona hurried home and went straight to the rabbit pen, where she pulled out a rabbit by the ears, stretched it across a wood stump, and raised her ax. As the ax fell, she said with great determination, "I'm going to get me that red dress if I have to raise rabbits until doomsday!"

The ax fell, and she was five cents closer to having her red dress.

Two nights later Augustus half-stumbled through the quarters door, looking foolish with a big grin. When he produced a package wrapped in tissue paper, Selona grew suspicious.

"What are you up to?"

From his pocket he produced a set of fresh stripes; he laid them over his corporal stripes. "We've been promoted to sergeant."

She howled with glee and threw her arms around him and kissed him. Then he held her at arm's length and said, "There's a party tonight for First Sergeant Tyler. He's retiring, and I'm moving up the line."

She took the package sheepishly, then unfolded the tissue with slow deliberation, noticing that Augustus looked about to faint. Then she saw the red dress and, to her surprise, found herself yelling at Augustus.

"Man, are you crazy! This dress had to cost at least two dollars! We get a raise in pay and you're already spending the money." Then there was a change in her tone as she stripped and slipped into the dress. A coy change, the way she spoke when she was pleased. "Too bad they didn't promote you to general. You might've come home with a pair of shoes to go with this dress."

She was teasing, of course, twirling around the room in her new dress.

Then she saw Augustus look at her bare feet, shamed by the oversight.

His big hands rubbed harshly at his face. "I'm sorry. I thought—"

She threw herself into his arms and squeezed him with all her strength. "That's just me talking, honey." She whispered, "I'm so proud I could bust." She kissed him passionately, and he could feel the heat from her body burning through the cloth.

"You'll wrinkle my dress," she said with a giggle.

He shook his head. "I'll keep you dancing so no one will notice."

They made love standing against the door. Later that night, no one noticed that she danced without shoes, and no one noticed the wrinkles in her dress.

27

G uilty!"
    Lieutenant Colonel William R. Shafter, now commanding Fort Davis, read the two charges decided by the special court-martial authorized and convened to try Lieutenant Henry Ossian Flipper, A Company, 10th Regiment of U.S. Cavalry (Colored).

The second of the two charges brought against Flipper, who was now standing before him at attention, was conduct unbecoming an officer.

The first charge was that of embezzlement. "Not guilty," Shafter had read solemnly, and the disappointment in his voice was obvious.

Lieutenant Flipper stood ramrod straight as the second verdict was read. When asked if he had anything to say before sentence was passed, he replied, "Never did a man walk the path of uprightness straighter than I did. But the trap was cunningly laid and now I am to be sacrificed. My only question is . . . how could my conduct be 'unbecoming,' when I have been found innocent of the criminal charge?"

There was no answer. Shafter read the sentence: "You are

*to be dishonorably discharged from the service of the United
States Army. The sentence is to be carried out forthwith."*

*On that hot day of June 30, 1882, Lieutenant Henry Os-
sian Flipper, the first Negro graduate of the United States Military Academy at West Point, class of 1877, was stripped of
rank and privileges.*

*It was a significant moment in United States military his-
tory. Flipper, a former slave, was the first—and only—Negro
officer in the military service of the United States.*

"Officer's trousers," Selona snorted, fishing from her kettle
trousers with a stripe of gold cloth running the length of the
outer seam. "Probably belongs to one of the men who sat in
judgment of Lieutenant Flipper."

That morning, as the trial of Lieutenant Flipper had ended,
there wasn't a person within two hundred miles—white or
Colored—who didn't know the truth.

"I told you them white men would find a way to get rid of
that young man," said Vina, standing at one of her kettles.
"Just a matter of time. Never should have gone ridin' with that
white woman over to Fort Concho. Uh-huh. Colored man out
here's got to watch himself like he was still a slave." Her husband, Darcy, was now a corporal, and she was pregnant with
another child.

"Don't matter what I think. I got washing to do and rabbits to skin."

Selona threw another stick of wood on the fire and looked
around, her eyes searching until she saw Adrian and David
scurrying through the brush with their slingshots. "Y'all watch
out for them rattlesnakes. I got enough on my mind without
young'uns getting snake bit!"

Selona watched them for a long time. How fast they had
grown! Time was moving faster than she realized, and she was
beginning to feel as though she was falling behind.

Augustus was on patrol and wouldn't return until the next
day, so it meant another night of worrying and waiting. The
threat of Apaches was now over, for Victorio's band had been

annihilated in Mexico two weeks after the battle at Rattlesnake Springs.

A large Mexican army led by Colonel Joaquin Terrazas had
killed the old chief on November 14, 1880, and scattered the
remnants of the Mescaleros into the mountains, ending the last
of the Indian wars on the Trans-Pecos. Now the 10th was protecting the stagelines and the railroad approaching from the
south from bandits and Mexican revolutionaries.

Frontier life was more civilized, but the Buffalo Soldiers
stayed in the saddle, constantly on patrol. There were more
Colored families in the area now, but only the families of
laundresses lived on the fort. There were at least thirty families now living in the nearby village of Chihuahua, and the
wives had formed a small social group that met once a week,
just like the officers' wives at Fort Davis.

Colonel Grierson had moved the headquarters of the 10th
to Fort Concho, and Colonel William Shafter was now the fort
commander. It was no small rumor he had little respect for
Colored soldiers, and many felt the real reason for Lieutenant
Flipper's dishonorable discharge was Shafter's prejudice.

Selona finished the wash, hung it out to dry, then went inside to begin supper. At the hearth she looked up at the empty
pegs and shook her head.

God! she thought. I'm so tired of being alone!

Toward sunset Selona was sitting in Marie's rocker on the
front porch when she heard hooves cracking against the hard
ground. Her hope that it just might be Augustus vanished
when she saw the rider approach. He was tall, his feet hanging nearly to the horse's knees.

Selona stood and walked toward the horseman. He was
dressed in civilian clothes. It was the first time she had seen
him out of uniform.

The horseman stopped and bowed to Selona just as the
boys appeared. To the west, the sun was nearly down; to the
north, Sleeping Lion Mountain was barely visible as the dust
and setting sun folded a blanket of darkness over the land.

He tipped his hat. "Good evening, ma'am."

"Good evening, Lieutenant." She immediately bit her tongue.

He paused. "I'm afraid that is no longer my rank, ma'am."

Henry Ossian Flipper was a big man, she thought, big as Augustus. He had a gentle voice and friendly eyes; she remembered that from the regimental cotillion, though his eyes were shadowed now by his hat. She suspected they were filled with sadness.

"You're Sergeant Sharps' wife, aren't you, ma'am?"

"Yes, sir. I'm Selona." She pointed to the boys. "These are our boys, David and Adrian."

"They're fine-looking boys."

She could see the white of his teeth as he spoke. Porcelain gleaming within the blackness of his skin; the darkness of his shape.

Flipper spoke while turning toward the western horizon. "Your husband is a fine soldier, Mrs. Sharps. I know he's on patrol, but I thought you might extend to him my farewell."

"I will."

There was the raucous sound of a man's laughter from one of the non-com quarters down the Row. Flipper shook his head and laughed and released a long sigh. The sigh seemed to carry from him his last bit of strength. "I'll miss this place." Flipper touched the brim of his hat and nodded. He was about to spur the horse when she stepped forward.

"Wait. Please, Mr. Flipper. Please wait." She ran into her quarters and went to the Dutch oven at the hearth. She took out several cornmeal tortillas, spread cooked rabbit meat, peppers, and onions onto them, folded them, wrapped them in a clean cloth, and took them to Flipper.

"For your journey." She reached up and handed him the food. He accepted the gift with thanks, then started away.

Something inside her cried to pull him back, to stop him from going into that emptiness with nothing but his sadness— his disgrace. She called to him, "Mr. Flipper, Augustus told me you could have got five thousand dollars from a white boy in Georgia for your seat at West Point."

The horse's muscles rippled, stirring the air and giving off the smell of dust. Flipper patted the shoulders of the horse, which she knew would be his only reminder of the cavalry: broken-down swayback.

"That's correct, Mrs. Sharps."

"Good God. A Colored man could have done a lot for himself with five thousand dollars. Why didn't you take it? The way things turned out?"

The answer came easy, without apology, without regret. "That's true. But some things aren't for sale, ma'am, and having the honor to attend West Point is one of them." He looked around as though trying to figure out where he was going; perhaps, where he had been. "As far as the way things turned out? I would take the same course again, even knowing the outcome beforehand. I would have done it the same way. More importantly, I believe others will follow. Henry Ossian Flipper will not be the last Colored man to graduate from West Point. There will be others. You'll see."

Flipper tipped his hat smoothly and rode off. She stood there watching him until he was gone, lost against the vastness of the west.

28

Marcia O'Kelly stood staring out the window. The silence of the morning was broken by the loud bark of a sergeant crossing the parade ground with a detail of troopers, then the thump of Captain Jonathan O'Kelly's heavy boots as he marched into the kitchen of their quarters on Officers Row.

"Good morning," he said simply, and dared say no more, as the coldness in Marcia's eyes cut across the room like an icy sabre.

Juanita Jackson picked up the coffeepot and poured Jon a cup as she had done every morning since becoming the O'Kellys' house servant the day after her marriage to Winston. She poured quickly, then went to the stove, where Marcia handed her a plate with eggs, fatback, and hot biscuits.

Now forty years old, Jonathan O'Kelly had been promoted to captain the year before, but still had not risen very high on the promotion ladder since his graduation from West Point in 1866, though there was no fault in his professionalism or his ambition. Rank was based on many factors, one of which was the opportunity to distinguish oneself on the battlefield. Fighting Indians and bandits was considered less than glorious.

Which meant that he had to seize every opportunity for distinction that came his way, even when it meant doing something distasteful.

Sitting on the court-martial board for Lieutenant Flipper was an assignment he could not avoid, especially when he had been personally selected by the post commander.

But Marcia had barely spoken a word to him since the decision. He hurriedly ate his breakfast and took his pistol belt and started for the door.

Her words caught him as he opened the door to a swirl of blowing dust. "What you did to that man was shameful, Jonathan."

He paused, clamped his hat onto his head, and marched out, saying nothing. Marcia watched him through the window until he reached the orderly room on the other side of the parade ground, and took some satisfaction in knowing that he knew she would be watching him every step of the way. When he disappeared from her sight she was drawn back to the kitchen by the voice of Rebecca, their one-year-old daughter.

She had long dark hair, bright blue eyes, and smooth features like her mother.

In the long hours of loneliness Marcia had grown accustomed to, Rebecca was the focal point of her life, and though she would love to have another child, she and Jon had tried without success. She assumed she was now barren and accepted that in the same way she had accepted other disappointments. But now she had found a new purpose that could no longer be ignored.

The trial was over now, and it was time to return to normalcy and think about the future. She went to her heavy trunk and immediately found what she wanted: four books joined by a leather strap. From inside one book she took an envelope addressed to her and carefully read the words she knew would bring about thunderous protest.

Selona was standing at her kettle, stirring in the hot sun, when she saw Marcia approaching, followed by Juanita, who carried her one-year-old son, Chihocopee. The boy was gorgeous, the blend of Seminole and Negro blood fashioning features that Selona thought were simply majestic.

Marcia was carrying her daughter, shading her with the bright yellow parasol that always announced her approach.

With a broad smile, Marcia pulled from her purse a folded sheet of paper. Triumphantly, she announced, "This came yesterday from Colonel Grierson."

The three women had conceived a plan some weeks before and Marcia, the wife of an officer, had assumed the mantle of responsibility.

Selona sensed from Marcia's broad grin that the news was good.

"We can start a school for the children," Marcia said simply.

Selona wiped her hands on her dress, saying, "Can I see the letter?"

Marcia handed her the letter and watched Selona unfold it carefully, as though it were Scripture.

"What does it say?" asked Juanita.

Marcia smiled. "This letter instructs the chaplain to allow us the use of the post chapel as a classroom. I will be the teacher."

Selona knew the chaplain used the chapel to teach the three *R*'s—"reading, 'riting, and 'rithmetic"—but only to the soldiers. The children of officers were generally sent back east to boarding school; the children of the enlisted went uneducated.

"All the Colored children can go?" asked Selona.

"All children five years old or older."

There was a sudden gleam in Juanita's eyes as she asked softly, "What about them that's older?"

Marcia understood, but played the game anyway. "How old?"

"My age?" Juanita looked at Selona.

Marcia laughed. "Anybody who wants to attend is welcome."

Selona looked off to the west. "I can't wait to tell Augustus."

Marcia folded the letter and put it in her purse and looked at Selona. "Jon has told me that your husband is one of the few soldiers who can read or write."

Selona nodded. "Yes. When he was a slave he was taught by the wife of his massah to help run the business."

"So he taught you to read?"

Selona nodded. "I can read and write a bit. But my writing isn't that good, because there's not much time for writing, and about the only book we have to read is the Bible."

Marcia gave this some thought. "Would you be willing to help in the classroom?"

Selona's eyes brightened. "I'd be willing to do what I can."

Captain Jonathan O'Kelly's voice thundered through the night air along Officers Row, and throughout Fort Davis there was not a soul who wasn't listening.

"How could you do this without my permission!" Jon shouted.

Marcia's eyes widened in mutual anger. "I don't need your permission."

"You wrote to Colonel Grierson without telling me! There is a chain of command in the army—a protocol—that has to be observed. First, you discuss the matter with me. I, in turn, discuss the matter with Colonel Shafter, the post commander, who then contacts Colonel Grierson—if he sees fit."

"That doesn't matter any longer. Permission's been granted by Colonel Grierson."

There was a strained look on his face as he asked, "Do you think it's proper that you teach Coloreds how to read and write? After all, it might be better if that was done by their own kind."

Marcia's eyes narrowed. "Do you think it's proper that you lead Coloreds as their officer! That should be done by their own kind. Of course, after yesterday, there aren't many officers left who are 'their kind.' "

He walked outside; moments later Marcia joined him. In her hand she carried his pipe.

"We've done enough fighting for one day, Jon." She handed him his pipe and watched him touch a match to the bowl. A thin blue haze drifted upward, and in the flicker of the match she could see his face relax as he exhaled a cloud of smoke.

Jon chuckled. "God, woman, you should have seen the look on Shafter's face when he learned about your school." He laughed aloud, then caught himself. The commander's house was not far away, and as it was a hot night, the windows would be open.

He whispered throatily, "I thought he was going to eat me blood raw."

She grew serious. "I do hope it won't harm your career. I would never do anything to harm you, Jon."

He took her in his arms and kissed her lightly. "I'm glad you did what you did."

A coyote barked in the hills as they walked back into the house.

Sergeant Augustus Sharps ignored the coyote, as did the four other Buffalo Soldiers—all young soldiers—in his patrol, as they slowly moved closer to the fort. He had covered nearly two hundred miles in the last week. His horse was walking head down, and there was no point in giving the animal the spurs for there was nothing left of its strength. It would probably be put out of commission by the next day's examination from the farrier.

By midnight the five had unsaddled and Augustus left for his quarters, while the four troopers went to the barracks. Augustus found Selona sitting in the rocker on the front porch, where he hugged her and kissed her for a long moment, then asked, "How are the boys?"

"They're fine."

He went inside, where she readied a hot bath behind the hanging blanket. He stripped down, bathed, shaved, then came outside, where he found Selona sitting in her rocker.

The night was quiet; he was tired, that was obvious by the heavy way he sat on the porch beside her.

Her hand went to his head, and she automatically stroked his hair. "I need to trim off some of that hair. You look like a buffalo."

He nodded, but said nothing.

"You done heard about Lieutenant Flipper, ain't you?"

He nodded. "The men are mighty upset, Selona."

"They should be. What regulation is there that says a Colored man can't be an officer?"

"It's not a regulation. It's a way of thinking. A way of doing things."

She nearly screamed at the houses on Officers Row, but instead laughed sarcastically. "Knowing all that, and you want to stay in the army."

He wasn't in the mood for her argument. He was bone-tired and had to get up at four the next morning. "I'm going to bed."

Selona stayed in the rocker, watching the shooting stars streak across the sky, listening to the coyotes bark, the sounds of the changing of the guard on the fort. She realized she was becoming increasingly critical of the army, and not having Augustus around meant her frustrations boiled to a head whenever he came home from a long patrol.

She would have to stop doing that, she told herself. Augustus wasn't to blame.

It was the loneliness . . . and more than half a married life spent in an empty bed.

29

The next afternoon Selona was leaving the cemetery after watering the flowers when she heard a voice call to her from behind, startling her with its suddenness and frightful familiarity.

"Where's headquarters located at this fort?" the voice howled like a cruel wind.

Selona shaded her eyes against the sun. She knew the speaker though she couldn't see his face.

Six men sat on horseback, their long dusters covering pistol belts and sharp knives.

"I asked you, where's headquarters?"

Selona could say nothing for fear she might faint. She could only point, then she ran.

The laughter from the men chased her all the way to her quarters, where she ran inside and slammed the door.

He was back!

Captain Jonathan O'Kelly was standing at a chalkboard, uneasily studying the duty roster. O'Kelly was now a troop com-

mander and the fort adjutant; Sergeant Major Brassard was
standing beside him sipping from a cup of coffee.

"Private Jackson and Corporal Haymes are two days overdue from their courier detail to Fort Stockton, Sergeant
Major." O'Kelly went to a map of their area of operations and
ran his finger along an imaginary line he knew Jackson and
Haymes would follow.

It wasn't uncommon for soldiers to be overdue from a patrol, but the fact caused apprehension for O'Kelly.

"They're good soldiers, sir. They can take care of themselves."

O'Kelly's eyes didn't move from the map. His finger traced
a line from Fort Davis to Fort Stockton, some eighty miles to
the east.

"Two days is too long, in my judgment."

Brassard had to admit it was unusual. "I can dispatch a patrol along the line of march they would follow back to the
fort."

O'Kelly started to reply when the door opened. Both men
stared as Captain John Armitage swaggered into the orderly
room.

Armitage silently handed a letter to O'Kelly, who read
quickly.

Brassard eased around to look over O'Kelly's shoulder.

O'Kelly folded the letter and gave it back to Armitage, saying, "It's from Colonel Grierson at Fort Concho. Captain Armitage and five of his Rangers are being posted here at Fort
Davis. We're to extend them every courtesy possible."

Brassard was flushed with anger and was obviously about
to say something he might regret when O'Kelly said, "Will you
see about that patrol, Sergeant Major?"

Brassard put on his hat and stomped out of the orderly
room, nearly bowling over the five Texas Rangers standing on
the front porch.

Augustus was at the rifle range when Brassard approached
looking fit to be tied.

"Jackson and Haymes are overdue from courier detail between here and Fort Stockton. I want you to take three men and scout along their line of march."

Augustus could see that there was something troubling Brassard besides two overdue soldiers. "Is there something wrong?"

Brassard picked up one of the Springfield rifles, jacked a round in the chamber, and took aim at a target one hundred yards downrange. He squeezed and watched the round kick at the dirt in front of the target.

"I never could shoot a rifle." He took out his revolver and fired at a target at fifty yards. The bullet struck the orange ball painted on the center of the target.

"That's better." He paused. "Wrong? Nothing's wrong. Captain O'Kelly's concerned. They should have been back by now and he wants a patrol. Is that explanation enough for you, Sergeant?"

It had been years since Brassard had tightened down on Augustus, and the man's tone sent an immediate warning to him. "Yes, sir. I'll get the men ready."

Augustus started to walk away, but Brassard called him back. "You're going to know soon enough, so you may as well hear it from me. Captain John Armitage and five Texas Rangers have been posted to the fort."

Augustus's fists balled and he felt anger rise that had been suppressed for many years.

Augustus hurried away. Brassard followed in close pursuit and caught up with Augustus near his troop's barracks. Brassard whirled him around. "You are a soldier, remember that. You can't go off looking for personal revenge. Not here in Texas. These crackers'll hang you for certain if you start a row with a white man. Especially a Texas Ranger."

It was then that Augustus realized it was nearly eight years to the day since a Ranger had led his fellows to rape and scalp Selona, eight years since the hatred he'd once carried for the Kiowa had transferred to one man on the earth: That man was Captain John Armitage.

Six months after the incident the governor of Texas had informed the army that Armitage had been cleared of all charges in the attack.

Now, in 1882, tensions were running high on the frontier between white settlers and the Buffalo Soldiers. Two troopers had been killed in a barroom brawl in Brownsville; at Fort Concho a sergeant was humiliated in a saloon, his buttons and stripes cut off his coat by drunk cowhands.

"Now is not the time." Brassard's voice seethed.

"When will it be the time, Sergeant Major? Maybe Selona's right. Maybe I am a fool to fight for white people that treat us like dirt."

Brassard's eyes tightened. "Don't you ever speak like that again, Sergeant. You have a duty to perform. If not to the country, then to yourself and your family. Not to mention your people. Getting yourself hanged won't change anything that's happened." His voice softened. "You just got to let it slide."

"To hell with that. You know as well as I do that Armitage was involved in the attack on Selona."

"But there's no proof, and the charges were cleared years ago. Now, assemble your men and follow your orders."

Brassard walked away and Augustus, holding his Sharps rifle, glared hatefully across the parade ground.

Armitage was standing there with the Rangers on the orderly room porch.

For some strange reason Brassard felt the hair stand up on his neck. He suddenly turned and felt the wind rushing from his lungs as he saw Augustus taking aim at Armitage.

Armitage saw Augustus and stood erect on the porch, not moving, his lip curled in an evil challenge.

A long moment passed; then Augustus lowered the rifle and walked into the barracks to assemble the patrol.

30

Augustus rode out of Fort Davis just before noon, followed by Gibbs and Bane. The three were still carrying the aches and fatigue of their last patrol, but Jackson and Haymes were their friends and they were overdue.

The trail to Fort Stockton, which was also the route of the stageline, did occasionally detour to avoid certain ranches where Buffalo Soldiers knew the settlers were unfriendly.

The heat was punishing, dry and still, except for the swirling alkali dust devils that seemed to stalk them along the way, then, in a burst of fury, pass among them with a swirling, cloudy vengeance.

The plan called for a three o'clock halt at a small creek to water their horses. Nearing the creek, Augustus suddenly raised his hand with the silent command to halt.

Augustus looked again to be certain his eyes weren't deceiving him, and seeing the black specks against the sky he slowly lowered himself from the saddle.

He motioned Gibbs off his horse and gave the signal to move on foot in a circle to the south; he ordered Bane to move to the north.

Augustus took his Sharps from the pommel holster and started working his way east between Gibbs and Bane.

Again he looked to the sky; again he saw the unmistakable shapes of vultures soaring overhead.

Then there was the smell.

When he found them he stared into their eyes for a long moment, recalling what they'd looked like when they were alive; wanting to remember them alive, not as he now saw them.

The piano-playing Haymes, with his harmonica keeping his comrades' thoughts from dying that night beneath the "horse fort" on the frozen plains of Kansas.

Jackson, whose quick smile had helped Juanita when she arrived at Fort Davis like so much baggage in the boot of the stagecoach. What would she do now that her husband was dead?

A tall barrel cactus stood like a monument at the edge of the creek where patrols stopped regularly; the Buffalo Soldiers often swam here to give their bodies momentary refreshment before moving on with the patrol.

Haymes and Jackson had been tied to the cactus with rope; this was no ordinary killing.

"They were used for target practice," Augustus muttered as he walked stiffly, each step a painful burden to body and soul, nearer to the dead men. He stopped, knelt between the two soldiers, and screamed, "The bastards scalped them!"

That's when Gibbs and Bane appeared, and the three knelt in front of their dead comrades.

When the grieving was over they cut the men down and draped them over their horses.

Augustus leaned heavily against his horse and softly patted the body of Haymes, then said to Gibbs, "Ride on to the fort and tell Captain O'Kelly what's happened. We'll walk in your direction and should meet up with you around dusk."

Gibbs swung into the saddle and rode off.

Augustus said nothing during the walk, and as the sun

began to set he pulled the horses into a stand of tall trees and he and Bane gently took both bodies down from the horses.

Augustus built a fire and made coffee while Bane shot a jackrabbit. The two ate in silence around the fire until they heard the sound of wagon wheels creaking along the trail.

Captain O'Kelly and Sergeant Major Brassard led the patrol, the sergeant major swinging heavily down from his saddle to the cup of coffee offered by Augustus. O'Kelly took his silver flask and poured two fingers of brandy into each cup and sat by the fire, looking occasionally at the bodies but not wanting to view them.

Not just yet.

Then the talk began, slow and deliberate. Augustus gave in perfect military detail what they had found.

"From the bullet holes, I'd say both men were shot at close range." Augustus took another sip of the coffee.

"Why do you say that?" asked O'Kelly.

Augustus walked to the bodies, took off the blankets, and pointed at several wounds. "The bullet holes are identical on each body. Both shot in each knee. Both shot in their elbows. Both shot between the eyes." Augustus paused, then said, "They were used for target practice after they were tied to the cactus."

"Then they were scalped," Brassard said flatly.

Augustus shook his head. "No. They were scalped while they were still alive. There's too much blood on their blouses and chests. Dead men don't bleed much after a scalping."

His bitter memories of Selona at Fort Sill suddenly became obvious.

O'Kelly spoke first. "Armitage and his Rangers passed along this trail earlier today."

Augustus had been brooding on that point since discovering the bodies. "My thoughts exactly."

A long silence followed. Then Brassard said to O'Kelly, "What are you going to do about this, Captain?"

O'Kelly said nothing. He just stared at the dead soldiers,

with the fire in his eyes burning hotter than the fire heating the coffee.

Juanita Jackson stood silent, holding Chihocopee, watching the coffin being slowly lowered into the ground. Then Haymes was interred, and the chaplain read from the prayer book, and the military honors of rifle salute and "Taps" followed.

The sun beat down mercilessly, and flies swarmed at the smell of the blood. There was a long silence.

Gradually the group of soldiers and civilians walked away to continue with the struggle of living, leaving just Selona and Augustus and the boys. Selona went to Marie's gravesite with her gourd and watered the flowers, then sat beside the grave and stared off into the distance. The boys sat, too.

"It's not right, Augustus. It's not right to be buried in such a lonely place. They don't even own the ground they're buried in."

Augustus replied, "They were soldiers, and they're buried in a soldier's graveyard. They expected no less when they joined the regiment."

Selona's voice rose above the graves in such a way that Augustus was shocked: "The regiment. That's all you men care about. The regiment. What about the children? What about the wives and the families? Don't you see what this is doing to all of us?"

Augustus shrugged. "What would you have me do, Selona? Get out of the army?"

"That would do for a start."

"And do what? Maybe get a job sweeping up at the sutler's? Or driving a wagon for ten dollars a month? If I can get that. Use your common sense."

"Common sense? What does common sense have to do with anything when we live in such a hateful place where even the people you are supposed to be defending are trying to kill you? Tell me the sense in that, Augustus."

Augustus shook his head. "I can't, except to say it will get better."

Selona stood and took the boys' hands, and as she started to walk away she said coldly, "It better, Augustus. It damn well better."

She walked away.

Augustus realized that this was the first time he had ever heard Selona curse.

In the early hours of the morning the sound of horses awoke Augustus and Selona. He pulled on his trousers and stepped outside to meet two troopers with an extra horse. They spoke briefly, then Augustus hurried inside and started to dress.

Selona sat up in bed. "What's wrong?"

"Trouble at the Adams hog ranch." He pulled on his boots, strapped on his pistol belt, and started for the door.

The troopers rode at a gallop with Augustus in the lead, making good time despite the darkness.

The Adams hog ranch was one of several whorehouses servicing the Colored troopers at Fort Davis. The women were Mexican and Indian girls recruited by the owner, Frank Adams, with the promise of making good money and maybe finding a husband.

Augustus tied off his horse and walked into smells of cheap whiskey and homemade tequila permeating the front room. Four troopers sat quietly at a table, playing cards with two Texas Rangers. The two Rangers sat behind a large pile of money; the troopers appeared nearly penniless.

At the bar stood only one man. Captain Armitage was leaning over a glass of whiskey; he laughed to himself as Augustus stepped to the bar.

"I don't drink with niggers," Armitage said softly.

"You don't have to," replied Augustus. He nodded to Frank Adams, a burly man with a flowing beard. Adams' eyes were wide with apprehension as he stood frozen behind the bar.

"Whiskey," said Augustus.

Adams' hand shook as he poured Augustus a drink. Armitage's arm flashed across the counter, raking the glass and bottle onto the floor.

Augustus stared at Armitage, then felt himself settle into calmness.

"I heard about your two boys getting killed." Armitage chuckled as he spoke.

Augustus clenched his fists. "They weren't killed. They were murdered."

"Your captain came around asking a lot of questions I didn't particularly like."

There was a roar of laughter from one of the Rangers at the table. "You going to bet, boy? Or you going to fold?" he asked one of the troopers.

The trooper was young and obviously scared to death. His voice cracked as he spoke, "I can't bet my hoss and saddle. They belongs to the cavalry."

Augustus recognized the ploy. It was a favorite used against the young Colored troopers.

Augustus turned to Armitage. "The boy's horse doesn't belong to him, Captain. Why don't you get your men and get out of here? We don't want no more trouble."

Armitage chuckled again. "Don't talk to me; talk to your boy. All he's gotta do is call the wager."

"He can't call the wager and you know it. He'll be court-martialed if he loses his horse in a poker game."

"That's his problem, now ain't it, Ser-geant." Armitage's hand went to his glass. As he started to drink, Augustus' big hand closed around Armitage's hand. Augustus guided the glass to his lips and slowly, forcefully, tilted the shot glass and drank Armitage's whiskey.

Armitage's free hand went for a pistol but Augustus slammed the hand holding the glass onto the bar. The glass shattered, slicing the Ranger's hand wide open along the palm.

Armitage howled, staring incredulously at his own blood. He went for his pistol just as the two Rangers stood from the table and reached for theirs. That was when the windows suddenly exploded; from outside two Springfield rifles appeared, trained on the two Rangers.

Augustus kneed Armitage in the stomach, then slammed the butt of his pistol against his ear. There was another howl, then

Armitage's heavy body crumpled to the dirt floor.

Augustus pointed his pistol at one of the Rangers. "You boys drop your weapons through the window. Nice and easy. We don't want any more trouble."

The Rangers dropped their pistols through the window and huddled against the adobe wall.

Augustus motioned to the troopers at the table. "You men get on back to Fort Davis. Report to your company commander after roll call. You understand?"

The troopers nodded, then slowly eased away from the table and out the door.

Augustus looked at Adams. "Any more of our men in here?"

Adams shook his head. Augustus reached into his pocket and drew out a dime. He tossed the coin on the counter and, walking through the door, called over his shoulder to Adams, "Buy the captain a fresh drink."

Augustus arrived home shortly after sunrise. Selona came out and hugged him, then whiffed his breath.

"You smell like you been drinking."

Augustus smoothed his stubbed face. "I only had one drink, honey."

Selona grumped, "Must have been a doozy of a drink!"

A grin formed on Augustus' mouth. "It certainly was, Selona. It certainly was."

31

Need brings about yearning; yearning brings about dreams. Selona had had a dream she never spoke of because she knew it would never come true: to own her own business.

Then history changed all that with the arrival of the Southern Pacific Railroad.

By the summer of 1882, the San Antonio-El Paso Mail had been put out of business, the stagecoaches replaced by the Iron Horse, which rode on rails stretching as far as the eyes could see. This new entry into west Texas kept the Buffalo Soldiers out on the desert, protecting the various watering holes and the long stretches of isolated track Mexican bandits found ideal for train robbery.

Although the railroad bypassed Fort Davis, freight companies and the Overland stage line operated between the fort and the closest railroad depot at Marfa to the southwest, and other towns to the north and east.

The reason Fort Davis was important was water.

Selona was standing in the sutler's two days after Augustus' confrontation with Armitage, noticing the passengers idling about while the stage took on fresh horses. That's when the idea came to her.

The next morning Selona rose early and cooked an unusually large breakfast, a breakfast so large Augustus was astonished.

"God Almighty, woman. I can't eat all that!"

She merely said, "Eat your fill. We'll have the leftovers for dinner."

The table was heaped with biscuits, sorghum molasses, fried fatback, eggs, hot coffee, fried tomatoes from her garden, and a variety of tortillas stuffed with rabbit meat and venison. She had made two apple pies from apples purchased at the sutler's. When Augustus was full, he finished dressing and reported to the orderly room.

When he had left Selona selected a variety of the leftovers, filling two plates. She wrapped the plates and carefully placed them in a basket. She left Adrian and David with Vina and walked across the parade ground straight to the sutler's and stood in front of the counter.

Conniger could see there was something different this morning in the way she smiled. But first he went to his ledger, skimmed to her name, and noted her credit was up to date.

"What can I do for you, Mrs. Sharps?"

Selona placed the basket on the counter and carefully removed the plates. "I want to talk a little business with you, Mr. Conniger. But first . . . I want to show you something."

He eyed her warily, then looked at the plates. "That's a mighty fine-looking spread, Mrs. Sharps."

She smiled and handed him a fork. "My husband says I'm the best cook in the west. Judging by his size, not many will argue."

She watched Conniger begin to taste the various selections. Momentarily he was eating heartily.

"I have a proposition for you, Mr. Conniger."

Conniger nodded his head and kept eating, motioning with his hand for her to continue.

"Augustus can't stay in the army forever. That's just a natural fact. And you know Colored folks in the army can't save enough money to buy a piece of land. When he retires, and we own a piece of land, we'll have somewheres to go."

"A man should think about the future," Conniger agreed, wolfing down a biscuit dipped in molasses.

"So I was thinking, we like west Texas, and it's starting to settle down. There's land around here to be bought—"

Conniger interrupted. "Land takes money."

"Yes, sir, I know. That's why I'm here."

Conniger's mouth stopped. He wiped his hands on his apron. "Are you looking to borrow money, Mrs. Sharps?"

"No, sir. I ain't looking to borrow money. I'm looking for a business partner."

Conniger laughed. "What do you have to offer for your side of the partnership?"

Selona pointed at the plates. "You're eating it, Mr. Conniger."

That afternoon was the first meeting of the new school at Fort Davis.

Marcia arrived early, setting up chairs and washing the chalkboard; then she set out chalk and slates given her by the chaplain, and the primers used to educate the young troopers. She had not slept the night before, thrashing about and keeping Jon awake. He had wound up sleeping in a rocking chair on the front porch.

The atmosphere was childlike, though there were plenty of adults sitting in the back of the room; the six laundresses had worked furiously that morning to finish their washing before class. Selona had been the first to arrive, with David and Adrian.

"We'll begin with learning our letters, then our numbers. Once you've learned the letters you'll begin learning how to form words, and that will help you learn to read."

Marcia, chalk in hand, began scrawling the alphabet on the board. With each letter she would have the class repeat the letter aloud, then write it on their slates.

Exultation swept through Selona as she watched David and Adrian write the letter *a* on their slates. She realized that on that day she had done two things in her life she never dreamed she could do.

She had begun a small business and had taken her children to school.

That evening Augustus returned home to a surprise. He had to step over pots and pans, metal plates, cutlery, and several baskets filled with vegetables, eggs, and smoked hams. His eyes bulged as he tried to count the money he would owe the sutler.

Sitting at the table with Selona was Vina. Selona wore a Cheshire grin; Vina was her usual solemn self.

Before Augustus could speak, Selona was out of the chair, saying, "Now, honey, before you bust a gut, you got to hear me out."

Augustus was silent. He sat on the edge of the bed and nodded.

"I got me this idea, honey. I've been trying to sort through everything until it was ready before I told you."

"You got everything sorted through, Selona?"

She nodded.

"Then you can tell me why you've taken leave of your senses and bought all this food on credit. You have enough food here to feed the regiment."

"Not the regiment . . . passengers on the stage and the men who haul freight to the railroad."

Augustus stood and walked around the small room, studying the baskets of food. "Go on, Selona. I'm listening."

"This idea come to me. You said I was the best cook in the west."

"That I did. There's no doubt about that."

"I took Mr. Conniger some of my cooking. He loved it. I told him my idea was to set up a little stand at the stage depot. When folks come through on the stage they always get off and stretch their legs. Why not have food for them to buy? Good food. My food! The best in west Texas!"

Augustus started laughing and clapped his hands. "Girl, you have to be crazy."

"Crazy like a fox, Augustus. Mr. Conniger thinks it's a wonderful idea. He's going to supply the food. I do the cooking and we split the money. You know, when word of my cooking gets around we'll be swimming in money."

Augustus sniffed at a large onion. "What about the laundry? If you give that up we'll lose our quarters and have to move off the fort."

"I'll keep my laundry job."

He shook his head. "You're going to cook all day and wash at the same time?"

She shook her head and pointed at Vina. "Vina's going to do the laundry. She'll use my kettles and have my washing folks. We'll split the money."

Augustus looked worried. "That doesn't sound fair. She'll be doing all the work and you'll be getting half the money."

"Augustus, me and Darcy and the kids could sure use more money. I'm willing to take on the extra work."

Selona added, "She'll be my partner. Mr. Conniger suggested it to me. He said it's good business, just like me and him being partners."

Vina nodded in agreement.

"I make ten dollars a month doing the laundry. I'll make that every week with my cooking. In a few years we'll have enough money to buy us a piece of land."

This statement surprised Augustus. "What piece of land? You haven't said anything about a piece of land."

She patted him on the hand. "I was getting to that, honey."

"You best get to it real fast, Selona."

She started off slow. "All my life I've wanted a home. A place I could call my own, my own land, for us and the children. We ain't ever going to get that land off your army money. And what are we going to do when you're too old and tired to soldier? What will we live on?"

Augustus stood slow, wearing the look of shame. "Are you saying I can't take care of my family?"

She stepped against him and felt his back stiffen. Her voice was no more than a whisper, a pleading whisper. "No, honey, I'm not saying that. I'm asking you to let me help."

He pushed her away slowly and walked to the door. "I'm going back to the orderly room. It appears you don't need my advice."

Selona stood there, tears in her eyes, watching him until he disappeared through the front door.

Augustus had walked no more than ten feet from the porch when he heard the clatter of hooves thundering across the ground behind his house. He stopped and turned just as the silhouette of a man appeared in the darkness, riding at full gallop.

Selona had just closed the door when she heard the horse, then the sound of the glass in the back window breaking.

Her eyes filled with terror, then she screamed, "Vina . . . run!"

Augustus was nearly to the porch when Selona and Vina came running through the door, with Selona screaming, "Run! Run! Someone threw dynamite into the house!"

Augustus grabbed her by the hand as Vina ran past him, and started running, dragging her as far from the house as possible.

They ran and ran, stumbling; then, suddenly, Augustus stopped. He turned and looked at the house.

There was no explosion.

"Stay here, Selona."

"What are you doing?" Her frantic voice called as he started for the house.

Augustus said nothing as he stepped on the porch and carefully peered through the opened door.

A stick of dynamite was lying on the bed, but there was no fuse. He walked to the bed and picked up the explosive, noticing a piece of paper tied around the dynamite stick. He removed the paper and began reading as he heard Selona calling, "Are you crazy! Come out of there."

Augustus walked outside, where he found dozens of people had collected from Suds Row. Darcy was running, carrying his pistol in one hand while pulling up his suspenders with the other. He stopped next to Augustus and, seeing the stick of dynamite, said to the frantic Selona, "Nothin' to worry about, Selona. There ain't no fuse in the dynamite."

Selona collapsed to her knees, then Vina knelt beside her, and both women began trembling uncontrollably.

Augustus handed the dynamite to Gibbs, telling him, "Take this to the sergeant major. Tell him what happened."

Gibbs nodded and started off, but paused as Augustus unfolded the paper and read the message scrawled in pencil: *Touch a white man again . . . You die.*

Augustus crumpled the note and looked around. He saw nothing.

Sergeant Major Brassard read the message for the third time, then said to Augustus, "We got to get you off this fort. I'll transfer you to Fort Concho in the morning."

"Fort Concho!"

"You'll be safe there. Besides, there's an opening there for first sergeant."

Augustus's jaw suddenly set like it was made of iron. "I'll get out of the army before I'll let that bastard run me and my family like a dog."

"You better come to your senses, Augustus. You've got a wife and children to think about."

A hard glint came into his eyes as he stared first at Brassard, then to Selona, and said, "I am thinking about them. For the first time, maybe, and I'm thinking real hard. This is our home, and we're going to buy us a piece of land here for when I retire."

Brassard stared at him incredulously. "Piece of land! What piece of land?"

Augustus grinned at Selona. "Whatever piece of land we want."

Brassard pointed out the immediate problem with the idea. "That takes money. You can't buy a piece of land on a soldier's pay."

Augustus reached over and put his arms around Selona.

"Selona has her own business now. We'll get that piece of land, and there ain't no man on earth that's going to chase us off."

Selona went to the bed and picked up the red dress she planned to wear on her first day of business. She asked Augustus, "Now that I've got a business, do you think I can get a pair of shoes to go with this dress?"

Augustus laughed aloud, saying, "You can buy two pairs of shoes."

Both were laughing as Brassard looked around at all the food filling their quarters and said, "What you plan on doing, Selona, feed the whole regiment?"

Selona and Augustus looked at each other quickly, then burst out laughing again, and started dancing around Brassard, who could only stand there looking dumbfounded.

32

Selona sat up most of the night peeling sweet potatoes, chopping onions, preparing tortillas and a ham, then went to bed after midnight, only to rise before daybreak. She started a fire in her stove and, reminding herself that today was a trial run, cooked what she thought was the best meal of her life.

Vina helped Selona load her Dutch oven onto a travois. Wearing her red dress, Selona made the short walk to the stage depot, leading the horse, while Vina fired up the laundry kettles.

Selona set up her tiny kitchen near the small building next to the sutler's that served as a depot for the Overland stage line. Plates and cutlery supplied by Conniger were stacked neatly on a blanket; her Dutch oven sat filled with a simmering ham while fresh eggs waited to be fried on the skillet. She had built a fire the first thing, and with everything ready, she sat and waited.

By noon the stage was an hour overdue, and the wind had started to pick up, roaring in off the desert, stinging her eyes with gritty sand and covering her skin and dress with a white film.

It was two o'clock when Selona lifted the lid on the Dutch oven. The ham was dry as a bone and falling apart from being overcooked. The biscuits were hard as rock and the sweet-potato pie was cracked, looking more like baked desert.

"The stage must have run into some trouble along the way, little lady," a voice called from the depot building.

Selona looked up to see Bill MacCallister standing at the door. MacCallister was a former stage driver and now served as ticketman for the stage line.

He motioned to Selona. "Come on in here out of the wind."

Selona walked into the depot.

"I heard about what you got in mind. Conniger told me last night at the sutler's." He hawked and spat into a spittoon.

"Where's the stage, Mr. MacCallister? All that food's going bad."

"No telling. Could have busted a wheel, or had a horse to die, or even get robbed. It's usually on time, but sometimes it's late. You got to know that if you're goin' to do business with the passengers. You got to plan ahead."

"How do I do that?"

"A good businessman—or woman, in your case—always tries to know as much as possible about what's going on. Now, you see that telegraph key, right there?"

Selona looked at the telegraph key and nodded.

"All the stations have a telegraph. It lets us know when the stage left what station so we know if there's trouble along the way, and if there's going to be a delay."

Selona shook her head. "No, Mr. MacCallister, that costs too much money."

MacCallister licked his lips. "There's a way you can pay."

Selona's eyes narrowed suspiciously. "How's that?"

MacCallister rubbed his hands together quickly, and said, "Conniger says you cook the best spread he's ever tasted. I ain't married and can't cook nothin' but beans and fatback. You give me a plate of your food every time you're here and I'll find out on the telegraph when the stage'll be arrivin'. That way you don't have to sit here waitin' while your food goes bad. Why, I can even find out how many passengers are on the stage."

Selona thought about this and smiled. "You're a nice man, Mr. MacCallister. I'd be proud to give you some of my cookin' . . . telegraph or no telegraph."

She got up and went outside and started to prepare him a plate when the stage roared in, looking as though it was being chased by an alkaline cloud.

Three-fingers Johnny Braxton climbed down cussing, just as MacCallister came out of the depot office.

"What happened, Johnny?" asked MacCallister.

"Dad-blamed women, that's what happened. We had to stop for nearly four hours so's one of 'em could have a young'un," Braxton snorted.

At that moment the cry of a baby came from inside the stagecoach. Selona peered inside and saw a young woman, her face showing the wear of childbirth, holding a newborn baby.

"Here now, girl, you go on and get away from there," said Braxton.

Selona stared hard at him. "I ain't no girl. I'm a woman."

Braxton's eyes were fixed on her buffalo wig. "What kind of hair you got on your head?"

Selona didn't answer; she handed MacCallister the plate, then opened the door and climbed inside the stagecoach.

The young mother was pale, weakened by her ordeal and loss of blood, but she appeared majestic as she held her newborn child.

"Don't you worry, Missy," said Selona. "We'll get you and the baby over to the fort hospital, where the surgeon can tend you." She held out her arms, and the woman, though never having seen Selona in her life, handed her the baby, as though the bond of motherhood between the two had joined them as one.

A buggy was brought to transport mother and child to the post hospital.

Selona set about feeding the passengers, including three portions for Braxton, who, when finished, belched aloud and handed her his plate, saying, "Girl, MacCallister says you goin' to be here every day. Is that sure 'nough?"

"Sure enough, so long as you and the stage are on time."

Braxton said, "With vittles like this waitin', I'll be on time. Nothin', not even child bearin' or God Almighty Himself, will make me late again. I swear, that was the best plate I've ever eat."

An hour later the stage pulled out. Selona loaded her wares and went home. She sat waiting for Augustus, the excitement almost more than she could bear.

When Augustus came in, she jumped into his arms and kissed him wildly, then said, "Put this somewhere safe."

Augustus carefully counted the first day's revenue from Selona's cooking business: four one-dollar bills!

The next morning Selona woke to the smell of lye soap and the sound of someone hammering wood. She walked out to the back to find that Adrian and David had started the fires and were sorting britches and drawers into two piles, while Augustus was standing beside a small caisson, a two-wheeled cart used to carry artillery ammunition.

"I got this for you. You can load your cooking supplies in the back." He opened a compartment used to store cannonballs and powder charges. "It'll work better than that travois."

She smiled and started to say something, when they both looked up to see Vina Gibbs come running; she looked terrified.

"What's wrong, Vina?" Selona asked. "You look like you've seen the Devil."

Vina pointed down the Row. "Juanita's gone, and so is the baby."

With the death of Winston Jackson, Juanita and Chihocopee had been told to leave the fort. That was army policy. But she was given thirty days, another policy, to make plans for the future.

"She said she was going back to her people in Piedras Negras. But it's not like Juanita to leave without saying goodbye," Selona said thoughtfully.

Vina shook her head worriedly, saying, "She didn't take anything except the clothes on her back."

Selona repeated, "She wouldn't leave without saying something."

"That's why I'm worried."

They searched Juanita's quarters and found what little property she and Winston had owned.

But Augustus looked at the wall and noticed something missing. "You two go on about your business. I'm going to look into something."

Augustus made the short walk to the stables, where he found a farrier shoeing a horse.

"Have you made the morning count?"

The farrier shook his head. "No, Sergeant."

"Come with me. I want every horse on this fort accounted for."

For the next hour a detailed count was made of the stalls and stable; finally, the farrier reported to Augustus.

"The count shows we're missing one horse and one saddle."

"Find the sergeant of the guard from last night and ask him to report to my quarters."

The farrier hurried off. Within fifteen minutes Sergeant Josiah Tubman reported to Augustus, looking as though he had been awakened from a deep sleep.

"Sergeant, did you give one of our horses to Juanita Jackson last night?"

Tubman looked momentarily worried, then said, "She told me she was going for a ride in the desert. You know she loved to ride at night."

Augustus knew that to be true. "Did she have her son with her?"

"Yes, sir. Had him wrapped onto her back papooselike. Then they rode off."

"Which direction?"

"Can't say for certain, but she looked to be going west."

"One more thing—did she have a Spencer rifle with her?"

Tubman nodded. "You know she always carried that old Spencer rifle whenever she rode at night."

Augustus dismissed Tubman and went to Juanita's quarters, where Selona and Vina were still waiting. By now the other laundresses were all there, and Augustus came straight to the point, saying, "Juanita and the boy are gone. I don't think we'll see them again."

Selona said what the women all knew. "Juanita's with child, Augustus. She can't ride two hundred miles by herself. You've got to do something."

"With child!" Augustus barked; then he knew what had to be done. "I'll talk to Captain O'Kelly." With that he left. The women began lighting their laundry fires, while Selona started on the day's cooking for the stage line.

By noon two small patrols had been dispatched to look for Juanita and Chihocopee, one sent due west, the other southwest. Selona was at the depot, waiting for the stage, which MacCallister claimed would be on time. She had set up her tiny mobile kitchen when there was the sound of hooves thundering from the west as the stage appeared on its return leg to Pecos from Alpine.

Braxton and the shotgun guard were yelling and shouting and pointing to the rear of the stage.

Augustus hurried to the depot and pushed his way through the crowd of soldiers and found Selona standing at the boot, wearing an enormous smile.

"Somebody sure fixed his wagon," one of the troopers said.

Captain John Armitage lay tied to the canvas cover of the baggage boot, his big hat clamped down tight over what was left of his head and face.

"Looks like somebody shot him right through the back of the head," said Braxton. "We found him lying in the road about two miles west from here."

"What about his horse?" asked Augustus.

The driver hawked and spit. "Whoever killed him took his horse." He reached and pulled off the hat. "And they took something else for a souvenir. Must have been Injuns."

"There ain't no Injuns left," said MacCallister.

Selona spoke softly, saying, "It appears there's at least one."

Armitage's scalp had been cleanly removed. Augustus smiled.

He squeezed Selona's shoulders firmly, then whispered into her ear, "You best get on about your business if you want that piece of land."

Augustus went back to the orderly room and from one end of Fort Davis to the other his laughter was heard; then, as the news spread, there was more laughter, until finally, the entire regiment was laughing themselves silly. Augustus knew that Juanita and Chihocopee Jackson would never be seen nor heard from again.

The body of Captain John Armitage was removed, and there was nothing at the depot to remind Selona of his presence except a splotch of gore on the canvas boot where Juanita Calderon Jackson had once ridden onto the grounds of Fort Davis.

Staring at the splotch, she was reminded of what Marie had said to her that painful morning in the Indian Territory, Fort Sill: "Don't let those butchers win, baby. If you die, they win. If you live, you got more than what they got right now."

She looked again at the splotch, then smiled and said to the passengers, "Y'all eat your fill. No charge. This meal's being paid for in the memory of that dead Texas Ranger."

She went home that night, the only night she would not see a monetary profit on her cooking business, but when she came through the door Augustus knew she had acquired something greater than wealth:

On her face was the smile of victory.

PART 4

1885: FORT GRANT

33

Selona and Augustus had done well for themselves by January 1885. Selona's cooking business had earned them more than five hundred dollars, and Augustus had built a small wooden building next to the depot to house the eatery. This new prosperity gave them added pride. Both were becoming respected in their own right on and off Fort Davis.

But it all meant more work for Selona, who was juggling the cooking business, laundry service, and childrearing at the same time. Adrian and David were growing like young saplings and had become her helpers, pulling the caisson on the daily journey to and from the depot.

Selona was proud of the man she had watched grow from a former slave to a leader of men. Augustus pursued his responsibilities with vigor and was a centerpiece of pride for the troop and the regiment. But he was a soldier, and the life of a soldier could always be shaken by the sound of alarm.

The three years following Augustus' promotion to sergeant had been quiet for the most part, except for an occasional renegade attack.

Everything seemed to be going their way as spring approached, and that was when she noticed Augustus began to grow quiet, often spending his evenings at the orderly room or with his men. Something was gnawing at him, and while the wives of the other soldiers began to notice the same in their men, there was no warning before the alarm finally sounded.

Vina Gibbs was standing at her kettle, eyeing Selona as though waiting to share some great secret. Selona noticed.

"You all right, Vina?"

Vina kept stirring the kettle, looking into the lye foam as though some demon might pop out of the suds. She shook her head. "You ain't heard, have you?"

"Heard what?" asked Selona.

"We going to be moving." She kept stirring, kept staring.

Selona gripped Vina's elbow. "What are you saying?"

Vina stopped stirring and wiped her hands on her dress. "Last night Darcy was corporal of the guard. A rider come in late asking for Colonel Grierson. He brung him a message. The colonel sent Darcy for all the company commanders and they had a big meeting. Darcy was standing outside the office and heard what they said."

"What did they say?"

There were tears in Vina's eyes. "Colonel Grierson told the officers the regiment's moving west to fight the Apaches."

"Apaches! The Mescaleros were wiped out in Mexico. Old Victorio himself is dead."

"Ain't Mescaleros. They called Chiricahua."

The news hit Selona like a burst of lightning. No wonder Augustus had been moody, often standing outside in the cold, talking to Gibbs and other men living along the Row. She had heard some of the conversations, but only smatterings of names she didn't understand. Names like Chatto. Nana. Mangus. And the name the men spoke in low voices, as though afraid to say it aloud.

Geronimo.

Selona marched across the parade field and into the orderly room. Augustus was sitting at his desk and looked up, surprised. She was through the doorway and standing in front of his desk before she realized it was the first time she had set foot in there.

Their eyes met for a long moment. "How long you known about this?" Selona asked.

Augustus rose from his desk and took her outside. From the stables behind the barracks the sounds of men and horses rumbled like an approaching storm.

"Is it true?" she demanded. "Are we moving?"

Augustus looked off toward Officers Row. "Orders came last night. We—"

Selona cut him off. "Is it true, Augustus?"

He nodded. "The regiment has been ordered to pack up and be ready for movement in two weeks."

Selona's eyes nearly exploded from her head. "Two weeks! Are you and them other men crazy!" She suddenly grew frightened. "What are me and the children supposed to do? Run alongside you like a pack of dogs? Or hadn't you thought about us? And what about our business? Have you forgot about that piece of land I've been working myself to death for?"

"I haven't forgotten. You can start a new business in Bonita."

She thought Arizona was bad enough, but now it was Bonita! "What's Bonita?"

"It's a town about five miles from Fort Grant. That's where the company will be stationed." The words froze on his lips; it took a few seconds for their meaning to become clear to Selona.

"You mean we're *splitting up?*"

"Just for a short while. Fort Grant isn't fit for men, much less women and children. Besides, there's no quarters there except for the families of officers. Once this trouble with Geronimo is settled I'll be back home with you and the children."

Something inside her seemed to dissolve; she had never expected this.

"You can still buy you that piece of land, Selona. Maybe in Arizona. Maybe we'll go to California when I retire."

Selona shook her head mechanically; Augustus seemed to
have an answer for every question.

"What about Mr. Conniger? He's my partner. All my uten-
sils?"

"I'll get us a wagon. We'll load everything up. You won't
need a partner in Arizona. You have enough money to start
your own business."

"A wagon?" Sparks of incredulity showered from Selona.

"The families are going to follow the regiment in wagons.
Colonel Grierson's making the arrangements."

Selona remembered, as a child, her and her mama following her father from post to post on the Kansas frontier.

"I done been scalped once, Augustus. Now you men are
going to get us all killed and my children scalped."

The air suddenly darkened from the dust boiling into the
air as a squad of soldiers rode out. Then another squad, and
another, until the parade ground was filled with the full com-
plement of the troop. Corporal Darcy Gibbs rode up, leading
four saddled horses. Augustus stepped off the porch and
mounted.

"I've got to go to formation. We'll talk tonight."

The door of the orderly room flew open and Colonel Grierson, followed by Sergeant Major Brassard, who had come
out of retirement to become an army scout, marched to their
waiting horses.

Grierson mounted and started to turn his horse when his
eyes found Selona. There was a sadness in his eyes; a sadness
that lasted only a moment before fading into that invisible
armor worn by men of duty.

Selona could only stand there and watch as Grierson read
the orders that would change all their lives forever.

It was late when Augustus came home. Selona was awake, sitting in their bed, as Augustus stripped off his heavy pistol belt.
He hung the curved sabre, as always, over the small hearth on
the two wooden pegs driven into the hard adobe. He stood
there for a long moment, staring at the Sharps and the sabre,

but she knew he was feeling the silence from their bed.

Augustus sat at the small, roughly hewn table, his arms spread like great eagle wings. He stared at a plate covered with a cloth, then lifted the cloth and tucked it into his collar. Selona had cooked a rabbit that night, the way she always cooked rabbit, first fried lightly, then baked in the Dutch oven in a thick gravy made from flour and rabbit grease. Juanita Jackson had taught her this technique, which tenderized the meat.

He ate in silence, sopping biscuits in the gravy, chewing methodically, carefully, wasting nothing, as a man does who has known prolonged and deep hunger. When he finished, he sat back in the chair, allowing his eyes to roam the room as though taking inventory.

Or was he saying good-bye? wondered Selona.

"Are you going to talk to me now, Augustus?"

He stood by the hearth and slowly ran his fingers along the stock of the Sharps. "I wanted to tell you sooner, Selona. But I couldn't."

"Why? For God's sake, I'm your wife. Don't I have a right?"

"Of course you do. I was just following orders."

"Orders." She snorted. "What kind of order keeps secrets between a man and his woman?"

"Army orders, Selona."

"God never intended secrets between a husband and his wife."

Augustus laughed sarcastically. "God never served in the Tenth Cavalry."

"Don't blaspheme." Selona rose and came to Augustus' side. "Now . . . you tell me what we are going to do." She had accepted the situation. They lived in a world of limited choices, and this was not a matter of choice.

"The regiment has been ordered to New Mexico and Arizona." He kept talking, ignoring the sudden rush of breath from Selona. "We'll be posted along the railroad. The Apaches are stirring up such a ruckus, the army is bringing in a whole bunch of troops. White and Colored."

Selona shook her head. "Them rich white men ain't satis-

fied with all the Injun land they done stole. Now they got to
get what ain't been took. Maybe get me, my children, and my
man killed in the taking."

Augustus released a long, helpless-sounding sigh. "Colonel
Grierson says I'm next in line to be promoted to first sergeant."
There was a quick brightness on his face; she tried to smile,
but couldn't.

"My, my. You are coming up in the world, Augustus
Sharps." There was a quiver in her voice and a wetness in her
eyes that gleamed in the firelight.

"I'm sorry, baby." He wrapped her in his arms. "I'm sorry."

She trembled, then said softly, "I come back after seeing you
and I sat here and had my cry. That's enough for now. No
more tears. No more sadness. I done accepted things because
I know I can't do anything about it. I can't do anything but
roll with the times and believe in you and God Almighty."

He looked around, then softly touched the buffalo skin wig
on her head. "I know life hasn't been fair to you, Selona. I
know you love this place. That you want a piece of land in
these parts. That we're safe here. But it's the army way, Selona.
When the bugle calls, a soldier's got to answer."

"I know," she whispered into his chest. "I know about life.
I know about fairness. I learned a long time ago that life is fair
. . . that everybody's going to get their heart broken somewhere along the way."

34

On April 1, 1885, twelve companies of the 10th Cavalry gathered at Fort Davis for deployment to the west. It was the first time in the history of the regiment that all troops, consisting of thirty-eight officers and 696 enlisted men, were joined together at one time beneath the regimental guidon.

Including newly appointed First Sergeant Augustus Sharps.

Though she hated to make the admission, it was a magical sight to behold, Selona thought.

The line of march paralleled the tracks of the Southern Pacific Railroad, ribbons of steel winding from west Texas through New Mexico and Arizona to the western horizon.

Except for those around Fort Davis, Selona had never imagined mountains of the size and majesty that she saw during the journey. Nor had she ever imagined that the heat of west Texas could be outdone by any other place. She spent most of her time driving the team of mules that pulled her wagon, an old hospital ambulance Augustus had managed to acquire due to his rank. It was their home; a rolling, jostling, creaking contraption that suggested collapse each and every moment. Like the soldiers riding ahead in a long column, she, too, was learning the discipline required on a long march.

The soldiers rode to the front, the wagons with the families in the rear. The families of the white officers naturally rode to the front of the Colored family wagons; at night, they camped off to themselves, forming a defensive perimeter with the wagons. The Colored families did the same, accepting the segregation for what it was. Despite shared hardships, there were some lines that could never be crossed.

With one exception: Marcia O'Kelly drove her wagon with the Colored families, and when camped at night continued her school classes by campfire.

During the day, Adrian and David ran alongside the wagon and quickly became the scourge of every rabbit within twenty yards.

By the end of April, the column had begun to dwindle as various troops reached their stations at key locations along the railroad. This frightened Selona, for the deeper they drew into Apache territory, the fewer were the troopers, the more the vulnerability. It was only at night that she felt safe, when Augustus rode into camp with the other non-coms, dirty, tired, and saddle sore.

Sentries were posted, campfires lit, and each night the circled wagons would throb with festivity as the families celebrated surviving the day.

Shortly after passing through Fort Bowie, Arizona, where the remainder of the regiment split once again, Selona and Augustus tucked in the children and left the wagon for a walk.

The night sky was carpeted with stars; the moon bright and full.

Selona pointed at the moon. "Look there. That old moon's still smiling." She giggled. "That old moon's got secrets on us. Remember those nights in the piñons? Lying there, making love beneath that old moon?"

"We do that now, some Injun might sneak up on us. Or one of the patrols might come onto us."

Selona laughed. "Ain't no Injuns here." When Augustus didn't answer, her voice tightened. "Are there?"

"Them Injuns are probably watching us right now."

That frightened her. "Are you telling me the truth?"

Augustus nodded. That was when she noticed the flap on his holster was open. "Maybe we best be getting back, then."

Augustus looked to the west. "I hear horses. Walking slow."

Selona's eyes widened, and for the first time since her scalping she again knew fear. Deep, soul-freezing fear; fear he had known most of his life but never mentioned. A fear much greater than when she was attacked by the Rangers.

"Let's get back, Augustus."

Augustus shook his head. "The horses are shod. Injun horses aren't shod."

She heard the hooves drawing closer, the sharpness of steel against sun-baked ground. The closer the sound drew, the more frightened she became, until she was ready to run for the wagons.

She looked toward a dune, where she saw the shadows of riders. She was almost ready to scream; Augustus' hand went to the butt of his Colt.

"Let's go back, honey." She was nearly hysterical, pulling on his arm. He eased out of her grip with little effort, keeping his eyes on the shadows. Now there were three. Four. Then he heard another sound. A sound he had heard before; a sound brought on by fear.

Then she felt him relax and his hand fell away from the Colt, finding her shoulder.

"Hello in the camp." The voice was low, husky, but casual.

"First Sergeant Sharps," Augustus replied with the same casualness.

Four troopers appeared as though from nowhere. Selona recognized them; they were with H Troop. They talked for a few minutes, then the troopers rode on, continuing on their assigned picket patrol.

Augustus and Selona walked back to the wagons. When she reached the inner perimeter she released Augustus' hand and raced for the wagon. "I'll check on the children."

Augustus said nothing. He understood. She would hurry to the wagon, find a clean dress, and change before he arrived.

He walked slow, giving her time, remembering only minutes before, hearing her wetness splashing off the hard earth. He wouldn't mention it tonight; but one night he would tell her it had happened to him before.

35

*　*　*

The troop arrived at Fort Grant, Arizona, in April; the fort sat on a grass-covered plain in the shadow of Mount Graham, the tallest of the Pinaleno Mountains. Once known as the worst fort in the U.S. Army, it had gradually improved over the years, yet still lacked proper accommodations for the families of the non-commissioned officers.

Augustus spoke with Major Van Vliet, the commander of the squadron that included the men of D, E, H, K, and L troops of the regiment. Colonel Grierson had decided to establish headquarters at Whipple Barracks, north of Fort Grant.

"Sir, me and the men with families would appreciate it if I could ride into Bonita and get them settled for the night."

Van Vliet nodded. "I regret there are not adequate quarters here for your families, First Sergeant."

"They'll make do, sir. We will be back by daylight."

Augustus saluted and he and four troopers rode off while the 10th set about establishing their presence at Fort Grant.

*   *   *

Augustus rode at the head of the little caravan of wagons, now reduced to only a few.

"Beautiful country," said Augustus, waving his arm toward the mountain. "And smell that air. It's as fresh as flowers."

Selona was driving the lead wagon. She was tired, dirty, and wanted a bath, a luxury no one had enjoyed in several weeks.

"Mean-looking country, if you ask me. People in town probably going to be mean, too. They ain't going to be used to seeing Colored folks around here. Probably going to hate Coloreds as much as they hate Injuns."

Augustus spurred his horse, yelling to her as he rode out on point, "You said the same thing about Fort Davis."

Selona stood and yelled back, though there was only a trail of dust to the front. "Fort Davis had Coloreds before we got there."

"So did Fort Grant. The Ninth Cavalry was stationed there for years," he yelled back and then rode harder, as though her tongue were an Apache arrow.

She sat down heavily, gripping the reins angrily. She stared at the rumps of her two mules and turned to Adrian, who sat behind her with David. "I been staring at them rumps for weeks. Soon as I get me a house I'm going to make mule rump roast."

The wind picked up, whipping the sand off the desert as the tiny caravan moved away from the mountains on a supply trail. She started to get uneasy, fearing she and the others might become separated in what she realized was now a sandstorm.

"Adrian," she shouted into the back. "You and David get under cover. Get a bandanna over your mouth and cover over with a blanket."

She stopped the wagon and worked her way to the rear, where she could see Vina Gibbs sitting in her wagon, a Spencer rifle cradled across her lap.

"Vina . . . I can't see. Augustus rode ahead and there's no telling where he's at."

"What we going to do?" Two more wagons pulled alongside, joined by the troopers from the flanks.

Corporal Darcy Gibbs dismounted and took his rope. He tied it to the rear of Selona's wagon, then to one of the mules pulling the Gibbs wagon.

"Tie off all the wagons to mules," Gibbs shouted to the troopers. "Get back inside the wagons. This'll blow through soon, then we'll move on."

"What about Augustus?" Selona asked. He was alone in the sandstorm in hostile country.

Gibbs shook his head. "Get in the wagon. Don't worry about the sarge. He knows what to do. He knows what we're doing. We've done this before."

Gibbs climbed into the wagon and pulled out a blanket. "Cover the eyes of your mules, else the blowing sand'll cut their eyes to pieces and they'll bolt."

Selona climbed through the rear and took a blanket. She made sure Adrian and David were secure, then she covered the eyes of the mules, fighting to keep her balance and her wits. She started back for the wagon, then froze. She felt the presence of something close.

Staring through the haze, she saw shapes faint and ghostlike; then there were more.

Eight men sat on horses; eight men with long hair and faces covered with bandannas. They carried rifles and were draped with bandoliers of ammunition.

Apaches!

She remembered wetting herself that night in the desert, but she had been with Augustus. Now, alone, she had her children only a few feet away. She raced for the wagon, climbed quickly to the seat, and pulled out the Colt pistol. She snapped back the hammer and pointed the horse pistol, but she saw nothing but the blowing sand and heard only the howl of the wind.

Minutes passed and still there was nothing; then she saw another horseman and took aim.

"Selona!" the voice of Augustus shouted. He was riding toward her, his head bent, his face covered. When he reined beside the wagon she saw the eight riders following. She started to raise the pistol, but his hand pushed the barrel down.

"They're White Mountain Apache scouts. They won't harm us. I ran into them just after the storm hit." Augustus motioned to the scouts. They dismounted, forced their horses to the ground, then covered the animals' eyes. Each of the eight took a blanket and lay between a horse's legs, covering himself. Gradually the scouts and horses disappeared under a layer of sand.

Augustus was in the wagon, tying the front flap and using his large body to protect Selona and the children. He used a blanket to make a tent inside the wagon, which was now filling with sand.

An hour later the storm had passed and the sky was clear. All the Negroes came out of their wagons and began to shovel the sand. Selona watched the scouts rise and shake themselves.

She noticed how much darker they were than the plains Indians. And fierce looking! Their eyes seemed to shine like black diamonds.

"Why are them Apache scouts for the army? I thought we was out here to fight the Apaches. They'll probably kill us in our sleep."

"They're reservation Indians," replied Augustus. "They'll push on to Fort Grant from here."

"They don't look like reservation Injuns to me."

About that time one of the scouts approached Augustus, then stopped suddenly. He was tall, sinewy, and carried his rifle with the ease of one carrying a small stick. He stood staring at Selona for the longest time, until she grew uncomfortable.

"What's he looking at?" she asked Augustus.

Augustus followed the Apache's line of sight, then burst out laughing. "He's looking at your wig!"

Selona reached up and grabbed the wig and tore it from her head. She shook the buffalo fur at the Apache, whose eyes were as round as her dinner plates.

"Here. Take it. You're probably going to get it one day anyhow."

The Apache pulled back into the group of other scouts, all

of them jabbering and pointing at her scarred head.

Selona clamped the wig onto her head, tied it down with her calico scarf, and, with pistol in hand, climbed into the wagon and snapped the reins.

"Hiyah, mules."

The caravan pulled away one wagon at a time, leaving the mystified scouts staring at Selona as she passed into the golden sunlight of Arizona, now unafraid, for she had met the Apaches and scared the living hell out of them.

36

It was dark when the wagons reached Bonita, a town of roughly one thousand inhabitants in mining country, and the only street leading through town was lined with saloons and drunk miners, as well as drunk white soldiers from the 1st Infantry, also stationed at Fort Grant. Seeing that, the troopers and their wives fell silent.

The wagons creaked and groaned through the street, and the deeper into the town they drew, the more drunken onlookers gathered.

That's when Selona heard a loud voice shout, "The niggers are here!"

Yet more miners began stumbling into the streets, waving whiskey bottles and shouting racial slurs. The mules, excited, kicked one miner, sending him tumbling into another group of drunks, and the shouts grew angrier. The situation was moving toward something Selona had never experienced before. She had known brief moments of racial confrontation, but only moments, except when she was attacked by the Rangers.

This was a large mob now, and she could feel the hatred.

"Git on back south!" shouted a voice.

"Find a rope!" shouted another.

Selona reached to the floor of the wagon, pulled up the pistol, and cocked the hammer back.

Augustus rode looking straight ahead, as did Gibbs, who was beside Vina's wagon. They didn't show weapons, only stony faces that turned to neither side.

"Augustus, what are we going to do?" Selona pleaded.

"Just drive the team. Don't pay any attention to them. We'll camp outside of town."

The deeper the caravan pushed through town, the larger the mob grew, until the wagons were forced to stop or plow through a human wall.

Augustus sat ramrod straight in the saddle, as did Gibbs. They knew better than to go for their weapons, but wished they didn't have the women and children along. They could ride, shoot, cut through the mob with their sabres, but with their families they had no choice.

Selona couldn't believe this was happening. In the wagon next to hers, Vina gripped the reins as though holding onto the edge of the earth, and muttered that she couldn't remember where she'd put the Spencer after the sandstorm.

David was fascinated by the sight; he had never been in a large town before. "Why are the miners so hateful, Mama?"

Adrian held his slingshot at the ready, a large pebble in the web in case they charged.

There was a loud explosion. Then another. Then a shout from the rear of the crowd.

"Get back. All of you! Get back. Clear a path and let these people through."

A tall man stepped into the street. He carried a double-barreled shotgun and wore a holster and pistol. On his coat was a badge; at each side he was flanked by two men wearing badges.

The five men pushed and shoved through the crowd, the sheriff reloading as the crowd parted, never taking his eyes off Augustus. When he reached Augustus he turned and directed the shotgun toward the men, saying, "I'll kill any man who lays a finger on these people."

There was a rush of grumbling, and Selona thought the man had to be either the bravest she had ever seen or the most insane.

When one miner tried to challenge the sheriff there was the flash of the shotgun, then the sickening thud of the stock crashing against his head. The miner tumbled backward among the crowd's scurrying feet as another blast from the shotgun shook the night air.

"Clear the street. All of you. Go on about your drinking and leave these people be. Do I make myself clear?"

As the crowd dispersed, Augustus eased down from the saddle and stood shoulder to shoulder with the sheriff.

In a matter of minutes the street was clear, and the sheriff turned to Augustus. But he wasn't looking directly at Augustus; rather, he reached to the pommel and patted the stock of the Sharps.

"I want to thank you, Sheriff. I think you probably saved a lot of lives."

The sheriff smiled. "That's the least I could do for you, Sergeant Sharps."

Augustus looked dumbfounded. "How do you know my name?"

"We've met before." He reached into his pocket, then said, "Open your hand."

Augustus did so and the sheriff dropped a familiar object into his hand.

A single Sharps cartridge.

As Augustus stared at his palm, his memory tumbled back through the years to a young boy in the Indian Territory.

The sheriff extended his hand. "I'm Ernst Bruner."

Ernst Bruner had grown into a tall, handsome man who, after a hitch with the 4th Cavalry, had remained in Arizona Territory to seek his fortune.

"I tried mining, but the gold played out. I thought about

ranching, but there's too many dangers from the Apaches."

They were all crowded into the front sitting room of the Bruner house, a stone structure on the edge of town. The night air and the stone made the atmosphere cool and pleasant.

Elizabeth Bruner was blond, with twinkling blue eyes, and heavy with child, but she had insisted on cooking for the man who had saved her husband's life. Selona and Vina were with her in the small kitchen, the first they had been in since leaving Fort Davis.

"You go and sit down, Miss Elizabeth," said Vina. "Selona was the best cook in west Texas, and she's more at home in a kitchen than a bird in a bush."

"That's right. Besides, you've got that baby to think of."

Elizabeth sat down near the iron stove, the first Selona had ever seen. "Ernst has spoken so many times about Augustus and how he saved him and his two sisters from the comancheros. He often wondered what had become of him. He thought their paths might cross when he was in the army, but they never did."

Selona looked past Elizabeth to Ernst, who was sitting at a table with Augustus and Darcy. Adrian and David and Vina's children were romping around outside, calling noisily to one another.

"He sure is a fine-looking man," said Selona. "Between the two of you, I expect we'll be seeing a fine-looking baby."

Elizabeth blushed slightly. "He's a good man."

From the corner of her eye Selona had caught Elizabeth staring at her wig. This didn't bother Selona, for she had learned to live with the stares and had found that addressing the situation squarely took the edge off the tension. She said, "You can't help but notice my hairpiece. That's what I call it. Augustus calls it a wig, but to me it's a hairpiece."

Elizabeth blushed again. "It's the most extraordinary hairpiece I've ever seen. What is it made of?"

"Buffalo fur. Augustus made it for me after I was scalped."

The house suddenly fell silent. Elizabeth sat frozen; having overheard, Ernst rose from the table and came into the kitchen.

"Dear God," Elizabeth said, her voice apologetic and sad. Then the tears began to well up in her eyes.

Selona came over to her and put her arms around her and held her like a child. "It's not so bad. At least I'm alive. I've got a good man and two good children." She looked at Vina. "And good friends."

"Life has been so cruel to you, Selona."

She shook her head. "Life's been better to me than to most Colored people."

Aside from being killed by Apaches, bitten by rattlesnakes, or lynched by miners, the greatest fear Selona had had during the trip was worry for the money she had saved from her cooking business. She had hidden the gold eagles at the bottom of a flour barrel, sleeping near it at night with her pistol in hand.

"So that's where you put your money." Augustus laughed.

It was the next morning, and Augustus and Gibbs were preparing to return to Fort Grant.

"The first thing we got to do is find a proper house to live in," said Selona, bouncing the leather pouch of coins. "Vina and me done decided that we're going to live together. That way we can look after each other in case them miners come around."

"If we can find a house they'll let Coloreds live in," Vina said, looking apprehensive.

Ernst spoke up. "I know a man who'll rent you a house for a fair price. It's clean and sound. I'll take you to his business when I go to the office. But first, I think you should take your money and put it in a bank. Bonita's filled with the worst kind of thieves."

Selona shook her head. "A bank! Banks get robbed."

Ernst grinned. "Not in my town."

Sheriff Ernst Bruner that first morning informed the people of Bonita that the Sharps family and the Gibbses were very special. With Selona wearing her red dress, he escorted the Sharps down the plank sidewalk of Bonita in full view of the people who the night before had threatened the new arrivals with violence.

Ernst's escorting her made quite an impression on Selona, who had never really trusted white people, other than Mrs. O'Kelly. When they reached the bank the surprise on banker Frank Carson's face was obvious, but seeing the glint in Ernst's eyes, and hearing that the big Colored sergeant had rescued Ernst and his sisters from the comancheros, he became as congenial as a heel hound.

They began by filling out an application, and Carson expressed surprise at how well Selona could write. Most Coloreds he had met were illiterate.

Finished with the formalities, Selona looked Carson straight in the eye and asked, "Where you going to keep my money?"

Carson led her to the vault. He opened it and swept his hand proudly to the interior. "This vault was made by Wells Fargo. It's German steel and has a time lock. That means it can't be opened except at the time set the day before."

Carson was a rotund man with red cheeks and small hands that seemed to never quit moving, which made Selona a little nervous at first, but after getting a full tour of the bank she took the leather pouch from her purse and handed it to Carson.

The banker took the money from the pouch and carefully counted it: five hundred dollars. Then he gave her a receipt and something new in banking.

"This is a checkbook. If you need to buy something around town, you merely write out the amount on the check and sign your name. The person receiving the check comes by the bank and can draw cash against your account."

Selona looked at him in utter astonishment. "You mean I don't have to pay with cash?"

"This is as good as cash. Besides, you don't want to walk around carrying cash. There are thieves, you know."

Selona nodded. "I know."

Ernst said, "Now let's find you a house."

*   *   *

The short, squat Chinaman was named Lo Ping, and after leaving the Southern Pacific Railroad, where he had worked as a laborer, he took his savings and invested them in his future.

In 1885, five years after walking away from the railroad, he owned several pieces of property in Bonita: a small restaurant, three houses, and a business that Selona understood better than most.

The local laundry.

Lo Ping had met a lot of hostility when he first walked the dusty streets of Bonita, and might not have survived that first day were it not for a young sheriff named Ernst Bruner. Therefore, when Bruner brought Selona to his laundry, which served as his main operation, Lo Ping was quick to help her.

The house Selona chose was not far from the Bruners', on the north end of town. It had a full view of the main street. There was a kitchen, four rooms for sleeping, and a sitting room.

"Lord have mercy," Vina breathed at her first sight of the house. "This place is big enough for the regiment."

"Big enough for us," Selona said. She walked out back and began to visualize where she would put the rabbit pens and the washing kettles. The laundry would be picked up and delivered at the fort every three days, and Vina's wagon and two mules would be used for transportation.

Selona already had plans for her two mules.

37

The next few days found Selona and Vina scrubbing and cleaning the house, arranging the few furnishings they had, and building a new rabbit pen. Eight of Selona's rabbits had survived the trip from Fort Davis.

Lo Ping's restaurant was more a hole in the wall than a proper eating place, as Selona had seen right off. This observation brought her to his office on the fourth day with a plate of rabbit stew.

"Mr. Lo Ping, I've noticed that your cooking business is doing poorly."

Lo Ping nodded. He took his first bite of the stew; then his eyes widened with delight.

"I had my own cooking business in west Texas, and folks said I was the best cook west of the Pecos."

Lo Ping nodded. He took another bite.

"I still have all my cooking equipment, and I believe we could make some good money if you and I was to become partners."

Lo Ping's mouth stopped working momentarily as he digested the notion; then he smiled, and swallowed. "You cook rabbit stew only?"

Selona shook her head. "Anything you want. I'm told there's lots of deer, antelope, quail, wild turkey, and cattle in these parts, and venison and beef would be easy enough to come by. I raise my own rabbits, and we can get some chickens and cook eggs, raise a few hogs for bacon. We can do anything we want."

Since first meeting her, Lo Ping had been intrigued by her wig. He pointed at her head, asking in pidgin English, "What kind hair that?"

She pulled off the wig and dangled it in front of his nose. "Buffalo fur."

Lo Ping nearly choked on the stew and stared wide-eyed at the wig, then at her disfigured scalp. He had known misery and seen torture in his life; and he certainly understood ambition. His instincts told him he could trust this woman.

Lo Ping nodded. "You be partner. But must wear buffalo fur in restaurant."

She plopped the wig back on her head and adjusted the calico rag, then stuck out her hand. "We'll serve the best food in the Arizona Territory."

"I hope you know what you're doing." Vina Gibbs was standing behind Selona that afternoon near the small stable at the rear of the house.

Selona pulled back the hammer of the pistol and took deliberate aim. "I know what I'm doing." She started to squeeze the trigger, but the mule she had dubbed "ornery" turned and looked at her down the barrel of the pistol. Augustus had taught her to shoot with both eyes open, and now she stood locked eyeball to eyeball with the mule. She realized she had never really looked in the mule's eyes; for weeks she had only stared at the other end.

She lowered the pistol.

"I knew you couldn't shoot that mule, Selona." Vina was grinning while stirring one of the boiling kettles. "You and that mule got history with each other."

Selona growled. "History. I was planning on using that mule right off for my cooking business. Now I got to think up something else."

The sound of wagon wheels grinding to a halt in the front made Selona raise her pistol again; she could still hear and feel the hatred from the miners. Seconds later, she lowered the hammer on the pistol as a familiar face came around the corner of the house.

"Good Lord, Miss Marcia! What have you done to yourself?"

Marcia's long hair had been cut short, and she wore a calico shirt and a pair of old army trousers. She resembled a man, especially with the floppy hat she wore.

"At Fort Davis all we could do was sit around the fort." She swung her arms around, saying, "Look at all this beauty! Tall mountains, rivers and creeks. It's a paradise compared to Fort Davis. And I'm going to start enjoying it."

Selona had to agree. How she had hated leaving Fort Davis, but now she was glad the move had been made. The flowers— the trees!—were everywhere. She had never in her life seen such natural beauty.

"What do you have in mind?"

Marcia pointed to Mount Graham in the distance. "I propose we go pick berries and have a picnic lunch."

Selona looked at the mule, then at Vina, who said, "You go on. I'll take care of the laundry."

Selona hurried inside and shouted for Adrian and David. At nine, the boys were strong as young oxen, and she figured it was time they started becoming young men.

When she came out she had the boys following, and she was carrying Vina's Spencer rifle.

"What's that for?" asked a startled Marcia.

"For Injuns . . . or venison. Whichever comes along first."

*   *   *

Mount Graham rose like a giant anvil, more than two miles above sea level, and a mile above nearby Bonita.

The buggy ride to the base of the mountain was marked by budding cactus, wildflowers, scampering jackrabbits, and swaying golden hay in the field of a local farmer.

"It is beautiful, Miss Marcia." Selona sat beside Marcia, Spencer cradled in her lap; the boys rode in the back, shooting their slingshots at any creature that dared move.

They reached the base of the mountain an hour later, spread a blanket on the ground, and feasted on the picnic Marcia had prepared. When finished, Marcia said to the boys, "Let's go for a hike." She asked Selona, "Do you want to join us?"

Selona shook her head. "You go on. I've got work to do." She patted the butt of the Spencer. "Your walking around might just scare up a deer or antelope."

Marcia and the boys headed up a steep trail that gradually wound to higher ground. They would not stop until Marcia needed a rest, for the boys seemed immune to physical exertion.

Selona found a clump of mesquite and hunkered beneath a limb to wait. From where she sat she could see the mountain and the three specks of Marcia and the boys slowly creeping up the trail to the mountain wall. Selona squinted, then shaded her eyes, trying to see more clearly.

Suddenly, she saw a large boulder moving from above, rolling directly at the three specks.

Her heart nearly stopped as she watched the three specks scramble, and stumble, and fall as they tried to get out of the way. Then she saw tons of rocks slam into one of the specks while the other two escaped, and the speck pushed off the trail to plummet to the base of the mountain.

Then she ran. And she ran. And she ran.

Too frightened to notice that her hairpiece had flown off.

The suddenness of Marcia's death was almost more than Selona could stand.

The cemetery at Fort Grant sat a half mile from the fort in an arid area without grass, plants, shrubs, or trees. Each marked grave bore a number and the name of the dead soldier, though there were dozens of graves that were not marked.

Selona stood watching the casket lowered into the ground, and thought that while life begins in secret—not giving a woman notice that she's carrying life for weeks, or months—with death there is no secret. Her eyes roamed the cemetery and she recalled her mother's grave, and the wagon wheel sunk into the ground as a marker; a white board marked her father's grave, and one marked Marie's. Markers that would not withstand time and would one day vanish, as on the unmarked graves in this cemetery.

Lieutenant John O'Kelly stood with his daughter and showed no emotion. He had ridden all night from near Wilcox, where a courier had arrived late the night before with word of Marcia's death. How Selona wished Augustus was here right now. Not that he could do anything for the lieutenant; it was she who needed him.

That thought had plagued her all morning as she helped wash and dress Marcia's body and prepared her for burial.

This was the first funeral Selona had ever attended without Augustus. And there had been so many.

When the burial was over and the grave filled, she stayed until everyone was gone. She went to her wagon, took a wooden box filled with flowering plants, knelt by the grave, and carefully planted the flowers along the outline of the grave. Then she soaked the flowers with water from a bucket she had brought.

Legend around Bonita said flowers wouldn't grow at the Fort Grant cemetery.

Selona meant to see that legend disproved.

38

The first three days of their new restaurant venture were a disaster for Selona and Lo Ping, who believed the only reason he had suffered financial failure with the earlier restaurant was the color of his skin. He had hoped that would not be the case with Selona as his partner.

He was wrong.

The miners, gamblers, and painted girls of the saloons and hog ranches stayed clear, even though the smell coming from the kitchen was the finest Lo Ping had ever encountered.

The only customer was Ernst Bruner, who managed to convince the town council to buy meals for his jail from Selona's restaurant, which she had named "Selona's Kitchen."

She was sitting at a table with Lo Ping, drinking coffee, thinking that his misery equaled hers. In the kitchen waited a roasted ham, rabbit stew, several loaves of fresh baked bread, potatoes, and two dozen hard-boiled eggs.

"Augustus was right, Lo Ping. There ain't much opportunity out west for a poor person of color."

Lo Ping shook his head. "Not true. Much opportunity. But must be lucky."

"Lucky? I ain't ever been lucky."

Lo Ping's eyes drifted to her buffalo fur wig. He smiled softly.

Selona felt uncomfortable. "Well. Maybe a little lucky. But not all-the-time lucky."

"Luck not come all the time. Luck come when time important. That's why called luck."

Selona thought about the rock slide, and how the boys could have been killed. She stood and said, "Well, I best be getting home. There don't appear to be much reason to stay."

She went into the kitchen and began loading the food into the baskets she used for transport from her house to the restaurant.

That was when she heard Lo Ping scream, and heard the sound of a gunshot.

Selona raced to the dining room to find the door open. Lo Ping was on the front sidewalk, jumping up and down, shouting in Mandarin. When she went through the door she yelled, "What's happening?"

Lo Ping pointed toward the bank.

Two men were coming out of the bank wearing masks. Ernst Bruner, who was making his rounds, pulled his pistol and fired, hitting the first robber as he tried to mount his horse. The second robber fired, striking Ernst in the leg, and he fell in the street as the robber started riding north out of town.

Selona's eyes widened. The robber was carrying a sack that must be filled with money.

Her money!

The robber rode right past her, and even nodded and held out the sack, as though to say he knew her money now belonged to him.

She saw a saddled horse tied to a hitching post at the saloon next door. She dashed to the horse, reached up, and pulled a Winchester rifle out of the saddle boot.

The robber was at the edge of town when she stepped out into the street and jacked a round in the chamber. She took aim, centering on the robber's back, then shouted, "You better come back here with my money!"

Selona's finger squeezed around the trigger, the way Augustus had taught her on the rifle range. The Winchester barked, and kicked so hard she was thrown backward to the ground.

Fifty yards away the bullet struck the robber dead center in the back, pitching him forward and onto the hard ground not ten yards from her house.

Selona straightened and walked slowly toward the robber, her heart pounding so loud she thought she would swoon. When she reached him she saw his blue eyes staring emptily over the mask, a look she had seen before. He would cause no more trouble.

She pulled at the sack, but his fingers were locked in a death grip. Again she pulled, and this time the sack came away from his hand.

Selona hoisted the Winchester onto her shoulder and started walking back toward town. Her hairpiece had slipped slightly, and ignoring the people coming out to line the street, she paused, took off the wig, made the adjustment, and continued walking.

Miners, gamblers, bartenders, and prostitutes watched in silence as she paced down the main street and disappeared into the bank.

Ernst Bruner was sitting in a chair, and Frank Carson was using a towel to apply pressure to the bullet wound.

"Ernst, are you all right?"

Ernst grimaced. "It's only a flesh wound. No bone broken."

Selona looked at Carson and extended her hand with the sack, saying, "Mr. Carson, I brought our money back."

Both men stared in utter astonishment.

The next morning Selona rose at dawn and loaded her cooking supplies for the short walk to the restaurant. Heading along the main street, the sun barely climbing over the eastern horizon, she could see there was a crowd of people in the street. As she came closer, she realized they were standing in front of the restaurant, and her heart nearly stopped, for fear something had happened to Lo Ping.

Reaching the front door was a long line of miners and townspeople that meandered like a moving snake.

"Good morning, Miss Selona," a rough-looking miner said. He had held the rope the first night they arrived in Bonita. "I'm so hungry I could eat a bear."

Selona laughed. "I ain't ever cooked a bear. But you bring me one and I'll try."

"How about ham and eggs and coffee?" He had taken his hat off and was speaking with good manners.

"Come on in. I'll start cooking."

He was followed by several more until the dining room was full. The customers stayed until she had fed them all, many standing outside until it was their turn.

When the last customer left they had made a fistful of money. Lo Ping, after making the count, gave her her share and said with a sly laugh, "Luck come sometime when time important."

Augustus and Darcy rode in that night from Wilcox, south of Bonita on the Southern Pacific Railroad. They had been on patrol since the morning they reported for duty and had no idea of what had happened until they began their ride through town.

One miner, recognizing Augustus, shouted, "That's some feisty little lady you've got, soldier."

A bartender stepped from a saloon and handed each of them a bottle of whiskey.

Augustus and Darcy were dumbfounded by this reception, but were stunned when they rode up to the house.

The yard was filled with townspeople of every walk and way. Ernst Bruner was on the front porch in Selona's rocking chair, his leg propped on a wooden box, grinning like a jackass eating briars.

Augustus could hear voices inside the house, then saw the boys come running out. What surprised him was that they jumped into the saddles of two horses tied at the hitching rail. Fine mounts, too, Augustus judged.

"Boys, get down off them horses."

David grinned. "He's mine. Ain't he, Sheriff?"

Ernst waved casually and replied, "Bought and paid."

Augustus eased down from his saddle. "What's going on here? Who paid for these horses?"

Ernst rocked forward, saying, "Two bank robbers that won't ever ride another horse or rob another bank."

Augustus walked into the house to find a sea of visitors standing about; all white, except for Lo Ping. Selona was sitting in a chair he had never seen before, and there were furnishings that made his head spin.

God! He thought, Selona's gone crazy from the sun and spent all her cooking money!

Selona saw him and dashed into his arms, hugging him wildly.

Augustus felt embarrassed. All the whites, many of whom had threatened him and his family, stood around grinning.

"Selona, what's going on here?"

A man stepped forward and said, "I'm Frank Carson, the banker. Yesterday two men tried to rob the bank. And would have, if it weren't for your wife. Why, this little lady shot one of them right out of the saddle and saved the money of every person in Bonita."

Ernst hobbled in on a crutch fashioned from a tree limb. "The folks of Bonita brought the furniture, some from the general store. It's their way of saying thanks."

"And that ain't all, Augustus." Selona had a look in her eye that he had never seen; a shining light brighter than that of the night they had waltzed at Fort Sill.

"What more could there be, Selona?"

She held out a piece of paper to him.

He took the paper and unfolded it, then carefully read every word, his grin growing broader with each line he read.

"That's called a deed," she said proudly.

Augustus nodded, then swept her off her feet and shouted, "You finally got yourself that piece of land!"

39

The very mention of the name Geronimo struck fear into the hearts of every man and woman in Arizona. The army was furiously searching for the war chief and his followers, who had jumped the reservation at San Carlos, stolen horses and guns, and were on a rampage throughout Arizona and New Mexico. Ranches had been burned, stock driven off, and the army was having little success in engaging Geronimo in an open battle. His tactic was hit-and-run guerrilla warfare, with the railroad one of its prime targets.

The 10th Cavalry was posted along the long stretch of track and, as in Texas, the troopers were used primarily as guards in isolated places where nothing could live but Gila monsters, rattlesnakes, and the Apaches.

As the new first sergeant of H Company, Augustus' primary duty was to inspect the outposts, making certain supplies, ammunition, and water were delivered to the troops, who, after more than a month in the field, had yet to encounter any hostile Apaches.

Twenty miles east of Wilcox, Augustus and a squad of seven troopers arrived at the eight-man outpost commanded by

Darcy Gibbs, who was now a sergeant. The outpost was nothing more than four tents surrounded by a stone wall to give the troopers some protection in case of attack; a corral had been built on the outside of the wall, made of wooden poles latticed to form a square.

Augustus slid from the saddle and shook hands with his old friend. The first words from Gibbs' mouth were to ask about the two families.

Augustus found a shaded spot and sat on the ground, fanning himself with his hat, and told him the news, ending with the piece of land outside Bonita. "Selona's building her that house she's always wanted." He thought for a moment, as though trying to recollect something important. "I'd imagine that house is about finished as we sit here talking."

"How's Vina and the children?"

"Vina's doing most of the laundry. Selona's got an idea she'll be discussing with you when you get back."

"What's that?"

Augustus grinned. "She says that piece of land's big enough for two houses. Yours and ours."

Gibbs sat beside him and laughed, saying, "Them women are always full of surprises." Then he laughed again. "Lord, Augustus, I wouldn't want to be the poor soul in charge of building that house. I'd wager Selona's counted every nail, board, and bucket of adobe mud being used."

Augustus was roaring with laughter, knowing it was true. "That's the tightest woman with a dollar I've ever seen, Darcy. I swear, one day back at Fort Davis, I saw her pay old man Conniger his share of the day's business, and when she gave him the money—a double eagle—she held on so tight to that coin, not wanting to let it go, I do believe I heard that old eagle scream."

They laughed for what seemed the longest time, the kind of laughter that can be heard only between friends who know all of each other's secrets. Full, deep, unapologetic laughter.

Then the conversation turned to the troopers and the boredom of the duty they were assigned.

"The men are restless, Augustus. Just the way they were in

Texas. It seems this regiment ain't ever goin' to be doin' anything but guardin' roads and waterholes."

Augustus tossed a pebble against the stone wall. He knew the frustration the men were feeling; all along the line there was the same complaint. Each outpost had a five-mile stretch of railroad to scout east and west, watching for sign of Geronimo. At various towns along the line troops were billeted to react at a moment's notice and board the train in pursuit of Geronimo. But in the mountains, where he was likely hiding, the white cavalry was being used to pressure the Apache into coming out for a fight.

Augustus gave Darcy the same reply he had given the others. "Colonel Grierson's doing the best he can, Darcy. General Crook thinks by having us along the railroad we'll know if Geronimo's on the move."

Gibbs stood and stretched, and was about to say something when there was the sound of a rifle shot.

Augustus jumped to his feet as Darcy slowly turned and faced him. There was a peculiar look on Darcy's face, a mixture of pain and astonishment.

Augustus looked at Darcy's chest, and saw the red blood begin to spread around the bullet hole.

The air filled with more gunshots, then the yelling and shouting of the troopers as they grabbed their weapons and raced to the north side of the stone wall.

Gibbs crumbled into Augustus' arms, the look of disbelief still on his face.

From the hills nearby, the Apaches were racing on foot from their rocky perch in a horde. Augustus pulled Darcy to the wall, grabbed his Sharps, and took aim at an Apache who was running toward the wall.

Augustus could see the hatred burning in the Indian's black eyes, framed by long hair and white and yellow war paint. Augustus squeezed the trigger. The Apache pitched backward, backflipped onto his stomach, then lay motionless.

Gibbs tried to speak, but Augustus put his hand over his mouth, saying, "Lie still, Darcy. I'll be back directly."

The Apaches numbered around thirty, Augustus figured, as

he now moved along the wall, directing the defense of the outpost. For most of the troopers, this was the first engagement
with hostile Indians.

"Don't fire too fast. Hit your target. Take your time and
take good aim."

One young trooper was huddled against the wall, his face
buried in the rocks, his body shaking wildly.

Augustus grabbed the trooper and pulled him around, saying, "We need you, son. This ain't no time for being scared.
You can do that later, but right now we need you!"

Augustus took his rifle and eased it over the top of the wall
and guided the trooper into the stock of the weapon. He put
the young man's finger through the trigger housing and fired
into the empty sky. The discharge seemed to bring the trooper
out of the cloud of fear, for he nodded, jacked a round in the
chamber and rose and fired.

Twenty yards away an Apache fell dead in the sand.

"Prepare for volley fire!" Augustus shouted, and the troopers took aim. The Apaches were now down from the rocks and
coming at them on the dead run.

"Fire!" Augustus ordered. The volley cut a swath through
the Apaches, but downed only seven Indians.

"Reload!" Augustus commanded. He opened the breech
and shoved a cartridge into the chamber and was ready to
command another volley when the Apaches turned and raced
back into the hills, where they took up positions among the
rocks and crevices.

The Apaches began sniping from the rocks, and though returning fire, the troopers' bullets didn't find the well-hidden
Indians. The fight now became one of keeping low, raising and
firing, then lowering again and reloading. The sun, beating
down on the 10th troopers, was to Augustus a greater threat
than the Indians. He turned and looked at Darcy, then his eyes
widened.

"Darcy! No!" Augustus shouted.

Sergeant Darcy Gibbs was standing on his feet, trying to
open the flap on his holster, his movement slow and slurred
as though he were drunk.

Augustus half-ran, half-crawled toward him, getting within a few feet of Darcy when he felt the sudden impact that threw his body forward onto the ground, then the hot, searing sting of the bullet, and the deep ache of the broken bone in his right shoulder where the bullet had exited. Instinctively, he rolled toward the wall, and through the haze of dust and pain he saw Gibbs suddenly straighten, then pirouette wildly and fall to the ground, his face inches from Augustus', who could only stare helplessly into the dead eyes of his friend.

Augustus tried to reach for Gibbs, but his arm trembled and became numb, his body weakened, then the face of Darcy Gibbs suddenly faded as Augustus felt his body seem to lift from the ground, as though flying through the sounds of gunfire, the shouts of desperate men, and what he thought was the sound of a bugle. Then there was nothing but blackness.

Augustus had no idea how long he was unconscious, or how confused his brain had become, but he knew there was something different.

It was the sound: not gunfire, but voices. He heard laughter, and the rattle of cavalry accoutrement. When he finally opened his eyes in the bright sunlight of the hot afternoon, he was staring into the deep blue eyes of a young cavalry officer.

Augustus looked at the officer's shoulder bars, and said, "Good afternoon, Lieutenant."

Lieutenant John Bullis, 4th U.S. Cavalry, smiled softly, then said, "You rest easy, First Sergeant. We'll be getting you out of here shortly."

Augustus tried to rise but was driven back down by the shaft of pain that struck his body.

"I said lie still, First Sergeant. That's an order."

Augustus turned his head slowly to the right, and there, lying on the ground near the stone wall, was a body covered with a blanket. Then he looked up to see the young trooper who had been frozen with fear at the wall; the trooper knelt by his side.

"These Fourth Cav boys say we done real well, First

Sergeant." The fear was gone from his eyes. They now shone with confidence and courage.

"What's your name, Trooper?" asked Augustus.

"Trooper Robert Calvin, First Sergeant."

Trooper Robert Calvin was a short young man, with narrow facial features and a broad mouth.

Augustus swallowed. "What happened?"

Calvin laughed, the defensive laugh one hears after a battle. A laugh designed to show that the soldier wasn't as scared as might be thought. "Them Apaches had us pinned down right good. Then we heard that bugle, and looked up, and here comes the cavalry. Them old Apaches just took off up into them hills like scared jackrabbits."

Augustus nearly laughed. "Trooper Calvin, Apaches don't get scared. They just decided to move on so they could fight another day."

Bullis returned, saying, "We're pursuing the Apaches, First Sergeant. They've finally come down out of the mountains and we're on their trail. I figure they hit your outpost for any supplies they could get their hands on, which means they must be hurting for rations and ammunition."

Augustus forced himself to the sitting position. "You mean—"

Bullis interrupted, "Yes, First Sergeant. You were attacked by Geronimo's main body. The wily rascal was up there in the hills directing the attack. But you and your boys—" Bullis stopped, then said, "You and your men stopped him cold against overwhelming odds. Geronimo's now running south for Mexico, but we'll box him up before he crosses the border." Bullis rose, then saluted, saying, "Your men did an excellent job, First Sergeant."

Augustus glanced at the blanket-covered body of Sergeant Darcy Gibbs, then said softly, "Did you hear that, Darcy? 'An excellent job.' "

The piece of land Selona had been given lay west of Mount Graham, and the site chosen for the house was surrounded by tall cottonwood and thick buckbrush, the landscape painted a myriad of colors by the wildflowers that spread like an ocean. The house, made of wood and adobe, was now finished. Fifty yards away another part of the property was receiving its first resident.

The few soldiers who could be spared stood in silence as the chaplain read from the prayer book. Then "Taps" was sounded, and Sergeant Darcy Gibbs was lowered into the ground. Vina Mae Gibbs stood with her five children near Augustus, Selona, and their children.

Ernst and Elizabeth Bruner stood in the background, along with Lo Ping.

When the mourners withdrew to the house, where food was waiting on a long wooden table, only Vina remained at the grave.

Augustus' arm was in a sling and he had lost weight from the ordeal, but the bone was mending, and the feeling had returned to his hand.

Selona looked up from the table, then toward Vina, as a curious thought came to mind. "Why is it folks always want to eat after a burying, Augustus?"

Augustus had no idea. "I don't know. Maybe it's to remind the living that we still got to take care of ourselves."

Selona shook her head slowly. "Seems like me and you spend half the time we have together in graveyards."

Augustus thought about that for a moment. "I guess we have spent a lot of time in graveyards." Then he looked up from his plate and said, "The company raised a good piece of money for Vina. More than enough to build her a house over near them cottonwoods."

Selona shook her head slowly. "She ain't staying, Augustus."

Augustus was caught off-guard by this revelation. "What are you saying, Selona?"

"Vina said she don't want no more to do with the west. She's planning on going to New York City and live with an aunt. She don't want to be here without Darcy."

"New York City! My God, she won't know how to live in

New York City. She's a frontier woman, not a city woman."

Selona stood and went to a wooden box; in the box were several flower plants, a small spade, and a gourd of water. She walked to the grave, and she knelt. Moments later, Vina knelt beside her.

Beneath the hot sun, the two women planted flowers along the edge of the grave of Sergeant Darcy Gibbs, H Company, 10th U.S. Cavalry (Colored).

That night Selona awoke to an empty bed. She walked around her new house carrying a lantern, first checking on the boys, who were sleeping in their own room, then the room where Vina's children were sleeping. Vina's bed was empty, and Selona didn't know what to think until she went to the kitchen window and saw the light of a lantern at the gravesite.

Selona walked to the grave, where she found Augustus standing with Vina. They said nothing, just stood there in a long silence, looking at the ground as though they expected Darcy would appear, laughing, and telling them this nightmare was nothing but a horrible joke.

But the ground didn't open up. Darcy was dead, and that reality was now forever a part of their lives.

Finally, Augustus spoke, saying in a low, pained voice, "I never properly thanked him for saving my life on the Republican that time up in Kansas."

Vina reached and took his hand and kissed his knuckles gently, and said, "Yes, you did. In more ways than you'll ever know. You were his friend. That was thanks enough."

Selona heard him lightly choke, then raised the lantern, and for the first time in all her years of knowing Augustus, standing beneath the stars that had followed them all from Kansas to the Indian Territory, from the Indian Territory to Texas, from Texas to Arizona, over hard ground and through hard times:

She saw tears streaming down his cheeks.

PART 5

1899: THE WILD WEST SHOW

40

T he men should have been mounted on horseback when we
made that charge, instead of on foot like infantry."
Theodore Roosevelt snorted.

"The jungle was too thick," said William F. Cody. "Besides,
most of your horses either died on the trip from Tampa or
drowned getting off the ship."

It was February 1899, and Roosevelt was pacing the pres-
idential suite of the Willard Hotel in Washington, D.C., his
fists balled, punching occasionally at the air. San Juan Hill last
July was still fresh in his mind, still clouded by the fact that
his men, all cavalrymen, made the charge on foot. Except
Roosevelt, who, wounded in the elbow, his glasses shot off,
had stayed in the saddle to lead his men into glory.

William Frederick Cody was sitting at the dining table, listening patiently, as he always did to Roosevelt. He was dressed
in fringed buckskin. Now fifty-six, his beard was long and
white, like his hair, his eyes still youthful though set within a
face that appeared ancient.

"By thunder, they'll not be afoot in my charge!" Buffalo Bill
said. "They'll be mounted on Arabian stallions: gray for the

Rough Riders and black for the Coloreds of the Ninth and Tenth cavalries."

Roosevelt never had appreciated his First Volunteer Cavalry being referred to as the Rough Riders. But history had prevailed.

"I still don't like the idea of the Ninth and Tenth getting so much credit." Teddy had never given the Colored regiments their just due.

"They deserve it, and we both know it. You even had several Coloreds in your Rough Riders from the western companies."

Roosevelt nodded slowly, recollecting that fact.

"Stephen Crane told me that if it weren't for the Coloreds your Rough Riders would have been decimated in that blame fool charge of yours." Crane's observations had been written while he sat on an abandoned Spaniard bass drum on captured San Juan Hill.

"We were successful. Despite the fact no one knows to this day where the order came from. General Shafter claims he didn't issue the order. General Wheeler said the same."

"Wheeler. That old Rebel! Hell, he came onto a patrol of Spaniards and ordered his troops to 'Charge the damn Yankees'!"

Cody twirled his beard, staring at Roosevelt, that mischievous gleam in his eyes. "I suspect I know where the order came from. Nonetheless, whoever heard of men on foot charging uphill into a well-fortified enemy position? Against artillery, no less! It's a miracle you weren't shot dead."

Teddy clicked his teeth and grinned. "History was good to me on that day."

Buffalo Bill stood and waved his white Stetson about. "It'll be the showcase of my Wild West Show! Gallant troopers charging the entrenched Spaniards. Guns blazing! Horses storming! Ah, God, Theodore, the women and children will be delighted."

Roosevelt's look reminded Cody of a buffalo bleeding out. "Flanked by your Coloreds."

Buffalo Bill laughed aloud. "Flanked by my Coloreds."

Roosevelt shrugged and appeared to accept the notion. "I know you have Sergeant Webb leading the Rough Riders. But who is going to lead the Coloreds?"

"Could I make a suggestion?"

Cody and Roosevelt turned to a tall man standing by the window. United States Senator Ernst Bruner had made the charge at Santiago alongside Roosevelt at the head of an Arizona company formed under the command of former sheriff and mayor of Prescott, Arizona, Captain Bucky O'Neal. After O'Neal was killed, Bruner became one of the company's leaders and, upon returning to Arizona, had run successfully for the Senate.

"Who might that be, Senator?" Cody asked.

"A soldier of valor. An original Buffalo Soldier. I met him many years ago on the plains of the Indian Territory, and later in Arizona." Bruner paused, and there was a gleam in his eye as he said with obvious enjoyment, "You met him one day yourself, Colonel Cody. On the frozen plains outside Fort Wallace, Kansas."

Cody looked puzzled. Roosevelt looked intrigued.

"Who might that be, Senator?" Cody asked cautiously.

"It was in 1869, at Fort Wallace. Do you recall having a shooting match with a young trooper from the Tenth Cavalry? A young trooper who used a Sharps rifle? You were shooting for Custer and the Seventh."

Cody's mind tumbled back in time. He had had so many shooting matches. But he did remember the ones he could count on one hand: the ones he had lost.

"My God. He was black as coal and could shoot better than any man I ever saw."

Bruner smiled, then said, "His name is Sergeant Major Augustus Sharps, of the Tenth Cavalry. His son Adrian was with my company in the Rough Riders."

Roosevelt thought for a moment, then recalled Adrian, and remembered meeting Augustus after the battle at Santiago. "He was a big man. Certainly one of the bravest. White or Colored. But how do you know him from the plains?"

Ernst said, "It's a long story, Bill. But I know he can be reached in Bonita, Arizona."

Cody slapped his leg with his Stetson and grinned at Roosevelt. "Then we're in agreement. You support the idea of my having the Rough Riders in the show, and my playing your role in the charge."

Roosevelt nodded. "I do."

"And that includes the Coloreds."

Roosevelt clicked his teeth again. "That includes the Coloreds."

Sergeant Major Augustus Sharps sat at attention on a roan stallion named Shiloh in the predawn darkness of Arizona.

The stallion showed a momentary restlessness, throwing his great head forward, then tried to rear up until he was settled by the tightening of the reins. Shiloh snorted and tried to crane his head away from the empty air beyond the rim of the deep canyon.

"It's almost time," Augustus whispered.

Augustus was watching the eastern sky as the sun began to filter through the crackback ridges of the mountains northeast of Bonita. He wore a short-sleeved riding jacket and crisply starched pants that blossomed above his knees before disappearing into tall, highly polished cavalry boots. The dark blue cavalry hat he wore over his close-cropped hair was pulled down slightly at the brim, just above his dark eyes; eyes that seemed to shine from within the brim's shadow.

The saddle on Shiloh was a McClellan, which he still preferred, what with the open slot in the seat that brought the horse's backbone against his tailbone, giving him the sense he and the horse were melded to each other physically. His Sharps rifle rested in the carbine boot on the right side of the saddle tree; on the left was his three-foot-long sabre.

The sun broke over the horizon; a red flood of sunlight swept the land and flooded into the canyon, running like fast water across hard ground. A narrow trail could be seen in front of Shiloh, a path that disappeared over the rim.

Suddenly, Augustus' arm flashed up; his fingers touched the edge of the brim in a sharp salute. He spurred the horse, stood in the iron stirrups, and leaned back as the stallion bolted over the edge into the redness of the canyon.

Down the stallion plunged, speed building as Augustus's right hand held firm to the reins, checking the power of the animal, while his free hand drew the steel sabre rattling against the saddle. With a smooth movement he extended the blade toward the imaginary enemy that lay waiting at the bottom. At that moment the sun flashed off the burnished blade and he felt the tightness of fear when he realized he was leaning dangerously far over the neck of the charging stallion.

He pulled the reins taut, sat back as far as possible, and distributed his body weight evenly, winning for the moment against the forward pull of horse and gravity.

Down they drove, leaving a spray of dust too heavy to rise in the hot air. The deeper rider and horse descended, the thicker the sheen of red dust collected, until the two appeared as flaming apparitions. It was only in the final moments of the descent, when the horse dove over the last ledge, and he heard Shiloh's hooves crack against the hard floor of the canyon, that he commanded . . .

Charge!

The canyon came alive with the sound of Shiloh's pounding hooves, the rattle of the empty sabre scabbard, and the snort of the stallion in full charge.

Augustus stood in the stirrups, leaned forward while extending the sabre beyond the stallion's rising and plunging head, preparing to receive the enemy charge. At the precise moment he and the enemy would join in battle, the sword flashed forward, narrowly clearing the head of the stallion; then Augustus pulled on the reins, wheeling the horse into the opposite direction.

A scream burst from his lungs as he spurred the stallion to full gallop and again stood in the stirrups with the sabre extended. He slashed and cut, parried and thrust the blade at the enemy as though he were fighting a legion of demons, unaware that he was not alone.

On the ledge above the canyon, another rider sat on a horse, watching the mock battle as she had many times. She knew that he came here, to the edge of their small ranch, and made this ride whenever he needed to feel young again.

Finally, Augustus drew the horse to a halt and, sitting at attention, saluted smartly with the sabre, then returned the blade to its scabbard with one crisp move.

On the canyon floor there was only silence, except for the heavy breathing of the stallion.

Selona was standing at the table in their kitchen when he returned. She paused at kneading dough as he poured a cup of coffee and sat down at the table.

"I expect now you'll be running all over with that Mr. Buffalo Bill. Getting yourself into trouble," she said, pounding the dough onto the table.

"Selona, I'm not going to get myself into trouble."

"Humph! Big Colored man like you is always getting himself into trouble." She shook her head while remembering. "Remember that Texas Ranger at Fort Davis?"

Augustus grinned. "Yes, ma'am. I do remember that Texas Ranger at Fort Davis."

"You coming in all smelling of whiskey. You tried so hard to keep from laughing, I thought you was going to bust."

"That's a good remembrance."

"Well, I can see you've set your mind to this. So go on. Telegraph Mr. Buffalo Bill and tell him you're fool enough to do it, if he's fool enough to hire you. You're just getting in my way around here anyway since you retired from the army."

There was a sheepish grin on Augustus' face.

Selona saw through him. She said flatly, "You've already telegraphed Mr. Buffalo Bill."

Augustus nodded. "I knew I was getting underfoot. I thought you might not mind if I did this."

"You think this is important, don't you?"

"It is important. The people of this country need to know

there were Colored troops at San Juan Hill. Same as they need to know about the whites."

Selona shook her head. "You and your remindering. You going to remind everybody about Colored troops until we plant you in the ground. Even then you'll probably be remindering about Colored troops to Saint Peter when you go through the Pearly Gates."

"Or the Devil, if I go the other direction."

She put down the dough and walked over to him and cupped his face in her hands. She stared long and deep into his eyes, through a flood of memories. "Augustus, you've already met the Devil, and He knows to stay clear."

He kissed her palms and rose, saying softly, "I best get my McClellan and Sharps cleaned up in case Mr. Cody wants me to do some riding and shooting."

"I want you to do something for me when you're back east."

"What is that?"

She held up a letter she had received the day before. "This come from Vina Gibbs."

Augustus' face suddenly appeared pained, then he looked through the back window at the small cemetery. The area was fenced off with a neatly painted white fence, and he had built an archway at the entrance; suspended from the pinnacle of the archway was a cavalry sabre that had belonged to the second resident. It was now gleaming in the sun.

"Do you think the Wild West Show will go to New York City?"

Augustus nodded. "I would think so."

"Good. I'll tell her to see you when the show comes to town."

Augustus could feel something coming. "And?"

"Fetch her back here on the train. Tell her I'll pay for the ticket."

"What if she won't come?"

Selona smiled. "Tell her I'm feeling poorly and I need her to help tend to Darcy's flowers."

"Are you feeling poorly?"

Again she smiled; that mysterious smile he knew full well. "Just you tell her."

That night he was sitting on the front porch, watching the stars when Selona came out and joined him. She had brought two heavy buffalo robes, wrapping one around his shoulders, scolding him. "You'll catch your death sitting out in this cold without something to keep you warm."

His arm flashed out and he grabbed her, pulling her onto his lap. "I got you to keep me warm. That's better than some old buffalo robe."

She giggled girlishly, then asked him something she had wondered since the first night she met him. "Augustus, do you ever think about them?"

"Who?"

"All them buffaloes you killed back in Kansas."

He had wiped the buffalo from his memory as he had the painful months he spent as a captive with the Kiowa. "Not a single time."

She shook her head as she realized something. "All these years I lived with buffalo robes, Buffalo Soldiers, even got a hairpiece made from buffalo fur, and I never seen a buffalo. Not a single one, except maybe you when you come in from a long patrol."

Augustus' eyes narrowed, and he could see them now, as though a great herd were right to the front, grazing in the low grass of their ranch. "It was a sight, Selona."

"Old General Philip Sheridan said, 'Kill the buffalo . . . you'll kill the Injun.' " She cackled, "He sure didn't know much, now did he?"

Augustus' eyebrows rose as he said, "He wasn't far from wrong. There ain't no buffalo left, and there ain't many Injuns left."

A long silence followed, then she asked, "Do you hate them, Augustus?"

"The buffalo? No, I don't hate the buffalo."

"Not the buffalo. The Injuns. Do you hate the Injuns?"

"I don't hate them, Selona. They're just folks like us, trying to survive in a world that don't want us."

There was some meanness in her voice as she said, "They killed my daddy and Darcy Gibbs."

Augustus' face eased out from beneath the robe. "Do you hate them?"

She thought about that for a while, saying nothing, then she stood and went silently into the house. She returned carrying a lit lantern. "I believe we should visit Darcy and the sergeant major."

The second grave in the cemetery bore the headstone of Sergeant Major Roscoe Brassard, who had died in 1894 of a heart attack. After his burial, Augustus took Brassard's sabre and, with a piece of chain, suspended it from the archway. In the spring the ground above his coffin bloomed with lovely flowers, as did that of Darcy's, like Marcia's at Fort Grant, where Selona went weekly. Jonathan Bernard O'Kelly had retired from the army after the war in Cuba, and had gone to North Dakota, one of the two new states formed from the old Dakota Territory. Augustus had received a letter from him a few months back, informing him he was working for the Great Northern Railroad, which ran close to the Little Bighorn. Several of his West Point classmates were buried there, at the site Custer and the 7th Cavalry had met their fates.

Augustus and Selona stood silent, looking at the graves, the white headstones gleaming in the lantern light. Finally, she spoke. "My mama never had a headstone to be remembered by, Augustus."

He nodded. "I remember. Your daddy was upset about that. Said he didn't have the money." He started to say something else, but she turned and walked quickly to the house.

Augustus stood there for a time. Then he straightened, letting the buffalo robe fall to the ground. His right arm came up, his hand forming a salute, and he whispered, "Until we meet again."

*   *   *

The next morning Augustus rose at daybreak, dressed, and ate a quiet breakfast of eggs and fatback. He saddled Shiloh and went back inside the house. In the bedroom he knelt beside Selona, staring at her for a long moment, as though making certain her face was committed to his memory. He kissed her lightly and walked toward the front door, but paused at the hearth.

Above the mantel, perched on wooden wall pegs, was his long, curved military sabre. Blackened by time, dented in battle, the steel blade slid smoothly from the scabbard, cutting the air with a *zilch!* that stirred Selona from sleep.

Through the door she saw him take the sabre, then the Sharps rifle, and walk into a new life, carrying with him a reminder of where he had come from and what was waiting for him when he returned.

As always before.

41

Adrian Sharps was tall like his father, square shouldered and narrow at the hip. But he was clean shaven, unlike his brother, David, who sported the flowing mustache and pork-chop sideburns of the frontier cavalryman he was.

The brothers were distinct in facial appearance, size, and skin color. Only their ages were the same; both were now twenty-three years old.

David was short and stocky, with cinnamon-colored skin, unlike Adrian, whose skin was the color of polished ebony. Both young men had now served their nation in a foreign war: Adrian with the Rough Riders, one of only a handful of Colored soldiers. David had served with his father in the 10th Cavalry.

All three had seen Cuba from atop San Juan Hill.

Augustus had been watching Adrian simmer since the three met on the loading platform at the Willcox train depot.

Adrian's eyes drifted over to the old McClellan lying beside Augustus' feet. "You going to take that old saddle?"

Augustus nodded. "My backside and that old saddle have

come to know each other. When my butt hits the leather, it's like old friends shaking hands."

Adrian asked, "What about the Sharps? That rifle's so old it'll probably blow up in your face if you try to use it."

David stepped away from the two. When Adrian was on the prod, he wanted to stay clear.

"It didn't the last time. That was yesterday. Since then it's been cleaned and oiled." Augustus' eyes remained fixed on the horizon. *Might as well let him get it out of his system.*

Adrian pulled at his suspenders and stepped to the edge of the platform. He hawked and spat. Then he turned and started to say something but was cut off by his father.

"I know you're angry because Mr. Cody asked me to ride with the Congress of Rough Riders. But we were there, too. It might be called Rough Riders, but it's supposed to stand for all the men that made that charge. Not just Mr. Teddy's boys."

"But I *was* a Rough Rider, Pop."

"We was all Rough Riders," said David. Then he laughed. "Of course, none of us were Rough Riders at all. More like rough climbers and rough crawlers!"

Augustus laughed. "The Spaniards didn't see but one horse that day. Mr. Teddy was the biggest target on that charge. He kept the guns off all of us."

David grinned to himself. His father always knew how to turn a bad moment into something positive by finding something of value in the negative.

"I'm proud for you, Pop. But I still wish I was going with you," Adrian said. "I hate that damn laundry. The smell of soap and filthy drawers ain't what I had in mind to come home to from Cuba."

Augustus' mouth curved in a smirk. "Mr. Cody just might give you a job sweeping the stables. If I ask him."

"Stables!" Adrian roared, then balled his fists. He stepped forward as Augustus opened his arms to him. They embraced as the conductor shouted to board.

"I'll see what I can do," he whispered into Adrian's ear.

They shook hands, then David hugged his father. "You

boys look after your mama. When I get back I've got an idea I'll be needing some help with."

"What idea?" David asked.

"Horses."

"Horses!" Adrian moaned. "Folks won't be riding horses much longer. Look at that train. Won't be long and people will be riding in those automobiles we read about."

Augustus snorted. "Horses will always be needed in the west. Not those broken-down old cavalry mounts. But quality horses. Bluebloods from Kentucky. Leisure horses."

Augustus stepped into the passenger car marked COLORED ONLY, and waved to his sons. "You boys look after your mama. And think about those bluebloods."

The United States Supreme Court decision of 1896 regarding *Plessy* v. *Ferguson* had made little difference in the railroad accommodations since Augustus' first train ride.

The Negro was still forced to ride in the Colored-only accommodations.

Separate but equal was the decision, and recalling that the coaches had always been separate, he saw little "equal" in the present circumstance. He had grown to accept that years before anyone had ever heard of Plessy. Or Ferguson.

The Arizona desert drifted past in slow motion, turning to tall mountains, then plains and swaying grass, from Wilcox to El Paso, then Denver and Kansas City. Hundreds of miles of land pocked with the unmarked graves of fallen Buffalo Soldiers.

But not unmarked in his heart.

The train roared near the Old Smoky River in Kansas, and he recalled a battle with the Cheyenne, when it would have been so easy to run away.

But he'd stayed, as had his comrades, and carved into the land a permanence most people today took for granted.

Where other passengers saw only empty land, Augustus saw ghosts posted along the route, silent sentinels marking the places where brave men had passed.

42

Baltimore, Maryland, was something new for Augustus. Paved streets bordered with gaslight lamps; trolley cars that rumbled and danced through the city on ribbons made of steel. It was a wonderment, and he felt like a child going to his first circus, when he found his way to William F. Cody's Wild West Show on the edge of the city. For the occasion he had dressed in his 10th Cavalry uniform, wearing the kepi hat of the old regiment, crossed sabres on the cant.

Buffalo Bill Cody was standing in front of the tent that served as his headquarters. Cody studied him for a long moment, then said, "I've often wondered what became of that young man that outshot me at Fort Wallace, back in sixty-nine. Not many men ever did that. Not before, or since."

Augustus grinned. "As I recollect, if I'd won the toss of the coin and had the first shot, you'd have had my last shot figured out and won the match."

They shook hands warmly and sat down in chairs outside the tent. The air was fletched with the fading sharpness of winter: cool, but comfortable.

"I am pleased that you decided to accept my invitation, Augustus." Cody ran his fingers through his long beard, his eyes moving slowly over Augustus. "I understand you have a family."

"My wife, Selona, is fine. She has her own restaurant and laundry service in Bonita, Arizona. Doing right good. My oldest son, Adrian, served with the Rough Riders in Cuba. He's back now. So is my son David. He was with me and the Tenth in Cuba. Both boys are out of the army now. They work with their mother, but I know both of them want to join the regular army."

"The *three* of you were at San Juan Hill?" Cody said.

"Sure was. All three of us made it to the top. Crawling on our bellies like Apaches."

Cody looked thoughtful. "How serious are those boys about joining the regular army?"

Augustus shook his head. "Going to be hard. The Colored regiments are being trimmed down, now that the war is over and the frontier is settled."

Cody mumbled slightly to himself. "Yes, the taming of the wild Indian has ended an era for a certain breed of man. Ourselves included. I do believe that if it weren't for the Indian, I would probably be farming in Illinois, or driving a milk wagon in Wisconsin."

Augustus knew Cody's old friend and one-time adversary Sitting Bull had died in what most considered the final hostility, at Wounded Knee in 1891. Sitting Bull, who had given the great scout Cody the name Pahaska—"long hair"—had once toured with Cody's Wild West Show in the United States and Europe.

Cody suddenly stood and swept his Stetson from his head. The approaching woman, accompanied by a rotund man, brought a sparkle to his eyes. She wore a long dress and western boots, and though they had never met, Augustus knew the woman by her legend.

"Augustus, this is Miss Annie Oakley. Annie, Sergeant Major Sharps will be with the Rough Riders in the show."

Augustus removed his hat and bowed.

Annie Oakley was small, with long braided hair and laughing eyes. When she offered her hand to Augustus, he felt quite humbled.

"Welcome to the show, Sergeant Major. The Rough Riders should be an exciting addition."

Cody motioned to the man with Annie Oakley. "This is Major John Burke. 'Arizona John.' He's the press agent for the show."

Augustus offered his hand. "I've heard of you, Major Burke."

Burke was brusque, shaking hands quickly, then pulling Cody off to the side, where they had a short but high-tempered conversation.

Minutes later, Cody came back to Augustus, visibly angry, and told him, "Gather up your gear and report to Bill McCune." Cody pointed at a tent where a sign read, OFFICER OF THE DAY. "Bill will get you billeted and arrange for your rations."

Cody stormed off without another word, followed by Burke and Annie Oakley. Augustus reported to McCune, who assigned him to a tent shared by other Colored men who had served in Cuba.

Later that afternoon Augustus took a stroll through the grounds of the Wild West Show. He was totally flabbergasted by what he saw. Languages of the whole world were spoken, sounding like fresh music to Augustus. There were Cossacks from the Caucasus of Russia; Indians from the American west; German Garde-Kurassiers of His Majesty Kaiser Wilhelm II; Filipino Rough Riders; South American gauchos; and the Queen's own Sixteenth English Lancers.

But the most impressive to Augustus were the Riffian Arabs from Morocco.

The leader of the Arabs was a giant man named Sheik Hadji Tahar, as big as Augustus and nearly as black. They shook hands and the Arab bowed, speaking to him in a language Augustus had never heard before. They chatted in grunts and hand signals, as he had once done with Indians, and could barely understand each other until they found two points of common ground.

The sheik rode a magnificent Arabian stallion that was as white as snow. On the saddle hung a long sword, longer than Augustus' sabre. The sheik offered the sword to Augustus, then motioned him to mount the horse.

Augustus climbed into the saddle, which he found comfortable, but not as good as his McClellan. He started off at a canter, then galloped along the tents and turned into the practice arena. He gave the stallion his head, guiding him in a wide circle, then a tighter circle, leaning with the long blade. With a sudden urging, he charged, leaning in the saddle with the sword extended.

He felt young again as the cold air washed against his face; the horse's breath matched his breathing, both snorting puffs of frosty air.

At the edge of the practice arena, Buffalo Bill stood with Arizona John. They watched, both impressed.

"I'll say one thing, Bill. Your Coloreds can certainly ride. This one especially." He poked a cigar at the figure of Augustus. "How did you come to know this fellow?"

Cody's eyes seem to fade slightly as his thoughts tumbled back to the Kansas plains.

"We met on a rifle range" was all Cody would say.

43

☆ ☆ ☆

On March 29, 1899, Buffalo Bill Cody's Wild West Show opened the season in New York City's Madison Square Garden before a sold-out crowd . . . in a manner of speaking. To be sure of a full house, Cody had supplied free admission to many orphans and asylum inmates.

Sitting in the COLORED ONLY section were hundreds of Colored people from the burgeoning Negro population of New York City.

Augustus Sharps sat aboard a black Arabian stallion saddled with his McClellan; in his hand he gripped the wooden staff bearing the regimental colors of the 10th Cavalry. He and the other Congress of Rough Riders performers sat nervously outside the main arena, waiting for their moment of entry.

The Rough Riders would follow behind Mexican bandits who attacked a Pony Express rider, an artillery demonstration, Annie Oakley's shooting demonstration, the grand review, and "The Star-spangled Banner."

Cody eased his horse alongside Augustus. "Well, old friend, this is the moment you've been waiting for. The chance to show the world about America's Colored troops. I hope you feel as proud as I."

Augustus extended his hand. "Mighty proud, Mr. Cody."

Cody, dressed to resemble Teddy Roosevelt, shook hands warmly, then said to the others, "Remember, boys, twice around the arena, then we'll hold up on the 'road.' We'll do some shooting, then make the charge."

On July 1, 1898, in Cuba, the road was Santiago Road, or the Camino Real—the Royal Road—that led toward San Juan Hill. Deep jungle separated the Hill from the road; between the Hill and Kettle Ridge, where the Spaniards were dug in, there was more thick jungle, which took the troops six hours to penetrate. All on their bellies. A bloody Hell beneath the guns of Spanish snipers and artillery.

"Remember that road, Augustus?" asked Bill Drees, the only other Colored in the Wild West Show. Drees was an original member of the 9th Cavalry, formed in 1866.

"I swear I do, Bill."

Drees was short, stocky, with a flat face and the expected flowing mustache that swept into pork-chop sideburns. The two men bunked together with the show and had become friends, having never previously met although they had fought on the same battlefields for nearly half a century.

"I seen Colonel Roosevelt get his spectacles shot off. He just grabbed another pair from his pocket and put them on. Then he yells, 'Charge!' and before I know it, we done all reached the top of Kettle Ridge."

"Yes, I seen him, too, waving that big pistol he carried. I'd been told the pistol belonged to one of the officers killed aboard the *Maine*."

"I heard the same, so it must be so."

Loud applause came from the crowd as the Pony Express rider flew on horseback from the arena.

"Gentlemen, are you ready!" shouted Cody.

The Rough Riders straightened in their saddles, then came the announcement: "Colonel Theodore Roosevelt and the Congress of Rough Riders from San Juan Hill!"

Cody shouted, "Charge!" waving the sixteen Rough Riders forward with the very pistol carried by Teddy Roosevelt in the famous charge.

The Riders stormed through the opening to the tumultuous roar of the crowd. Augustus had never heard such noise in his life. Nor such fanfare.

It was glorious!

And for the first time in his life, he felt that he truly was what he was supposed to portray: an American hero!

He thought of himself as a soldier trying to defend his country on the one hand, and hold his family together on the other. Medals of valor had meant nothing, although he wore many on his left breast.

And in that moment, as the flag whipped and the children's faces became a blur, as the Rough Riders circled the arena, Augustus stood in the iron stirrups, gripped and extended his sabre, and made the mounted charge that he and the others at San Juan had been denied.

44

The following afternoon, Augustus was currying his horse for the next show when a young boy appeared in the stables, staring wide-eyed at the tall cavalryman. He wore a hat that said WESTERN UNION.

"I'm looking for Sergeant Major Augustus Sharps."

Augustus laid down the brush and stepped forward. "I'm Augustus Sharps."

The boy stared, "Are you in Buffalo Bill's show?"

"Yes. I'm one of the cavalrymen in the charge at San Juan Hill."

The boy extended an envelope. Augustus took the telegram, put on his spectacles, only recently purchased, and carefully read the message. When finished, he folded the telegram and handed the boy a nickel.

"I'd rather have a ticket to the show," the boy said.

Augustus smiled and reached into his pocket, removing one of the complimentary tickets Cody gave performers for friends and family. "Come to the last show. It's the best!"

The boy walked away slowly, looking back until he disappeared from the stables.

Augustus sat on a bale of hay and read the telegram again.
His eyes grew wet as he read:

AUGUSTUS,
ME AND CHILDREN IN NEW YORK CITY.
HEARD YOU WERE IN WILD WEST SHOW.
WOULD BE PROUD TO HAVE YOU FOR
SUPPER ON SUNDAY.
VINA

The telegram added her address.
It was time to visit a painful part of the past.

Harlem was a teeming sea of black faces. Augustus had never
seen so many Colored people in one place at one time, not even
when, in 1885, the entire 10th Regiment assembled for the
move from west Texas to Arizona Territory to fight the
Apaches.

Riding in a horse-drawn taxi for the first time in his life, he
watched Harlem roll past; tall buildings, taller than any he had
ever seen. He was dressed in his cavalry uniform, wearing his
greatcoat bearing the gold chevrons and rockers of his rank.
By his side lay his sabre, which he wanted the children to see.
It represented a real part of his past, and theirs.

The taxi stopped in front of a brownstone, where Augustus paid the fare, then straightened himself and walked up the
steps. He climbed two floors to the familiar smell of ham and
lima beans cooking on a low fire, the way Vina always fixed
them.

The door opened and she stood there, a short, stocky
woman with cinnamon skin. Her face was old; her hands appeared like twists of dried grapevine. The years, Augustus
thought, had not been good to Vina Gibbs.

Not since Darcy Gibbs had been killed by the Apaches.

But her eyes were aglow as she stepped into his gigantic hug.

"Oh, Augustus," she whispered. "Good Lord, it seems
ages."

He held her at arm's length, saying softly, "It *has* been ages."

"Out west, Colored men are called 'boys.' Just like during slavery. White men are called 'men.' When you hear 'cowboy,' you're talking about Colored men who work on ranches with cattle. The white men who work with cattle are called 'cowmen.' "

Augustus sat in a large chair in the middle of Vina's apartment, looking at the children and grandchildren of Darcy and Vina Gibbs. The children had either forgotten much of the true history of the west they had lived or chose not to remember. Either way, it was the grandchildren of Darcy and Vina Gibbs to whom he was speaking. They knew very little of their heritage in the settling of the western frontier.

Augustus meant to see that was changed.

"In September of 1868, Colored troopers of the Tenth Cavalry rode hard through terrible heat and hostile Indian territory to relieve the fifty-one frontier scouts of Major George Forsyth and Lieutenant Frederick Beecher, of the Third Infantry, to a small island on the Arikaree Fork of the Republican River. This was called the Battle of Beecher's Island, where those men held off a Cheyenne war party of more than seven hundred braves for nine days. They would have all died without the Tenth Cavalry. Lieutenant Beecher, by the way, was the nephew of Harriet Beecher Stowe, the lady who wrote *Uncle Tom's Cabin.*

"Colored troopers of the Ninth Cavalry protected Texans from Mescaleros and comancheros. Some of those white people were former slave owners of the very troopers who were braving Apache bullets to protect them. I know. I was born a slave in west Texas, and years later, I fought for those folks when I was with the Tenth Cavalry.

"Colored troopers of A Troop, Tenth Cavalry, crossed the Staked Plains—the "Illano Estacado"—under the command of Captain Nicholas Nolan, and established the first military watering holes in the region.

"Colored troopers of the Tenth Cavalry later drove off the Apache war chief Victorio at Rattlesnake Springs. I know. Me and your granddaddy was there with Colonel Grierson.

"Colored troopers of the Tenth Cavalry helped capture Geronimo in Arizona, where your granddaddy was killed by the Apaches, and I was wounded . . ."

One of Darcy's grandchildren asked, "Does it hurt to get wounded?"

"Naw," Augustus said jokingly. "It just slows you down a bit."

Another of the grandchildren said, "I hear that Geronimo was evil."

Augustus shook his head. "No, child, he was just a man fighting for his country and family, not understanding he no longer had a country to fight for. He was brave. And noble. The way an enemy should be. He wasn't evil."

Augustus continued. "Colored troopers of the Ninth Cavalry helped with the fight against Sitting Bull's Sioux warriors at the Battle of Milk River in the Dakotas, with the Seventh Cavalry, and brought to an end the Indian wars on the frontier. In doing so, they brought an end to the Indian, and for a time, the end of Colored troopers.

"But the Spanish-American War brought the Colored soldier again to the battlefield for the United States. We were there with Mr. Teddy Roosevelt at San Juan Hill, and that's what I do in Mr. Cody's Wild West Show. I remind America that the Colored soldier—and his family—have served and fought for our place in these United States."

The children were enthralled. They had heard a little of this from Vina, but hearing it from this big sergeant major made it real.

Afterward, they ate a lavish dinner of ham and lima beans, greens, and cornbread dipped in buttermilk.

When supper was over, Augustus asked, "Where's the toilet?"

Vina showed him to a room down the hall.

Augustus was shocked. "An indoor toilet!" It was disgusting.

"Times do change, Augustus."

A little later, the two sat alone in front of a warm fire as they had done with Darcy and Selona on the plains of Kansas and the deserts of Texas and Arizona.

"They're fine children, Vina. Darcy would be proud," Augustus said.

She shook her head. "He would be ashamed and you know it's the truth. They're nothing but city children now. Don't know nothing about nothing. Indoor toilets and streets with gaslight lamps. Not like us, with campfires and—Lord!—the stars overhead. Can't even see the stars in Harlem." She paused, then laughed, and changed the subject. "How's her business doing?"

"Doing just fine. Still got her restaurant with Lo Ping, and since they closed Fort Grant she's his partner in the laundry service."

"That Selona. I swear, she could make a partner out of a stranger."

"That's the truth. Their restaurant's the only place around that serves chitlins, chili, and chow mein on the same menu, and they'll wash your drawers while you eat!"

Augustus thought that might stir a laugh, but Vina didn't smile. There was something lost about her, he thought. She stood up and walked to the window, wrapping a shawl around her shoulders, and Augustus realized she was no longer the woman who had served beside her Buffalo Soldier.

In ways he could not articulate, but in ways he understood, she had died the day her husband was killed.

"I hurt, Augustus. God Almighty, I hurt so much. I miss all that hardship. All that loneliness and even the emptiness—because I knew it would end when he came riding in, that hoss a-trompin', that sabre scabbard rattlin'—that heavy hoss scent. That man who smelled of courage!"

He rose and put his big arms around her, holding her the
way a friend holds a friend, keeping her close but not too close,
just enough to keep her from falling off the edge of the earth.

"I know," he whispered. "I miss that, too."

"But you got your Wild West Show. You got Selona. What
have I got? I'm just a broken-down old Colored woman in
Harlem, New York, with children that don't want to be
proud."

"Come home, Vina. To the place you helped build. You
didn't help build Harlem. That's for folks different from us.
Come home. You do remember home, don't you?"

She nodded; tears ran from her eyes as she took the train
tickets he pulled out. "How can I do that? I ain't got the
money."

He hugged her again, then whispered, "Don't you worry
about the money. The money don't mean nothing. What
counts is you . . . and coming home."

When Augustus left, he chose not to hail a hansom; rather, he
wanted to walk in the cool night air, and found himself stopping at a church where rejoicing voices drew him inside.

The eyes of the minister widened. His hands urged the congregation to continue singing as he walked down the aisle and
extended his hand to Augustus.

"Welcome, Mr. Sharps."

Augustus was surprised that the short, stocky man in the
rumpled suit knew his name.

"You *are* Sergeant Major Augustus Sharps of the Wild West
Show, aren't you?"

Augustus nodded. "How did you know my name?"

The minister laughed. "I'm Reverend Homer Sanders. I saw
the show yesterday afternoon. It was splendid." He guided Augustus to the front pew and motioned him to be seated, then
returned to the pulpit, where he quieted the singing.

"We have a special guest tonight, friends. Sergeant Major
Augustus Sharps. Mr. Sharps is a performer with the Buffalo
Bill Wild West Show."

Excitement rippled through the congregation as Augustus stood and bowed.

The completion of the service found him surrounded by adults and children excited at seeing an authentic Indian fighter of the western frontier.

Augustus found these children excited and curious, asking the questions that only children can ask. Innocent questions whose answers prompted painful memories at times, but mostly pride.

"Have you ever thought of writing down your memories, Sergeant Major?" asked a young woman in her early twenties. She reminded Augustus of Selona at that age.

"No, ma'am. I've never given that any thought."

"I know you have a wealth of memories that Colored people would love to hear. You might even find a publisher. I happen to know several who would jump at the opportunity." She handed him a card with her name. "I work for a newspaper here in Harlem. If you ever decide to write your memoirs, I'd be willing to help in any way I can."

Augustus took the card and placed it in his pocket. He left an hour later to the farewells of dozens of people standing in front of the church.

He caught a hansom for the ride to the fairgrounds, but stopped along the way to send a telegram to Selona. The telegram read:

VINA AND EIGHT CHILDREN AND GRANDCHILDREN WANT TO
COME HOME. PLEASE SEND MONEY FOR TICKETS.
LOVE, AUGUSTUS

Augustus was thoughtful when he returned to the showgrounds. Never had he imagined he was interesting enough that people would want to read about him. But, he thought, telling Colored people about Colored soldiers might be a good thing to do.

He was strolling toward his tent when he heard raucous voices coming from the tent housing a group of cowmen.

Nearing the tent, he froze at what he saw. Several cowmen

stood swaying drunkenly in the dim light in front of their tent.

"Good throw, Bennet," shouted one.

The cowman, Jim Bennet, from Abilene, Kansas, recovered his lariat.

He had thrown it around Bill Drees, who sat tied to a chair.

The cowmen were using the Colored soldier for lariat practice.

The blood boiled in Augustus' veins; he marched quickly through the cowmen. Just as he reached the chair, a lariat draped around his chest, and he felt the rope tighten.

"We got us another one, Jim," a cowman shouted, as he tightened the lariat onto the saddle horn, then jumped down from his horse and approached Augustus.

Augustus stood frozen for a moment, staring at Drees, who had obviously been dragged by a horse before he was tied to the chair.

The moment Augustus felt the lariat tighten, his hand went to the hilt of his sabre. He pulled the blade from the scabbard and cut through the rope. With a catlike move he stepped forward and swung upward with the blade, striking the cowman with the flat of the blade across the temple. The cowman fell; Augustus returned the sabre to the scabbard and prepared to meet the oncoming cowmen.

Three stumbled forward, with Bennet, a tall, lanky fellow with red hair, at the lead.

"I'm going to cut you for that, nigger." Bennet pulled a long, sharp knife, an 'Arkansas toothpick,' from his boot.

Bennet lunged with the knife, barely missing Augustus' neck. Augustus stepped forward and drove the heavy sabre hilt into the cowman's stomach. A rush of air exploded from Bennet's lungs as he dropped to the ground. Augustus whirled and swung and heard the sickening sound as the heavy scabbard crashed against another cowman's skull.

The last cowman turned and ran into the darkness. Augustus quickly untied Drees and hoisted him to his feet. "Can you walk?"

Drees forced a laugh. "I can run, if need be."

"We don't have to run."

They started off to their own tent, but Augustus stopped. "Go on ahead. I'll be right along."

Augustus picked up one of the lariats and walked to the fallen cowmen.

The next morning, when the sun rose, the three cowmen were found tied together in the cold mud in front of their tent, shivering in their drawers.

45

The next few days found the show preparing for the trip into the heart of the south. Augustus had never been south, and he had a sense of foreboding as he sat in the train, watching the countryside roll by. The show was headed for Richmond, Virginia, the one-time capital of the Confederacy.

He took out the writing tablet he had purchased and sharpened a pencil with his pocketknife. The lady in Harlem had suggested he write about his memories; he thought he would try. Now that he thought things over, he was amazed at how much had actually happened in his life.

There were so many memories, and he wanted to write about the pride of his service; the service he and other Buffalo Soldiers had given to the nation that still treated them as second-class citizens.

He began to write.

Good memories, thought Augustus, as he walked the streets of Washington, D.C., in April 1899, where the show was stranded by a train accident. While they waited for repairs, he chose to walk the streets of the city from which so many orders had been issued that had affected his life. And the life of his family.

The thought of going south, to Virginia, West Virginia, and Tennessee, still bothered him.

"Smells like Harlem," Augustus said softly. The familiar aroma of ham and lima beans seemed to float on the air in this section of the city where Colored people lived.

He passed out of the Colored neighborhood and turned a corner, where a drunk stumbled against him.

"Goddamned nigger Yankee. Get out of my way!" shouted a man Augustus' age, a man dressed in an old, tattered Confederate uniform.

"Excuse me," Augustus said. He walked on, ignoring the insult, when he felt the man grab his arm.

"Goddamn you! Don't turn your back on me." The drunk swayed slightly, then righted himself momentarily. "And you damn best well call me 'sir.' Do you hear me, boy!"

Augustus nodded. "Yes, sir. But don't call me 'boy.' I'm a man just like you. I was a soldier just like you."

The Secesh's eyes widened into two challenging fireballs. "You call yourself a soldier? You ain't nothin' but a fieldhand wearin' a Yankee blue coat."

Augustus turned to leave when lightning exploded in his head; there was the sound of glass breaking and the warmth of blood. He touched the side of his jaw. The flesh stung where the liquor seeped into the gash caused by the broken whiskey bottle.

The Secesh came at him, the broken bottle's jagged edges gleaming. Augustus stepped back, preparing himself, not about to run even if he had known where to run.

The edge of the bottle snaked toward him and Augustus could see the man was about to lunge when—suddenly—there was the glimpse of wood and the sound of a skull being crushed. The Secesh stood staring for a moment, his fiery eyes now like muddy water. He crumbled slowly to the ground, falling against Augustus' knees.

Augustus turned quickly to the alley behind the building. An ax handle appeared in the thin darkness, waving. Then there was a voice.

"Get in here, man. What the hell's wrong with you?"

The voice was that of a heavyset Colored man with the arms of a weightlifter, who was now climbing into the driver's seat of a beer wagon. His head was shaved bald, his face covered with a heavy beard.

"I said come on. Get in here. Are you crazy?" The man repeated, motioning Augustus with the ax handle.

"What about him?" asked Augustus.

"What about him? He was going to kill you. Now, come on, or get left to explain to the law how a nigger had to defend himself against a white man."

Augustus climbed into the beer wagon and held tight as the man—Benjamin Williams, he said his name was—snapped the reins and the team raced through the streets.

Thirty minutes later Augustus was at the railroad station. He was shaken and confused. He offered his hand to Williams. "I appreciate your help, Mr. Williams."

Williams shook hands. "You ain't been in these parts before, has you?"

Augustus shook his head. "Never before."

"Then you best be warned that a Colored man's got to walk careful. Especially one dressed in an army uniform. White folks don't take kindly to high-tone niggers. Even here in Washington, D.C. We might have been set free by the war, but in ways we still slaves. Still got to act like the white man's better than us." Without another word he skipped the reins off the horse's back and drove away.

Augustus returned to the train, where he sat staring out the window toward the lights of the capital.

Finally, he took out his pencil and paper. This time he didn't write about his memories; rather, he wrote a note he would take the next morning to the telegraph office.

He knew he could no longer be alone. Campaigns had separated them in the past, even foreign war, but that was never their choice. This had been a choice he had made, one he now regretted.

He knew he had broken his vow to Moss Liberty to always look after Selona.

46

Selona sat at a small table in the cooking area of the restaurant, staring at the four telegrams that lay on the table. One was from Augustus. Another was from Vina Gibbs, saying she was coming back to Arizona and would arrive within the week. The other two had been delivered at the same time.

She swept the telegrams into her hand and walked through the back door, crossed the alley, and entered the rear of the laundry she operated with her old friend Lo Ping.

Lo Ping was standing over a tub of boiling water, stirring clothes with a paddle. He smiled as Selona came in, his round face dark from the Arizona sun.

"Lo Ping, where are Adrian and David?"

"David go to bank. Adrian on delivery," he said. His English had not improved.

"Tell them I want to see them both when they get back."

She went back through the alley to the restaurant, opened the cashbox, and removed a twenty-dollar gold piece.

If she was going to go east, she would have to have some new clothes. And a hat. Especially a hat.

Folks back east might not understand her hairpiece the way they understood in the west.

But first she would have to prepare for Vina's arrival.

Selona found Asa Broadhurst, the big carpenter who had built her house, and told him, "You get busy on building a new house, out there by them cottonwoods. It's got to be big enough for nine people. Five grown children, three of them with young'uns, and one bedroom for their mother."

Broadhurst sat down and came up with the figures. Selona studied them with a wary eye, but didn't dicker. For the first time in her life, she let the eagle fly without a single holler.

"How soon can you have it ready?" she asked.

Broadhurst was surprised, having done business with her before. "Two weeks."

Selona grunted. "Have it ready in one and I won't make no argument."

Broadhurst smiled, then said, "One week it is, Miss Selona."

An hour later Selona was slicing onions while Adrian and David sat watching in silence; when she finished she reached in her apron pocket and pulled out her telegram. "You might as well know," she said, shoving the telegram across the table to her two sons. "Your daddy wants me to come back east for a while and traipse around the country with him. Seems like all I've done my whole life was follow around behind that man."

David laughed. "You loved every minute of it, Mama."

Selona giggled. "I reckon I did." Then her face grew serious as she took the other two telegrams and pushed one to each of her sons. "You might as well go on and read this. They're for you."

Adrian opened the telegram, noting that the seal on the envelope had been broken. "You've read this, Mama?"

"Of course I read them. They both say the same."

David looked with irritation at the telegram lying in front of him. "Then why don't you just tell us what they say?"

Selona smirked. "That Buffalo Bill wants you two to join

your father in his Wild West Show. He said you'll be the only father-and-sons act in the whole show. I expect the pay won't be too bad, and I know you're both itching to get away from that laundry."

David and Adrian nearly jumped from their chairs with excitement.

"Buffalo Bill!" David shouted. He nearly ripped his envelope open; he read the message with eyes flashing.

"We can go together, after Vina comes and we get her and the children settled," Selona said, but neither of the boys heard a word she said. "I don't like traveling all that way by myself."

Vina Mae Gibbs arrived ten days later in Willcox, and Selona was waiting.

Their embrace was long and deep, these two women who had known each other for nearly three decades, followed their husbands halfway across the west, and buried the ones they loved.

They were more than friends. They were sisters in history, bound by love, blood, fear, and tears.

Selona had hired three buggies for the trip back to Bonita, Adrian and David driving the other two while the two women rode beside each other, talking as the afternoon turned to dark. They rode into the night as though there was no fear, for they had known greater fear and survived.

"You remember them mules?" asked Vina, who started laughing before she finished the question.

"I was going to shoot them mules."

"Why didn't you?"

Selona grumped. "Would have ruined my restaurant business. Them mules was harder than a yard dog's jawbone. Even Lo Ping wouldn't have served them mules."

Vina knew the truth.

The night was growing long and the stars bright, and the children and grandchildren of Darcy Gibbs found themselves sleeping beneath heavy buffalo robes as the small caravan reached the house near Mount Graham.

Selona took Vina by the hand and led her to the cottonwoods, carrying a lighted lantern. Vina's jaw dropped as she
saw the house, but she didn't go inside.

Not just yet.

"Don't you want to see the house?" asked Selona.

Vina dabbed at her eyes, then took the lantern. "I truly do.
But I'd be grateful if you and the boys would get the babies
inside."

She said, "First I'd like to visit Sergeant Gibbs."

Three days later, Selona and her two sons took the stagecoach
to Flagstaff, where they boarded an eastbound train. Her sons
didn't quite understand their mother's reasoning in going
through Kansas by way of Denver, but they found themselves
changing trains at Bent Fork, Colorado, for Denver, where
they boarded another train traveling east.

Taking Selona back to her past.

It was not until they reached Wallace, Kansas, where the
train stopped for several hours, that they understood why they
were taking such a roundabout route.

"Come on," she said to her sons. "There's someone I want
you to meet."

Wallace was still a small town and not unfamiliar with Colored people, so they went unnoticed. The fort was gone, but
so were the Indians, except a few from the reservation who
lay drunk in front of the only saloon in town.

They walked the snowy street to the edge of town, to the
small cemetery. A wrought-iron fence had been erected around
it since she was last there. Outside the fence, in disrepair, were
dozens of graves with crude markers, unlike the white people's
granite markers inside.

"They wouldn't let Coloreds be buried beside white folks,"
she said acidly, walking through the tall prairie grass. The air
was chilly. The boys could see she was determined to find
something.

Then she saw it, rising from the tall, snow-covered grass. A
wagon wheel was stuck in the earth, most of the spokes gone

or broken. She knelt by the wagon wheel and said, "Hello, Mama. It's Selona. I brung you your grandchildren. Remember? I promised you I would."

After nearly an hour they made the short walk back to the station, stopping only once. Selona went into the only funeral parlor in town, where she paid the mortician twenty dollars and gave him the inscription to put on the granite marker:

HERE LIES DELLA LIBERTY.
1830–1869
Wife. Mama. Grandmama.
Woman of the west.

As the train pulled out of Wallace, Selona pointed out the window. "I used to live there when I first met your daddy. Back then the place was called Buffalo Bottoms."

Only an empty field lay there now; gone was any sign that Colored families had once lived there.

"I'm glad we stopped here, Mama," said Adrian. "I always wanted to visit her grave."

Selona nodded. "I only wish I could have visited my father. It's not right for family to be so far apart. That's one thing your daddy always wanted—for our family to stay together."

"We have," David said.

She shook her head. "It wasn't easy. Every time we would get settled, it seemed like we was picking up and moving along to some other forgotten place in the middle of emptiness."

"Where did you like being stationed the most, Mama?" asked Adrian.

Selona said nothing; her thoughts were suddenly drifting alongside the train.

After a few moments she said, "Wherever your daddy was."

47

Buffalo Bill Cody laughed until he thought he would bust. "I'd like to have been there, Selona, and seen you shoot that bank robber out of the saddle. That must have been a sight. A woman with a Winchester, and scared at that, ain't nothing for a man to take lightly."

Augustus chuckled, looking at Selona and his sons. "She made me proud, the way she stood up for what's right. She saved the money of every person in town. The banker even gave her a piece of land."

Selona was obviously content to sit quietly at the center of attention in the headquarters tent of Cody's Wild West Show. She was tired from the trip, but glad to be with her husband again.

She could see why Augustus held Cody in high esteem. He was colorful, no doubt; but he was a gentleman and moved with ease among the various cultures of the show, always willing to give his time where needed.

The next day was the first show in Richmond, Virginia, and Selona felt great pride as she watched her husband and sons perform together for the first time.

When the last show of the day was over she stepped into one of the mess tents, where the smell of open-pit cooking reminded her of her restaurant.

The mess tent was huge, with large tables established for the various groups of performers. The English and Germans ate together at table six; the Indians at table seven. The menu for each table was designed to provide the distinct cuisine of the particular nationality.

This gave Selona an idea.

"Go to work for Mr. Cody!" exclaimed Augustus.

"Why not? I can cook as good as any man."

Augustus shook his head. "You're supposed to be having a rest, Selona."

"I don't need to rest. Besides, I might learn something I can use in my restaurant back home. Imagine, Augustus. Exotic foods from all over the world in Bonita. Folks'll come from all around to my restaurant!"

"Folks already do come from miles around, Selona." But he could see she wouldn't be dissuaded.

Cody agreed and Selona started work the next morning. One week later she approached Cody with another idea, one he found intriguing.

"Yes, sir, Mr. Cody. I know the people who come to your show would enjoy tasting the food that comes from other parts of the world. Same as they enjoy watching the performers from other parts. I'll start out small. Just a pushcart and some samples from the mess hall. If it don't work, there won't be anything lost. If my idea works, that's all the better. I'll take my wages in commission."

Cody agreed. By the time the show reached Murfreesboro, Tennessee, her pushcart operation was ready to begin service. She found that what the people enjoyed the most was the exotic desserts, especially the cakes from Europe, the Middle East, and north Africa.

* * *

In Murfreesboro, Selona found something else, something shocking. She had lived her life in the west, not really understanding the south. Traveling aboard the train and staying with the performers, she had not seen much of the townspeople, except during performances. Now she found that southerners were not like westerners. There was a deep hatred in the south for Colored people, one she could not understand.

A hatred she saw boil to the surface one warm Sunday evening.

"You know I don't like to go to church," Augustus complained. She was fastening his collar in the tent they used as their quarters. Adrian and David were outside, beside a buggy they had rented for the occasion.

"A little church won't hurt you, Augustus Sharps. I'd expect you and the Lord have a lot to say to each other after all these years. Besides, there's a young preacher visiting here, and all the Coloreds in town say he's something special to listen to."

The buckboard drive to the little church on the edge of town was pleasant, the evening cool but comfortable as they came within range of voices singing hymns.

David tied the horse off while Augustus and Adrian escorted Selona through the door. They sat in the back row; all heads turned and stared at them.

An older minister was in the pulpit. He recognized the Sharps family and welcomed them, saying, "These folks have come all the way from Arizona."

The gathering murmured, staring again, making Augustus more uncomfortable.

There were more hymns, then the elder cleric introduced a young man who had been sitting in the front pew. "Reverend Phillip Dawes joins us tonight from Chicago. As you know, he's traveling through these parts, spreading the word of the Lord."

The minister motioned for Reverend Dawes to take the pulpit; the older man stepped back and took a chair.

Reverend Phillip Dawes was tall and thin; his dark eyes seemed to penetrate into the hearts of the congregation. To Augustus's surprise, his voice was deep and loud as he began to speak.

"The Colored people in America have come a long way in the history of this nation. We have traveled the road from the injustice of slavery to the present day of freedom. But the journey has not ended. It has just begun. Where once we lived in injustice—the moral justification of human bondage—we now live in the darkness of inequality. That, too, is now being morally justified as segregation of the races."

A wave of murmurs rolled through the church as Augustus turned and looked at Selona. "Did you know he was going to be preaching this kind of sermon?" he whispered.

Selona shook her head. Augustus rubbed his hands together. He had a sick feeling in his stomach. He glanced anxiously at Adrian and David, who also appeared tense.

"The white man would like us to believe that America has a Negro problem. I think that philosophy is wrong. I believe that America has a white problem! I believe that until white America is willing to accept the Colored people as equal, America will never reap the bounty of the freedom promised in the Declaration of Independence and the Emancipation Proclamation."

Augustus loosened his collar; he found the air stifling.

Then the door to the church suddenly burst open.

"Help me! For God's sake, help me!" A young black man stood at the door. He wore chains on his ankles; his chest was bare and he wore only tattered trousers. He collapsed in the aisle as screams erupted and people began to stand.

Another voice shouted, "They're coming! I can hear the dogs!" Indeed, the sound of baying dogs was coming closer.

Augustus slipped quickly from the pew and knelt by the man. He had ugly gashes in his ankles from the chains; deep cuts in his back bled profusely.

"He's been horsewhipped," Augustus said.

Then there was the bark of dogs outside, and the sound of hooves pounding into the churchyard, followed by an angry voice shouting from beyond the church door.

"Get him on out here, Preacher! Get him on out here now, or we'll burn the place to the ground."

Augustus watched the old preacher straighten his frock coat and walk toward the doorway, where he stood framed by the dancing light of burning torches. Augustus thought he looked like a man about to descend into Hell.

"Please, Cap'n. This is a house of God," the preacher begged.

"You got a boy in there that escaped from the prison gang. We want him. Now!"

The voice came from a big man riding horseback. Through the door Augustus could see the man, but not his face. He wore a sack over his head; two holes cut in the sack revealed only his fiery eyes. He saw a dozen more riders, all wearing the same covering on their heads.

Augustus walked to the door and stood beside the preacher. His big hands gently moved the preacher aside as Augustus walked out toward the men.

"Good evening, gentlemen. What's the problem?" asked Augustus.

The men snickered; the horses snorted.

The big man rode his horse around Augustus several times, then stopped, looking down, a torch in one hand, a shotgun in the other.

"You've got an escaped convict in there. We want him."

Augustus shook his head. "No, sir. That boy needs medical attention. I'll take him to a doctor. Then I'll send for the sheriff. He won't cause any harm."

Selona started to scream but it was too late.

The roar of a shotgun blast echoed through the church; then there was more screaming, and the hooded men rode their horses into the church and threw a rope around the injured boy.

Selona, frozen in horror, watched the boy being dragged

down the aisle, his head striking the edges of the pews, until he was gone, as though he were a momentary dream.

Screams and shouts filled the air as the congregation stampeded for the door; some broke open the windows and raced screaming into the darkness. Flight spawned by fear has a special sound, one of guttural desperation, and Selona could hear the sound all around her as the members of the congregation fled for their lives.

Then, as quickly as it began, the nightmare was over. There was silence as Selona and her two sons ran into the empty churchyard.

She stopped suddenly, then fell to her knees. Augustus was lying in a pool of dark blood; he appeared much smaller now, like a child sleeping beneath the stars.

Selona tried to scream, but her head began to swirl and she was swept away by a sea of blackness.

Adrian hurried past his fallen mother, shouting to David, "He's still alive! Get the buckboard!"

David hurried off as Adrian knelt beside Augustus. He quickly pulled off his belt and applied it as a tourniquet above the knee as David drove up with the buckboard.

"Let's load Pop first," Adrian said.

David looked down the road and spoke with contempt. "Those bastards. Those dirty bastards. Why'd they shoot him?"

"Because he stood up to them. That's not done down south."

They loaded Augustus into the back of the buckboard. "Is he going to make it?"

Adrian was helping Selona into the seat beside the driver, then climbed in and snapped the reins, saying, "He's going to make it."

"We'll go to the showgrounds. There's a doctor there. I don't want any of these cracker bastards touching him."

The buckboard flew through the night, rounding a curve where Adrian paused, swore viciously, then snapped the reins again.

David looked up from the back and saw what had enraged his brother.

The young escapee was hanging from a tree limb, his face contorted from the rope cutting into his neck.

48

He's lucky to be alive. But he'll never walk like a normal man," Dr. Samuel Pierce spoke in a low voice to Selona. She was in the hospital tent of the Wild West Show. "Lucky for him your sons knew how to handle the situation. Otherwise, he'd have bled to death."

For some reason Selona said, "They were soldiers. They know about gunshot wounds."

The next few days saw a gradual improvement in Augustus, but he wasn't the same man. Something besides blood and bone had been torn away by the shotgun blast. Part of his spirit had gone as well.

Selona looked up as the familiar figure of Buffalo Bill Cody entered the tent. He bowed, holding his Stetson over his heart.

"If there's anything I can do, I'm at your service," he said softly.

She nodded. "I'll be taking him home as soon as he's fit to travel."

Cody sat down heavily in a chair beside Augustus, watching the Buffalo Soldier's eyes stare aimlessly into nothing.

"This was no way for a man like you to be treated," Cody said.

Selona growled, "He wasn't treated no different than any-where else in his life. Only difference this time, he didn't have his Sharps. If he'd had his Sharps he'd have driven those Klansmen off like they was short-tailed rabbits."

"You'll be taking him back to your ranch?"

"Yes, sir. Back to the ranch."

"That's a long trip, Selona. Mighty rough trip for a man in his condition."

She shook her head angrily. "I'd rather see him die trying to get home than to sit here with these crackers. I won't let him die here and be buried in this hateful ground. If he dies he'll be buried on good ground . . . on our ground!"

Cody stood and patted Augustus on the arm. "I'll drop by and see you again, old friend." He added to Selona, "If there's anything you need, just ask. Anything at all."

"One of those chairs that's got wheels. I'd like to have one of those chairs. I can push him around and get him out into the light. A body'll die without sunlight."

"I'll have one delivered before the end of the day."

The wheelchair arrived that afternoon, but Augustus only stared at the strange contraption with contempt.

"You expect me to crawl around in that thing like some lizard in the desert?" He was sitting up on the edge of his cot, weak from the loss of blood.

"I expect you to act like the man I've always known. You've been wounded before and you never felt sorry for yourself. I expect the same from you now. We need you, Augustus."

He kicked at the chair, but missed and nearly fell off the cot. "There's not much need for a one-legged man in this world."

"Not if he don't think he's needed, Augustus. Not if he's give up. Have you give up?"

Augustus just sat staring at the wheelchair.

"You can get you one of them artificial legs as soon as the

wound is healed. The doctor said you can do anything a man with two legs can do."

Augustus looked up at her. She was shocked at what she saw. It was the second time in her life she could recall seeing tears in his eyes; not since burying Darcy Gibbs.

"You aren't going to let me have any peace, are you, Selona?"

She sat on the edge of the cot and cupped his face in her hands. "You don't need peace. You need me and your children. We're here, and here we'll always be."

He forced a smile, the first smile since being shot. "Now go on out of here. I have to get used to this contraption." He started to lift himself off the cot and nearly fell, but she caught him and righted him. He finally got into the chair and sat there for a long moment.

Finally, he said, "Well, at least it don't have to be fed and watered. And it sure smells better than a horse."

"It's a chariot made for a good, brave man," she said.

He laughed. "Brave? I'm not brave, Selona. That Kluxer shot me down like a dog."

She jumped to her feet. "A dog! Don't you 'dog' me. You and my sons was the only real men anywhere near that church that night. When them Kluxers saw you coming through that door—a big Colored man standing tall and unafraid—you struck terror in their hearts. Terror! While all them hallelujah house niggers was jumping through the windows and running off scared into the woods, you showed them what a real man looked like."

Augustus shook his head and laughed again. "What makes you think that Kluxer was terrified?"

She patted him on the shoulder. "If he hadn't been terrified, his aim would have been better."

EPILOGUE

1917: SABRE RANCH

*   *   *

"Why do we want to go to war with those Germans?" Selona asked. She was standing on their front porch, looking past Augustus at the two rising columns of dust approaching from the west.

She had no doubt what the dust meant.

Augustus was whittling, his artificial leg propped up on the railing. He glanced up at the approaching riders and smiled knowingly, then went back to his whittling. The artificial leg he'd purchased years before from a Chicago prosthetics clinic allowed him to walk, even ride, but each time he purchased a new pair of boots he had to make some adjustments on the foot. A whittle here, a whittle there, until the boot fit perfectly.

Selona said, "You buy another new pair of boots and you won't have a foot left. If that was a real foot you'd have already whittled off your big toe."

"Hush, now, Selona," Augustus said softly, slipping the boot easily over the artificial foot. "Why don't you fix me and the boys something to eat?"

She stormed into the house as Adrian and David rode up.
"You've heard?" David asked.

Augustus nodded. "A patrol from the Tenth passed through this morning. Sounds like there's going to be a ruckus."

His two sons were now in their late thirties.

"What's your plans?" asked Augustus.

"We're going to Fort Huachuca this afternoon," Adrian replied. "We're going to enlist. I expect the army will be needing some Colored troops."

Augustus grew serious. "I expect the army will be needing some Colored officers."

"Officers!" they chimed.

Augustus stood and walked off the porch toward the stable. The boys followed, leading their horses behind them. In the stable he saddled his horse and mounted. The three rode east into the desert.

Augustus told them, "Captain Lewis Morey was leading the patrol. He said the army is going to recruit non-commissioned officers from the Colored regiments to become officers. Right off he's recommending First Sergeant Houston and Corporal Queen of K Troop."

Adrian and David both knew the men. They had distinguished themselves nearly a year before during a punitive expedition into Carrizal, Mexico, when fifty troopers of the 10th had engaged more than five hundred Mexican cavalrymen. The 10th was soundly defeated, but its courage in the face of such overwhelming odds was a source of regimental pride.

"What about Theresa?" Augustus asked.

David shrugged. He had been married for nearly ten years and had three children. Adrian had married a year later, but his wife had died during childbirth. He had never remarried.

"She'll be fine. She understands."

"Your mama will want her and the children to stay with us," Augustus said.

David nodded. "I expect she will."

*   *   *

Augustus paused at the edge of the canyon. He stared out over the wide expanse. "Your mama thinks you boys are too old to be going off to war."

"General Pershing wasn't too old to fight in Mexico last year," Adrian said quickly.

Augustus nodded toward the canyon. "Maybe you best find out for yourself."

Augustus' right hand came up in a sharp salute and he spurred his horse over the edge. Down he rode, driving the horse furiously until he reached the bottom. He then spurred the horse to a gallop, charging the unseen enemy he had attacked so many times before. When the dust had settled, he motioned to his sons, who sat mounted on the rim above.

Adrian saluted smartly, then drove his horse over the edge, the reins tight as he pushed the stallion downward while holding the mount's strength in check. When he reached the bottom he made the same charge as his father, wheeled and made another attack, then reined in beside Augustus.

On the rim, David did the same, galloping down the steep ledge, following the trail cut by his father over the years. The trail the sons had ridden many times in their lives.

Augustus studied their faces for a long moment, as though he was looking at them for the last time. Then he spurred his horse and raced toward the mouth of the canyon, followed by Adrian and David.

The three horsemen rode out of the canyon and toward the ranchhouse. Augustus was in the lead, not knowing that his sons were holding back on their reins slightly, knowing the old Buffalo Soldier's heart was breaking because he would be left behind while younger men on strong legs rode off to war.

"Fort Des Moines, Iowa!" exclaimed Selona. "Why is there a fort in Iowa? There's never been Injuns or comancheros or

Mexican bandits in Iowa. Probably aren't any Germans, either."

"It's where the Colored Officers' Candidate School is located, Mama," Adrian replied.

Two months had passed since Adrian and David had ridden to Fort Huachuca and spoken with the fort commander. He'd accepted their application for enlistment and forwarded his letter to the War Department recommending the OCS appointment of Adrian and David Sharps.

"Probably do to you what they did to Lieutenant Flipper," Selona said acidly. "Colored officers don't do well in the army."

"Colonel Charles Young has done well for himself," David snapped back.

Charles Young, the third Negro to graduate from West Point, who had served in the late 1880s with the 9th Cavalry, was the first Negro officer to serve with a white cavalry regiment—the 7th Cavalry, Custer's old regiment. He was promoted to major during the Spanish-American War, serving with the 9th Ohio Infantry, and was the first Negro in the American military to be promoted to colonel. The newspapers had recently reported that he was riding on horseback from Ohio to Washington, D.C., to prove he was still physically fit to serve in Europe.

Selona ignored him. "Besides, I don't know why you would want to risk your life fighting white people in France who've never done anything to you. Why don't you fight for the Coloreds in America who are being murdered by white Americans!"

"Don't be unpatriotic, Selona," said Augustus in a stern tone.

"Unpatriotic! I'll talk to you about patriotism. Was it patriotic for you to risk your life for more than thirty years in the army and have some white man in Tennessee blow your leg off because you tried to stop white men from lynching a young Colored man? Now you're talking about my babies going to the other side of the world and fighting for white people's freedom, when their own people don't have freedom in this country! Damn you, and damn your patriotism!"

Selona ran from the house, slamming the door behind her.

Augustus rose slowly, the words more painful than the phantom pain in his amputated leg. "I best go after her."

They stood beside a tall cactus near Darcy Gibbs' grave in the hot afternoon sun, listening to the wind whip along the ground. His breath was labored by the old agony in his leg; her breath was angered by the agony in her heart.

"You could have stood by me, Augustus," she said softly.

He shook his head. "You were wrong, Selona. I won't abide you when I know you're wrong."

"Wrong? What's wrong with a mother wanting her children to be safe?"

"They're men, Selona. They're not children. They have to make a man's way—and a man's decisions."

"But France! God Almighty, that's so far from home." She stared off into the distance. "If they're killed, they won't even be brought home. They'll be buried in some foreign place where nobody knows them."

He touched her arm gently. "They won't die. They survived Cuba. They'll survive France."

"So many young men are dying in that war. I read that over a million men died at that battle called the Somme. A million men, Augustus. We ain't never lost a million soldiers in all the wars this country ever fought. That was in just one battle."

Augustus knew, and privately also feared, the incredible casualties of the war. "Sure must have been a ruckus."

She shook her head. "No. A slaughter. That's why I'm scared. Who do you think will be the first Americans they'll put in those trenches? Not the white regiments! They'll put the Coloreds up there first. Our sons!"

He said something he had said many times. "When the bugle calls, a soldier must answer."

She shook her head in anger. "You and that damned bugle. That bugle has killed a lot of good young men."

He turned and walked toward the house. Inside he found

Adrian and David sitting in the kitchen. He looked at them both affectionately; then to David he said, "I have something I want to do. But I don't want you to be offended."

David stood and put his arms around his father. "I think I know. I won't be offended."

Augustus walked into the sitting room and reached over the mantel, removing the dented, blackened sabre from the wooden pegs. He looked at Adrian, then held the sabre out in his upturned palms.

Adrian looked at David, who nodded with a smile toward the sabre.

"Adrian, I carried this in battle for over thirty years. I think it's only fit that the oldest son should carry this as a reminder of what our family has done for this country. I expect you'll do the same with your son one day if he has to go off to war."

Adrian took the sabre and hugged his father. David joined the embrace as Selona walked through the door.

She had tears in her eyes as she put her arms around the three men in her life, and whispered, "You have a long journey. I best fix you some food to take on your trip."

Then she did what she had done most all her life, knowing she was just one woman in a world always consumed by war:

She went to the kitchen and had her cry in private.

Afterword

The following is a list of some of the Buffalo Soldiers who received the Medal of Honor for Valor during the period of this novel:

INDIAN CAMPAIGNS: 1868–1890

9th United States Cavalry (Colored)

Sergeant Emanuel Stance	1870—Texas
Corporal Clinton Greaves	1877—New Mexico
Sergeant Thomas Boyne	1879—New Mexico
2nd Lt. Matthias W. Day	1879—New Mexico
Sergeant John Denny	1879—New Mexico
Capt. Francis S. Dodge	1879—Colorado
2nd Lt. Robert Temple Emmet	1879—New Mexico

Sergeant Henry Jackson   1879—New Mexico
Sergeant George Jordan   1880—New Mexico
Sergeant Brent Woods   1881—New Mexico
2nd Lt. George R. Burnett   1881—New Mexico
Sergeant Thomas Shaw   1881—New Mexico
Private Augustus Walley   1881—New Mexico
1st Sergeant Moses
    Williams   1881—New Mexico
Corporal William O.
    Wilson   1890—South Dakota

10th United States Cavalry (Colored)

Captain Louis H. Carpenter 1868—Kansas/Colorado
Sergeant William McBryar   1880—Arizona
2nd Lt. Powhatan H.
  Clarke   1888—Sonora, Mexico

Seminole-Negro Scouts

Sergeant John Ward   1875—Texas

THE WAR WITH SPAIN: 1898

10th United States Cavalry (Colored)

Private Dennis Bell   1898—Cuba
Private Fitz Lee   1898—Cuba
Private William H.
    Thompkins   1898—Cuba
Private George H. Wanton   1898—Cuba
Sgt. Major Edward L.
    Baker, Jr.   1898—Cuba

*   *   *

The author wishes to express his deepest appreciation to The National Medal of Honor Museum and Military Library, Chattanooga, Tennessee, for their wonderful support and assistance in compiling the names of the Buffalo Soldier recipients of this nation's highest combat decoration for Valor.